TRUE SHOES

Also by Doug Wilhelm

The Revealers
Falling
Raising the Shades
Alexander the Great: Master of the Ancient World

Choose Your Own Adventure books

Curse of the Pirate Mist
The Underground Railroad
The Gold Medal Secret
Shadow of the Swastika
Gunfire at Gettysburg
Search the Amazon!
The Secret of Mystery Hill
Scene of the Crime
The Forgotten Planet

I just looked at him. This was like Janelle apologizing, or Bethany turning into a decent human being. Something I never thought I'd see.

"We've ... pretty much been friends since she got here," I said.

"I know it," he said. "And what I want to ask is ..." He stood up straighter. "Will you watch out for her? Just keep an eye out. You can do that, right?"

"Sure," I said. "I sort of already do."

"I'm not saying *go* out with her. You understand."

"Not a problem," I said. "And listen."

"What?"

"You can stop by," I said. "Any time. To carve, or visit or whatever. Even stay. I know my mom would like to see you. I'd like to see you. Any time."

He nodded. And then he said it.

"Thank you."

He stuck out his hand. I shook it. We met each other's eyes. Then Richie looked past me, at her. One last time.

He turned, jammed his hands in his jacket pockets, and walked away.

Epilogue

If you've never heard the song "Someone to Watch Over Me," you should download it. It's completely old, but it's amazing.

At spring concert the next night, Cat's dad sat near us in a dark suit, with CC beside him in a very short dress. When I told Kennedy who that was, she raised an eyebrow.

"I'd say *she's* loaded for bear," she whispered in my ear.

"You mean for Cat's dad?"

"Well, it's just a guess," she added quickly. "Maybe all cute young women dress that way over there."

"He is single," I whispered back. "Or I guess divorced."

My mom leaned over me. To Kennedy she said, "What are you two gossiping about?"

"You *could* ask me," I said. "I'm right here."

My mom waved me quiet. Kennedy said to her, "I'll tell you later." They both sat back.

Elliot was sitting on Kennedy's other side. A few rows down sat Bethany's mom and her dad. Turner wasn't here — he was at his house working madly to put together all the pieces of our project for the deadline tomorrow. We were going there after the concert, Emily and Bethany and me.

Bethany was in the chorus, which sang before the band came on. Lauren Paine was in the chorus, too, but she hadn't shown up. Needless to say, neither had Serena or Cayenne. Also needless to say, by now everyone in school knew what Cat had done, standing up to Serena and taking her group down.

After the band did a couple of songs, the director, Mr. Foley, motioned to Emily and Cat. They'd been sitting in the front row on stage with their saxes, alto for Emily and tenor, the bigger one, for Cat. When the two of them got up and stood side by side with the band behind them, the cafetorium got very quiet.

Mr. Foley sat at the piano and started playing an intro that sounded, to me at least, the way it feels to be inside on a dark, very rainy day. Then, I can't really describe the song: it kind of doodled around at first, the two saxes weaving in and out and through each other. Then the melody built and built until it absolutely soared. It was really beautiful.

Just like her. She always would be beautiful, to me. No matter what.

When they finished, what happened I think amazed everyone in the jam-packed room. Sure, the girls had been good — they'd been *very* good; they had played together like their instruments were sisters who could finish each other's sentences. But the spring-concert crowd is usually, let's face it, fairly low-key. Its applause is polite, family applause.

Not this time.

As the last long, doubled note died, some kids in the front leapt up and started clapping really loud, pounding their hands together. This might not have been that unusual — after all, kids will make noise — but then others around them were standing up, and before you could think about what was happening, kids all over the cafetorium were on their feet, yelling and pounding their hands and stomping their shoes.

The parents looked around, puzzled; then they were up and applauding, too. The two girls on stage got so red-faced, they looked like they'd morphed into radishes.

The stomping could have been louder, of course, but all over the room kids were wearing the same kind of rubber-soled shoes. Emily and Cat had on nice dresses and leather pumps (*are* they pumps? I have no idea; I am a guy) — but elsewhere, as I looked around I could see that a whole lot of kids, even if they'd been forced by parents to dress otherwise decently, were wearing red, blue, yellow, purple, pink, plaid and patterned canvas lows. And highs. Every one was personal. And they were pounding and stomping their feet in those shoes on the floor.

In the clamor, Elliot leaned our way. "This is like the end of the first *Star Wars*!" he said. "I mean Episode IV of course."

He sat back. Kennedy nudged me.

"I thought you said he was dealing with reality now," she murmured in my ear.

"Well, you know. It's two steps forward and one step back."

She nodded, philosophically.

"I guess that's how we get anywhere," she said. "It's the same old story."

She reached for my hand. And we didn't say anything more.

Acknowledgments

True Shoes has been a labor of love — and of listening.

Several years ago, as I visited middle schools around the country that were reading *The Revealers*, students would often ask, "Will there be a sequel?" Or they'd just demand one. "There has to be a sequel!" And I would sort of shrug. "A decent story has to grow from an idea," I'd say. "I don't really have an idea for a sequel."

But on those visits I was also talking with and listening to young people whenever I could — in their classrooms, their cafeterias, their gyms and auditoriums and school libraries. And from those conversations, some ideas did begin to grow. A few came from passing observations, like when I spotted a boy who sat on the floor in the back of a multipurpose room, at a Massachusetts school, wearing all camouflage. (I never found out why. He did say he liked to cook.)

Then there was the eighth grader in a group I had lunch with, in a school library in Florida, who told me he was a filmmaker and had a site for his videos on YouTube. His friends all nodded. I pulled out my notebook and said, "I want to see your films!" He gave me the URL but said, "They're kind of weird." And they were, a little — but they were very interesting. That boy's filmmaking helped me to think about the newly opening avenues for young people's creativity in our Net-connected world.

As I talked with middle schoolers, and with their teachers, principals, guidance counselors and school librarians, I also heard more and more about kids' struggles to come to grips with the impacts of online meanness: the posting of embarrassing videos, of nasty messages, of websites designed to humiliate. I heard most of all about the spreading of rumors by text message. One boy approached me in a cafeteria, after this subject had come up in a discussion of *The Revealers*, to confide that some popular girls in his school were sending out rumors by text with the warning, "If you don't forward this, the next one will be about you." As we talked, as I asked questions and wrote in my notebook, other students came up to tell me more.

At a middle school in Vermont I met an eighth grade girl who, like my character Catalina, had recently moved to the U.S. from the Philippines. She was a high achiever, friendly and well-liked, and her background at home, she told me, was very traditional. I asked if I could seek her parents' permission to interview her at some length. It took weeks to get her mom's okay, but eventually we did the interview; and we kept in touch by email. When I had a new question about Catalina, about her country's customs, or about the tensions a teenage girl, new to the U.S., might face between American and Filipino social norms and expectations, I would ask — and Ihna would answer.

In these ways and many others that were similar, my ideas for a new story grew. And as I read fiction from the Philippines, as I asked American kids how it felt to be the subject of a quickly spreading rumor, as I listened to a high schooler tell me what it was like to be judged and misunderstood the way Richie is, my different threads of ideas were weaving together. Before long I was writing; and then *True Shoes* was taking shape, almost, it seemed, on its own.

But it didn't happen on its own. A book never does. For their help, kindness and advice to me during the research and writing of this one, I am grateful to more people than I'm going to remember. But I do want to thank Kevin Buchanan and Joseph Donarum, Vermont mental health clinicians, for sharing with me their insights about adolescents at the very start of this project. I'm grateful to Ihna Mangundayao, to Sam Whitney, to Zach Krasner and to all the young people who gave me advice and shared their own experiences.

Thanks to technology educator John Minelli, for letting me observe the introduction of a creative-multimedia project to students at the Hartford (Vt.) Memorial Middle School; to my nephew Henry Woodard, for helping with the wording of text messages; to John Kueffner for improving my description of an ambulance call; and to Wolfgang Mieder, professor and proverb expert at the University of Vermont, who sent me the oldest printed expression he has found, in an 1855 English sermon, of the saying about lies and truth that opens this book.

I'm grateful to Gail Hochman, my agent, who carefully reviewed two drafts of this manuscript, demanded that I cut them dramatically, then pointed me in the direction of independent publishing, where I'm very happy to be. And it's easy to see how much this book gains from the artwork of Sarah-Lee Terrat, who is my sister and has been a top-flight professional artist for over 30 years. Thanks also to Tim Newcomb, my longtime pal and frequent collaborator, for designing the book's cover and pages so expertly and well.

In this independent project I relied on a series of volunteer readers for the close, careful criticism that a writer normally gets from a professional editor. They did a wonderful job! I'm thankful to each of my readers: Vermont teachers Elaine Anderson and Laura Foley, New Jersey prevention specialist Becky Carlson and her daughter Anna, globe-trotting sportswriter Alex Wolff, and Patricia Worsham, who has been a close friend since childhood and today chairs the English Department at E.C. Glass High School in Lynchburg, Virginia. The final, expert critique of the *True Shoes* manuscript came from Patty and two longtime colleagues of hers, Diane Stroud and Betsy Garrard. Thanks.

In the end, I think this book came to be because I fell in love. Not long after I began working on it, I met Cary Beckwith, a lovely woman who somehow (this part is still a mystery) saw something in me. We were married on Labor Day weekend in 2009. Cary was the first reader of *True Shoes*, and as a mental health counselor for children and families she gave me expert guidance and advice at key stages of this project. With my son Brad and Cary's son Nate we have made a good strong family, and that to me is a source of gratitude and steady joy. It's to Cary that this book is dedicated, and for all the best reasons.

As I was finishing *True Shoes*, my sister Sarah-Lee, our brother Gordon and I lost our dad, Peter Wilhelm. Whenever kids ask me how I got started writing, I tell them first how I got started reading — and that was because my dad was the best reader I've ever known. Throughout my years of struggling to get books published, and mostly getting them rejected, my father never gave up on me. He only showed interest, and only gave support. I hope that in some small way, his spirit of inquiry, fellowship and humanity is reflected in this book.

Doug Wilhelm

TRUE SHOES

Doug Wilhelm

Cover art and illustrations
by Sarah-Lee Terrat

LONG STRIDE
BOOKS

Weybridge, Vermont

Published by Long Stride Books
Weybridge, Vermont

Visit Doug Wilhelm on the web at
www.dougwilhelm.com

Library of Congress Control Number 2011942967

ISBN-13: 978-0-615561-78-3 (Long Stride Books)
ISBN-10: 0-615561-78-0

Printed in the USA

A lie can travel around the world
while the truth is still putting on its shoes.

An old English proverb,
often attributed to Mark Twain

This book is for Cary

Contents

PART ONE

An Unstable Planet

1.

Our Time

The sound of her saxophone floated out all alone from the music room, like a lost goose calling in the sky. I was in the library, pretending to do homework. But really I was listening.

Band practice was over and everyone else in band, except for her, had flowed by chattering down the hall while I waited in here, the way I did every Monday, Wednesday and Friday after school. This was Monday. She liked to stay by herself a while, and just practice. She never ever felt she was good enough. I felt way differently — but I couldn't tell anyone.

It wasn't safe.

When her music stopped I packed up my homework and went into the hall. My locker was just outside the band room. I spun the knob, opened the locker and stood there, not really looking at the messy pile inside. This moment right now, when our time was about to start — I always liked this best.

The hall was quiet when Catalina came out, her backpack slung on her shoulder and her sax case swinging from its handle in her hand. I looked up, like I was surprised.

"Oh," I said. "Hey."

"Hi, Russell," Cat said, nodding in her kind way.

Oh, she knew. We never said one thing about it, but she knew. She could have shredded me with a look, with one roll of her eyes. A lot of eighth-grade girls eventually would have. But all this year, Cat never had.

I shut my locker and bent for the sax case. "I can take this."

She smiled. "Thank you." We started to walk.

"You're really playing well," I said.

"I don't know. I'm not sure I should try out next year."

"What? Why? It'll be great! The Parkland Marching Pirates." I did a dorky little high step, swinging my arms; but she was anxious. She was often anxious, these days.

"But," she said, "in high school you don't get to just *be* in the band. You have to really work, and really be good, and ..." She shook her head.

"You are good," I said. "You are."

She glanced at me sideways and smiled, and my insides came loose a little. I never knew what to do with how she made me feel.

"Are you coming to spring concert?" she asked.

"Well yeah. Of course."

Her lashes lowered. "I'm playing a duet. With Emily."

"*You* are? I mean ... you *are*?"

"Yes. In front of everyone."

"Whoa," I said as this sank in. "Wow."

If you mentioned music in our grade, almost anyone would think of Emily Behrens. She played and composed on like five instruments. She hardly ever said a word, but she could *play*. She was also going out with my friend Elliot Gekewicz.

This sort of killed me. I mean, here I was with this pathetic crush while Elliot, of all people, had an actual girlfriend. He basically spent as little time as possible in the real world. Outside school Elliot was generally in his basement playing Dominion Quest, one of those online life-substitution, I mean role-playing, games.

At lunch with our group, he and Emily sat together. Catalina never sat with us. She could never be seen sitting with me, or walking with me when people were around. It wasn't safe.

"I know," Cat said, looking down. "I have no business playing with her. I don't know why they asked me."

"They asked because they wanted you," I said. "You'll be great."

"She's great. I'm petrified."

Up ahead I could see the main hall. Our time was almost over. "So," I said — "what are you playing? Part of a song?"

"A whole song. 'Someone to Watch Over Me.' It's an older American song, by Mr. Gershwin."

Cat had a funny way of talking about anyone who was an adult. She told me once it was because Filipino people always showed respect. It was awkward, but cute.

"I was practicing it," she said. "Just now." She looked at me, hopefully.

"Oh," I said — "yeah. That was really pretty."

"You should hear her play it."

"I want to. I can't wait." When her face fell, I said, "I mean I can't wait to hear you both. Together. Playing it."

Oh god.

The fact that I was hopeless and said boneheaded things was, apparently, never going to change. I was a good friend to Cat, though. We'd known each other since not long after she moved here last year from the

3

Philippines, at the start of seventh grade. She was awkward and skinny, then. That was last year.

This year she was beautiful, tall and graceful the way she moved, with long dark shining hair. I loved to watch how her hair swung and caught the light as she walked, how it fell back from her face when she laughed. Basically I loved to watch her. I couldn't let anybody see this, it had to be an absolute secret. But it was true.

The main office was dark behind its glass. Cat turned to me. Her eyes were bright.

"I'm getting a *yaya*," she said.

"A what?"

"A yaya. It's like a housekeeper, but not really. Like a friend of the family who comes to live with you and take care of things. She's flying in tonight. From home."

"All the way?"

"Yes, Russell."

"Okay ..." I could see unsureness in her eyes. I said, "Is this good?"

"I ... hope so. My mom says she's a great cook. She'll make the things I've been missing *soo* much. And ... you know ..." She looked at the floor. "I've been home alone a lot."

"Yeah. I know."

Cat's parents were divorced. Her mom, back home, was Filipino; her dad was American, and he was always off traveling on business. So she'd been by herself a lot of the time since she and her dad moved here last year. It wasn't easy. She was an eighth grade girl, a long way from home.

"So this is good," I said. "I mean right?"

"I don't *know*. My mom's texting me stuff like, 'She's going to be my eyes and ears.' Like, 'I need to know what you're doing, you're representing our *family*.'"

"So ..."

"Russell, Filipino culture — it's different. This lady will watch every move I make. It's no joke."

I asked, carefully now, "Does your mom know about him?"

"No! Are you *kidding*?"

"O ... kay ..."

I was starting to get why she'd be stressed.

Cat started backing away. "I have to go." She glanced over her shoulder at the outside doors. "Don't come closer. He'll see."

At our school, the main hall and the office were not actually in the

4

front of the building — it was a strange old place — but over at one end, where the big doors were. That's where everyone went in and out. The upper halves of those doors were glass. If I came too close, he would see.

I stood there. This was the end of our time. I always just stood there.

"Later," she said, stepping backward. "I'll text you."

"Yeah," I said. "Say hi."

"What?"

"Tell Richie hi."

Her eyes got huge. "*What?*"

"I'm kidding."

But maybe I wasn't. I was a little tired of this.

"God." She shuddered. "Don't *do* that." Holding her hand against her stomach, she waggled her fingers at me. She always said goodbye that way — so he wouldn't see.

I stayed back and watched Cat's head disappear down the stairs. Richie would be out there waiting, the way he was every Monday, Wednesday and Friday after school. She was desperate that he never, ever find out that she and I walked and talked for just a few minutes, those same afternoons in an empty hallway before she went out to meet him.

I knew him. So I could understand why she was worried.

Richie Tucker was in high school now, a ninth grader. He was a loner, and he knew how to make you scared. I talked back to him a couple of times last year, when we were both in middle school, and I paid the price.

Now I stepped up alongside the doors and peered out. Richie was leaning against a tree across the street, watching as Cat hurried up to him. His hands were stuck in the pockets of his black army jacket. As she came up he held out one hand, low against his side. She slipped her hand in his, and they walked away.

2.

The Out Crowd

"I made Level 49 with my warlock darkwalker last night," Elliot announced brightly as he sat down with his tray. "I'm building up my levitation and telepathy powers. Had to battle swarmdwarves for skill training. Ugh, they're *disgusting*. I was up till two."

As he talked he started picking and tearing at his milk carton, not looking, just shredding it. Emily reached across our table and took the milk. She quietly opened it, then slid it back.

Elliot drank. Wiped his mouth. "Had a huge battle with some character from Iceland. Or Ireland. Somewhere."

I said, "You mean a game character, or a real guy?" I didn't understand these things.

"Hey," Janelle said — "he can't be too real if he plays that game all the time. Know what I'm sayin'?"

She grinned. Elliot, eating his cheese sandwich from home, didn't seem to notice. But Emily glared.

Janelle was a big girl, and she tended to dominate our table. She was one of only two African-American kids in our grade, and she had a way of telling you just what she thought. If you didn't like it, that was your problem. She also wore the same purple zipup sweatshirt every day, and I mean *every* day. If you didn't like that, the same deal applied.

Janelle took a big bite of her meatball sandwich, sat back happily, and chewed.

This was our group, most of it. We called ourselves the Out Crowd.

At our school you could pretty much map the eighth grade social hierarchy by the tables at lunch. We sat up front by the sandwich counter, Bun Appetit. This was not a status-rich place to be — in fact, it was the whole length of the cafetorium away from the ultimo table of the tip-top populars. But one good thing about our spot was that from here, in the bottom corner, it was easy to keep an eye on the whole room if you wanted to.

Today that was about to be an advantage.

The left side of the lunchroom, which started with us, was the cooler side (except for us), and it got cooler as you went. Halfway up were the tables of the athletes, in their sweats and warmups. The jocks were sometimes all right but tended to be full of themselves. They saw Parkland Middle School as "Us, the athletes," and "Who?"

On the other side of the center aisle was the social diversity. There were the tables, let's see, of the geeks and wizards, the arties, the skateboarder/alternatives and the theatricals (that's where Cat sat, with her friend Allison). The general mess of kids sat mingled in the middle.

The table right across from us had the kids with food allergies who, like Elliot, always brought their lunches; and the Asperger's kids (this meant that socially, whatever happened, they didn't get it); and the ones who were just ... too ... nice. Those kids could only socialize with each other. Most everyone else, in eighth grade, was just too casually cruel.

Speaking of cruel, perched at their table beyond the jocks at the head of the room were the tiptop ultras. This was an airtight clique of attractive and ruthless eighth grade girls who almost all looked alike, plus a few boys they sometimes allowed to hang around them. We called this group the Royalty.

The Royalty was headed by Lauren Paine, the blonde, excuse my language but it's true, bitch goddess of our grade — we called her the Ice Queen — and Serena Sunderland, the girl with the cleavage. Serena wore scoop-neck tops, and her long dark hair fell down there and sort of curled around. Except for her, the Royalty girls had to look and dress like Lauren. They had to be very slim, they had to have straight blonde or light-brown hair to their shoulders, and they had to wear these V-neck tops over a lacy undergarment that just barely showed above the V. (I have no idea what these things are called, okay? I'm a guy.) Anyway, that's what they wore lately. When Lauren changed her style, the others had to change too.

Often sitting with the Royalty was Jon Blanchette, our grade's golden boy. Jon's blonde hair fell just casually right, his clothes looked and fit just right, and he radiated a smiling ease that you could spend your whole life trying to copy and you'd only seem over-medicated. Jon was great at sports, a natural, but even he had no real authority at the top table.

The absolute, life-and-death social power at Parkland Middle School — known to the rest of us as Darkland, and for good reason — was wielded by the Ice Queen and Serena. Those two decided who could sit with them, go out with them, do errands for them or whatever, along with who in our grade would be the next chosen target for rumor and ridicule.

Less power was held by the teachers who stalked the lunchroom

7

aisles, glaring around to stifle any acting-up or outbreaks. We knew they'd rather be in the teachers' lounge with their coffee and pastries and their low-fat salads, and who wouldn't? Our cafetorium was like a zoo if all the cages got emptied out for a nice, shared meal. Survive middle-school lunch — survive middle school — and you're either strong for life or scarred for life. Or both.

Our group was a mishmash of ... let's say individuals. We had Janelle, looming large in her purple hoodie; little Emily, the musical prodigy who silently safeguarded Elliot as he babbled about swarmdwarves; and me, sneaking secret (so I thought) glances at Catalina, up with the theatricals (where she didn't totally fit, in my opinion — she was far too shy to be in theater). And we had Cam and Turner, who weren't here right now.

I wondered where those two were. Often they were up to something. Janelle sat back. "Everyone is *so* scared," she declared out of nowhere. I said, "What are you talking about?"

"Look around." She nodded. "Eighth grade is the age of fear."

"You're in eighth, too," Elliot said.

"That's how I *know*."

Elliot and Emily gave each other a glance, then started texting below the table. This was fairly risky. We could bring our cells to school, but if we got caught using them they'd be taken away. Of course everyone *had* to have a phone, and had to bring it everywhere. Last year in seventh grade, cell phones were still fairly unusual; this year, I bet half the kids had a smartphone. I just had a basic cell, but at least I had that.

Glancing down as Emily next to me thumbed under the table, I saw that her shoes were green today. This was something you wouldn't expect: quiet as she was, every day Emily wore different-colored sneakers. They were regular, old-school canvas lows. Tomorrow she might have on red. Or blue or orange. She was the only person I knew who did this.

"Oooh, I'm scared to do something *wrong*," Janelle said — "or wear something wrong, or say something wrong. I'm so *scared*." She wiggled, absurdly. But before we could react or answer, Cam came up and sat down fast.

Cam was the other African-American kid in our grade; he was new this year, actually new since the holiday break (it was early spring, now), and every day he wore camouflage. He was always competing, always pushing. "I'm stronger than you," he'd say, or "I can do that faster than you," or "I can take pain better than you." He had some kind of fire inside.

Now he leaned low over the table. "Watch," he said.

"Watch what?"

"You see White, right? By the jocks. Don't stare!"

Turner White, Cam's pal, was our crazy-serious filmmaker. He had a YouTube site called darklandramas where he posted his videos. Now he was moving slowly up the left-side aisle, by the athlete tables. He held his tray unusually low.

"He's got the Flip cam in his muff," Cam said, holding his hands like they were in the kangaroo pocket of Turner's black hoodie. (Turner always wore black.) The Flip was Turner's high-definition mini-camera, a powerfully cool little device.

"He cut a little *hole*, right? Camera's taped in there," Cam said. "*Don't look.*"

"But why?"

"Because we," he said, "are prankin' the Queen."

We gaped at him. "Sit *back*," he said. "Act normal."

Janelle laughed. "Oh right, *this* group? What you mean, prankin' the Queen?"

Cam grinned. "That girl always gets a blue Powerade. We know this."

"How do you know this?"

"We been watching her."

"Why?" Janelle squinted at him. "I told you not to mess with those people."

Cam ignored her. "So White gets in front of the girl on the lunch line, and I get in behind," he said. "When she's got that bottle on her tray and we're waiting to pay, White jerks around all dorky, like he forgot something — knocks the Powerade on the floor. So we know the girl's gonna give him the death look, I mean right?"

We nodded. The death look was one of Lauren's basic powers.

"While this is happening, I bend over and pick up the bottle," Cam said, "like this is my chance to impress this *fine* girl. But in my hand I have this."

Cam glanced around; then he laid his hand on the table, palm up. Gripped between the knuckles of his first two fingers was a pushpin, its sharp tip pointing up. Its plastic body was clear, so that if you saw the back of his hand you wouldn't tend to spot it.

Cam's grin spread wide.

"I punch a hole, right? Just above that blue stuff. When she takes a sip, it is going to *drib*-ble. Down that little outfit. When that happens and

9

she can't figure out *what's* going on, White films it."

Cam spread his hands. "Put *that* on YouTube. Blow the Barbie to pieces."

Janelle stared at him. "That has got to be the lamest idea for a prank I ever heard," she said. "You think that's gonna *work?*"

Cam ignored her again. His back was to the lunchroom, but I, across the table, could see. "Watch," he said to me — "but don't let 'em see you watchin'."

"You're just lucky this won't work," Janelle said to him. "If you did something embarrassing to that girl — to *that* girl — do you have any idea what she could do to you?"

Cam shrugged. "What's happening," he said to me.

"Nothing."

"Keep watching," he told me. "Don't be obvious!"

"Like you are with that Latino girl," Janelle said.

3.
The Stain

I started to fold up inside when she said that — but I couldn't show anything. Janelle loved it when she got to you. And that stuff was *secret*.

I watched Turner drift up the side aisle.

"It's gonna happen fast," Cam said.

"Nothing's going to happen," Janelle declared.

I couldn't see. "Hang on," I said, and picked up my tray.

I walked to the window into the kitchen where we slid our empty trays. I dumped my trash, pushed the tray through, then turned and watched as I slowly strolled back.

In his black hoodie and jeans, Turner looked like an alternative commando as he sidled toward the top table. Lauren was there listening with a bored expression to Bethany DeMere, who in seventh grade was queen but this year was one of the high-level wannabes. Last year, when Bethany ruled, Catalina and Elliot and I got some evidence of how she was spreading nasty rumors about other kids. We made that part of a truth-telling thing we did on KidNet, our school's computer network. That popped the balloon of Bethany's popularity, which she was still trying very hard to pump back up. She absolutely hated us. The feeling was mutual as far as I was concerned.

As Bethany talked, the Ice Queen gazed off and lifted the blue Powerade to her lips. I strode to our table. "She's gonna drink it," I said. Elliot spun around to look.

"Don't *do* that," Cam said. "Be *cool*."

But nothing happened. Lauren took a drink, set the bottle down, and spooned up some of the yogurt that was the only other item on her tray. She really was very pretty, in a starved blonde supermodel kind of way.

I sat down. "I don't think it worked."

"Of course it didn't work," Janelle said.

"What did you see," Cam asked.

I shrugged. "Not much. No leak."

"She drink it?"

"She drank. But no leak."

"Huh."

Janelle smirked. "You two ever stop to think she might pick up that drink from the other side? Oh, you planned this *way* careful."

We were silent. Then Elliot perked up. "On Level 38 my beastmagus character had to battle an omniclops," he said brightly. "Their eye socket goes all the way around. You can't come up on any side. So the way I defeated it, I ..."

"Beverage alert," I said as Lauren, at her table, lifted the Powerade again. "Quick. I need a tray."

Emily held up hers; I took it and stood to see Lauren start to drink just as Ms. Bender, a gym teacher in shiny black-and-gold Parkland Pirates warmups, moved in to bust Turner for loitering among the populars. Ms. Bender was blonde and slender like Lauren, but she could crank her voice up so loud we called her the Amplifier.

Turner saw her coming and backed up awkwardly, trying to keep his hidden camera pointed at the Ice Queen. While I watched the drama unfold I had a random thought. You know how you'll see news videos online of a car bomb or suicide attack, in Israel or Iraq or some such crazy place? Right after the explosion there'll be people running around, everyone screaming and sirens blaring and black smoke pouring up. We don't think about those videos; it's like they just happen. And sometimes they do, if it's a cell-phone video — but mostly they don't. Usually someone has to go into the danger zone to get the shot. Some cameraperson takes the risk.

Right now that was Turner. As the Amplifier tried to corner him, he kept hopping away, keeping his body angled toward the Ice Queen while he and the teacher did this odd, dodging little dance.

That's when something did happen.

Bethany must have seen it, because she stood partway up and tried to grab the Powerade out of Lauren's hand. But of course you couldn't *take* something from the Ice Queen, and Lauren's head jerked back in a shocked haughty way as she yanked the tilted bottle toward herself. This squeezed the thing and made the thin blue stream that was coming from it push out even harder. The two of them wrestled the Powerade back and forth — then Lauren stood up. Even from here you could see the blue zigzag widening across her ivory-colored top.

Bethany yelled, "Oh my *god!*"

Lauren stood frozen as people all over the cafetorium turned to look, then stood up to see. Ms. Bender pivoted away from Turner, who

12

moved in closer in the confusion as everyone, I mean everyone, leapt up and jumped on chairs in a sudden howling roar. Middle schoolers rise to drama like seals to a fish.

I hopped on my chair. Lauren stood motionless as people pointed at her, said things to their friends and even, the ultimate horror to a popular person, *laughed*. The Amplifier rushed in like a royal guard in her shiny outfit, shouting and waving her arms. "Sit down, people! Down! I want quiet *now*!"

Behind her, Lauren sat. Turner slipped in closer, stooped over his hidden camera like a dark question mark among the confused pretty people. The rest of us settled, more or less. Ms. Bender bent to say something to Lauren, who stood and turned her back on everyone. We watched in silence as she walked, straight-backed, out of the cafetorium.

The teachers were moving down the aisle now, controlling the crowd — but we were way up front, so I was still on my chair when I saw Bethany pick up the Powerade bottle and study it. Then she looked up ... at me. And she glared.

I hopped down. "Bethany's got the bottle," I said. "I think she found the hole."

"Oh yeah?" Janelle turned to Cam. "*Soooo.* How long you think it's gonna take those skinny girls to figure out who it was knocked that bottle off her tray? And who picked it up?"

Cam shrugged. Janelle said, "Do you *have* to get in trouble? Is it some kind of compulsion, or what?"

But that didn't make sense. Cam hadn't been in trouble since he'd come here, as far as I knew. But Janelle was agitated. "You do not know these people," she said. "They make bad things happen."

"Barbies on the warpath," Cam said. "I like it."

Janelle flopped back, shaking her head. "*Bad* things," she muttered again.

We were trooping out of the lunchroom when I saw Catalina threading toward us, against the flow of the crowd. She came up to me, smiling. I froze.

"Hi," she said.

Okay, this was just weird. Cat almost never spoke to me in front of other people. She was so scared about her boyfriend ever finding out that she and I were ...

Well, what? What were we?

Friends. That's all we were. Friends. And I knew she relied on our friendship — at night and on weekends, Cat would call my cell to talk, she would text me, but in public I had to act like I hardly knew her. She was petrified that word would get back to Richie that she was even talking with another guy, and then he would get mad. I didn't want that either, definitely not. But here Cat was standing in front of me, smiling with people all around.

"Uh ... hello," I said.

"That was crazy, huh?"

"What was?"

She tipped her head toward the top table. "That."

"Oh. Yeah."

"Would you like to come over today? After school?"

"Huh?" Today was Tuesday. No band. But still ... huh?

"I told Cecilia I was bringing my friend."

"Who?"

"Cecilia. My yaya, remember? She came in last night."

"Oh. Right."

"She wants to make *merienda*, her first day here," Cat said. "To be special. I said I wanted to bring my friend over, to share it. She thinks that's a nice idea."

Something wasn't right about this. Cat was talking a little too fast. I wasn't sure what didn't feel right, but something.

To explain, merienda is a traditional Filipino afternoon snack. It can have lots of different foods. Merienda's a big thing over there — Cat told us last year how she used to have it every day, with her mom. Food is really key in the Philippines. But why would she suddenly ask me over to her house? She'd never once done that. And why now, when this new lady had just shown up to keep an eye on her?

Cat was up to something. I knew her. She looked at me in a soft-eyed, melting kind of way ... and I melted.

"Okay," I said. "What time?"

4.

Merienda

After school I stood outside, blinking in the sunlight while people streamed by me down the steps. She'd said to meet here, but she was taking a while. I couldn't see her. Where *was* she?

Then she came out. The spring air had a chilly edge, and Cat's soft dark hair swung against the fluffy white hood that fell back from her jacket. Inside, I swayed; but she was agitated.

"I was at your locker!" she said. "I was *waiting* there."

"But you said outside. You said to meet here!"

"I did?" Her eyes were scanning past my shoulder. I thought, *She's looking for him.*

"I'm sorry," she said. "It's just that I usually see you there."

"But ... this isn't what we usually do."

"No." She nodded, seeing something. "There she is."

"She?" I looked around.

"Yes." Cat exhaled. "In *his* car."

"Whose?" Richie had a car?

"There," she said, pointing. Past the idling buses along School Street sat the usual line of parents' waiting cars. "See the red Audi? That's *our* car. I knew she'd do this. Come on."

She strode off as I stood there, staring dumbly.

I wasn't stupid, just easily confused at this time in my life. Physically it was like I'd been assembled from spare parts — I would stumble over something, then I'd look back and there would be nothing there. Also I was filled with feelings I did not understand, and I was way too embarrassed to let anyone know. Cat turned back and gave me a shrug, like, *Are you coming?* I took a breath and started to follow as she strode toward the red car.

I don't want to give the wrong impression about Cat — really she's a sweet person. Last year when she was new to America and our school, she wore big glasses, she was tallish and slender and awkwardly shy, and she missed her mom and home really badly. Then she became the target of a nasty rumor-spreading campaign led by Bethany, who had decided to destroy the new girl. That confused Cat. My mom said Bethany was threatened because she could see Catalina would be beautiful. That confused *me*. But it turned out that's what happened.

She was honestly gorgeous now, with her soft mouth, her shapely face and (she'd gotten contact lenses) her deep-brown, soulful eyes. Her skin glowed light-bronze, and when she walked she sort of flowed in this amazing way. She wasn't all skinny like the Ice Queen — "for one thing," she'd told me once, "Filipinos *eat*." She was just ... I don't know ... real. And most of the time she stayed in her house by herself.

Except for school, band practice and her secret meetings with Richie — times when I couldn't stand to think what they were doing together — Cat was at home studying. Academics are incredibly important in the Philippines. She and her mom texted each other all the time, and they Skyped; and lately her mom had been asking more and more pressuring questions. What was Cat doing, every hour when she wasn't in school? Who was she with? If she wasn't studying, then what?

I figured Cat had to be making up stories about her afternoons with Richie. If her mom found out she had an older boyfriend and was spending time alone with him, my impression was that one of them would be on a plane. Cat could get shipped back home in disgrace. It was no joke.

In our nightly phone calls, for a long time Cat never even mentioned Richie to me. But lately, she'd started talking about him — a lot. He was really stressed. He'd gotten mad at her because she was two minutes late coming out the school doors. "He was so strange today," she'd tell me. "He got so upset with me."

He. He. He. That was all I'd been hearing.

Now, as she stalked to the red Audi, I could see a dark-haired woman in the driver's seat. Cat stopped and turned back to me.

"Um, one thing," she said. "I didn't actually mention that you're ... you know."

"What?"

She shrugged. "Well ... a boy."

"*Huh?*"

"Well, it was late when she got in last night and she was all, 'Oh it'll be *wonderful* and I'll teach you how to make traditional food and I want to make merienda for you tomorrow after school.' So I said, 'Okay, I'm bringing a friend.' And she said, 'Well, sure. I want to meet your friends.' But she may be a little bit ... you know ... surprised."

And before I could wonder if this day could get any weirder, Cat had herded me into the passenger seat where I came face to face with a

16

youngish lady who was pretty, with shiny dark hair cut short, who looked almost Chinese but not quite, and who was suddenly and totally stupefied.

Cat opened the back door and slid in. "*Até*, this is my friend Russell," she said. "Russell, this is Até Cecilia."

The lady blinked at me. I said, "Um, hi." Cat crossed her arms, sat back and watched.

The lady blinked again. Then something happened behind her eyes. She sat up straighter and popped a big smile.

"It is nice to meet you," she said. "I have *heard* of you."

"You have?"

"Yes," the lady pronounced.

She put the car in gear and pulled out. She could barely see over the steering wheel. "You were Cat-a-lina's first good friend," she said, glancing in the rearview mirror. "When she was new in America."

"Well. Kind of."

"Yes." She nodded. "Catalina was having trouble with that nasty girl, and that girl's friends. They were saying very bad things."

"Yep. That's Bethany."

"She is still there? That girl?"

"Oh yes."

"Does she still do bad things?"

"Well, I'm sure she does when she can."

"But not to my Catalina."

I thought, *your Catalina? Didn't you just get here?* From the back seat came a snort.

"Uh ... no," I said. "Not lately."

"Please you can call me CC," the lady pronounced. "You do not need to call me Até." She glanced in the mirror again. "Because you are American."

"O ... kay ..."

"CC is what everyone calls me."

"All right. But what's ..."

The lady said, "Até?"

Then Cat cut in. "In Tagalog, it means older sister," she said. "A girl or woman who is older than you, who isn't your mom or aunt or your *Lola*, we call her Até."

"Lola?"

"Lola is your grandmother," CC said. "Young Filipinos use a word

17

like this when they speak to an elder." She looked in the mirror. "It is a way of showing respect, yes?"

I glanced back, expecting scorn, but Cat just nodded.

We were in some neighborhood of big houses when we pulled into a driveway. This house, of white-painted brick, looked like it had just been built.

"Here we are," CC said, switching off the engine. The two of them got out quickly, like they were competing to lead us in. Maybe they were.

The front hall was bare and the living room looked like it hadn't been used, but inside the kitchen were warm smells. A small white TV on the counter was playing a sitcom repeat. One of the walls held a picture of the Last Supper. There was fruit in a bowl on a round white table, by windows that looked out on an empty backyard.

Looking around, Cat shot out a sharp exhale. "You don't waste time," she said.

"You like it?" CC spun around. "Not all the way like home, but it's a start, yes?" She rushed over to the stove and got busy. Cat slumped in a chair and stared at the fruit. The bowl had a pineapple, oranges, and ...

"What're those?" I said.

"What?"

"Those." I pointed at two oblong rosy fruit objects.

Cat's eyes bulged. "You don't know *mangoes?*"

"He is American," CC said. "Don't make fun."

Cat made a quick, mocking face; then CC hurried over and snatched a mango. At the counter, she slit and cut and pulled something from the fridge. Then she set before us a plate of orange glistening chunks, and two forks.

"Mango with lime juice," she said.

Cat offered me the plate with eyes that were, suddenly, shining and soft. "Merienda," she said.

"That is only the beginning!" CC called from the stove, where she was busily working on more dishes.

I speared a piece of mango and slipped it in my mouth. It tasted like a luscious orange, but smoother, richer, and tangy from the juice. I said, "Whoa."

"These aren't even the good mangoes," Cat said. "You can't get the good ones here."

More merienda came out, and Cat's mood warmed with the smells that floated through the room. I remember a bowl of soft white things, like big flattened Rice Chex.

"These are *palitaw*," CC said. "They're very nice — just rice flour in balls popped in boiling water, then rolled in coconut and dusted with sugar."

"You *have* to like palitaw," Cat said, and she smiled.

I did like palitaw. It was warm and amazing. I also liked ... see if I can remember: *ensaymada*, warm little buns topped with sugar and melted cheese; and banana fritters, fried golden brown. I loved those.

"We buy these in the street, at home," Cat said. "You get them wrapped in newspaper."

I mumbled through a mouthful, "You have this every *day?*"

She nodded. "At home, every afternoon. But when I came to America ... no. I tried a couple times, to make it, but I didn't really know how."

"But now is different," CC said firmly as she slid two cups of whipped-to-a-froth hot chocolate in front of us. She stepped back and looked at Cat. "Now," she said to me, "she is in the eyes of home."

Cat, eating fritters, didn't answer. I asked, "Did you, like, know each other back home?"

"Yes, a little," CC said. "I am the younger sister of her cousin's husband. Catalina has been so far away — but still everyone at home asks about her, knows about her. Everything she does here, it reflects on her family. Especially it reflects on her mother."

Cat ignored CC, who kept on pretending she was really talking to me. "Maybe there are things in this country she can do that are okay," CC said — "but if she does them, people at home will say, 'Oh, her mother is bad. She is a *bad* mother.'"

Cat's head jerked up. "Maybe people shouldn't jump to conclusions when they don't *know*," she said.

"Oh yes," CC told me — "because this is what people do, no? For example, if a girl brings a boy home after school, maybe people will get a wrong idea. Even if the boy is a very good boy." She smiled at me.

Cat slapped down her fork. "Maybe you don't know about this country. Maybe a boy and girl could be friends, in *this* country."

CC said to me, "Of course. A boy and girl can be friends in our country, too — if he is a good boy." She nodded. "I think you are a good boy. I think you would not come here if you were not ..."

"But you don't *know* that," Cat cut in. "Maybe Russell just seems nice."

I thought, *What?*

"All right," CC said. She smiled at me politely. "Your parents. Do you have a big family?"

Cat went, "Huh! American families are *not* the same."

"It's actually just me and my mom," I said.

"Oh, I'm sorry," CC said. "I know too many American families have divorce."

"See? You're jumping to conclusions," Cat said.

"My dad passed away," I said. "When I was a kid. So it's my mom and me."

"Just you two?" CC's forehead crinkled, like she couldn't quite get this. "Sisters? Brothers?"

"No."

"But uncles. Aunts. Cousins."

"No. Not around here."

"What about grandparents? *They* must be here."

I shrugged. "Long ways away."

Cat said, "See? American families are *different*."

CC, nodding, said, "Yes, but you and Catalina. Do you do things with friends, or ... just you two?"

"Well," I said. "We don't really do much. I mean ..."

"Just us two," Cat said.

"Well ... yeah, but ..."

"Just us two," she said again, looking at me. "Right?"

"Well. I guess."

Now CC was glaring at Cat. "If I were to speak about this," she said — "to say that on my first day here you brought a boy home, to this *house*, what do you think people would say? Eh?"

Cat looked away. CC said, "I think they are right, what they say about you."

"What? Who says what?"

"They say you forget your culture. They say you forget how to act, because nobody has been with you, helping you."

"Oh, so you're here not even a day and you can *judge* me? I've been here almost two years, and who's helped me? Nobody!"

"How did you eat?" CC said. "What did you eat?"

Cat shrugged. "I get takeout. They deliver. And frozen dinners are really pretty ..."

"That is *food*? These things are not food!"

"You can't just come here and *take over!*"

They were nose to nose, now. "I am your elder," CC said. "I will feed you and care for you and you will show respect. And if you want to *shock* me ..." She motioned toward me. "This is a nice boy — and I think you brought him here just to shock me. Is this how you treat your friends in America?"

Cat looked at her and then me, and in a flash I realized: CC was right. This wasn't about me, it was about Richie. Cat had brought me here as a distraction. If CC got all flustered and upset about me, maybe she'd miss what was really going on.

I had been Cat's truest friend. Now ... I was a decoy.

Cat spun away and stomped out of the kitchen. We heard her pound up the stairs. A door slammed.

CC picked up the almost-empty plates. "Would you like some more?" she asked me, and she smiled. "Chocolate? Mango?"

"I think I better go home."

5.

Media

She makes me do my homework first. When my mom gets home, I've generally been online for a while (okay, so technically I do that first). She marches into the living room and — this is her battle cry — says, "All right! Everything *off!*"

So I have to turn off the TV, pause the iPod, pull out the earbud (I've only got one in, so I can also hear the TV), close up Facebook and YouTube and whatever other tabs I have open, and just ... do the homework.

Don't get me wrong; I do it. There's too much, but I do it. Still with my mom it's the same thing, every afternoon. "All I ever see is the top of your head! Why can't you be doing something else when I come home, just one time? Why can't you be, I don't know ..."

"Building a rabbit hutch?"

She smiles. "Yes. Or picking up your room."

"Huh!" This is our routine, hers and mine. Luckily we have humor.

"I could set up our old camping tent in the basement," I say. "Like a fort, right?"

"You could *clean* the basement."

Okay, I have humor.

"I could build a hang glider and jump off the roof with it! I saw this YouTube video, these insane guys in Norway — they build personal gliders out of some superfabric and they jump off fjords. Off *fjords!*"

"Homework," my mom says.

"They look like flying squirrels. They glide at about a hundred miles an hour — they fall down along the cliff's edge doing somersaults, then like soar over cars and roads and rivers. It's amazing! I'll show you."

I start tapping keys, but no.

"Stop right there. No Internet. *Homework.*"

I sigh.

I try to broaden my mom's perspective. But it's hard.

In an hour or so I had the homework done. My mom was around the corner making dinner. I checked Facebook to see what my friends were doing. Elliot was playing Dominion Quest, of course. Turner was working on a movie. My news feed said, "13 of your friends are now friends with ..." But I'd never heard of the friends they were friends with. I unpaused the iPod, flipped through TV channels, then started watching *The Daily Show* on my laptop. I kept checking back to see what was new, but nothing was.

Some people I knew had hundreds of Facebook friends. It could get depressing. I mean, I could have tried to be friends with these friends of friends that I didn't know, but mostly I didn't. I guess I wasn't a strong networker. My cell was by my laptop, but it hadn't buzzed (three buzzes for a text, four for a call) in a while.

I clicked up YouTube. My home page there showed my favorites, like ohnoyoufail, which was somebody who spliced together clips of people messing up at random things; and the muckdogs, two guys who made stupid but hilarious movies with plastic Army men and mutilated Barbies and monster puppets made out of paper bags and weird items from the dollar store — stuff like that; and this graffiti artist in I think Indonesia who called himself eyetagblind and who filmed himself doing these incredible spray-paint vandalisms on public walls in a city somewhere, and I always wondered if when he finally got arrested that would be on YouTube, too. So far, no.

All these people in the world were more creative than me. They were so much cooler than me. One disadvantage of the Internet is that it shows you so many people who are standing out for one reason or another when you're not. Sometimes I'd get frantically into it, maybe so I wouldn't have to think about that — and right now I was clicking up more videos, zipping around, hitting Share to send eyetag's fresh new thing to Turner, then flicking back to Facebook when my cell buzzed three times.

It was a text from Turner. Looked like he'd broadcast it.

Check out my YouTube site at 6 p.m. tomorrow — world premiere of my new film, THE LUNCHROOM INCIDENT

Turner's dream was to post a film that caught fire and got a million zillion hits before he was even in high school. You could go online and see his best work so far, like his video *Gag Me With a Fork* that showed these girls, one after another, with appalled and disgusted expressions (he'd gone up to them outside school and asked things like, "How would you rather die, drowning in a pool of mucus or sliding down a ten-foot razor blade?" Then he filmed their reactions).

Turner's other cool short film was *Sneakerspy*, where he put his mini-cam on top of his backpack when he was standing at his locker. It was down by the floor and it filmed people going by, at the level you'd see if you were a small dog. That video was great; it was all legs and shoes and noises. It made you see and hear things in a whole new way.

That was Turner, too, seeing things in his own way through his camera. Sometimes it got a little hard to tell him and it apart.

My cell buzzed three times. It was Elliot.

See Trnrs text?

I thumbed back:

Why didnt he post film?

He's WORKING on it

I wondered what it's like to have something special in your life, something intense like Turner's passion for making films that shook people up, when a message from Cam popped up in Facebook Chat.

Film is way cool! BarB in stains!

He'd been helping Turner work on it, no doubt. Those two were a pair.

My mom called out, "Dinner!" But I didn't absorb that because the cell buzzed again. This time it was Janelle.

double double trouble trouble!

We read *Macbeth* by Shakespeare in Language Arts last February. It starts with these witches, talking like that. Janelle *loved* those witches.

If he posts that video, fire n bubble n toily trouble!

"Dinner is *now!*"

This was the full-throated war cry of the clueless parent. My mom entered the living room, puffed up large. "Everything *off!*" She jabbed

24

her finger at me, then swept it toward the kitchen.

I sighed, shut the laptop, and flicked the cell to silent. Right when there was drama, I had to miss it.

Well, I thought, *that's okay. It's only getting started.*

6.

Shadows

After dinner I was into all of it again. The buzz over Turner's announcement was spreading, people were discussing it on Facebook, when our doorbell rang. This was such an alien sound that at the time I didn't hear it, not consciously. It's only thinking back that I can remember, *Oh yeah. There was a sound.*

My mom came into the living room. "You have a visitor."

I didn't answer. She puffed up: "Hel*lo?*"

"Uh?"

"You have a *visitor.* An actual human, in person at the door. Will wonders never cease."

I said, "Huh." I didn't get it. Who just comes to your door?

Then I did get it.

Once I had a wart taken off my finger, by the doctor quick-freezing it with nitrogen gas. It turned white. I mention this because now it felt like my whole nervous system had been quick-frozen with nitrogen gas — like I turned white inside. I only knew one person who did not text you, did not instant-message you, did not Facebook Chat you or call you or anything. When he wanted you, he came and found you.

I had been avoiding contact with Richie for months. Catalina had said to me, again and again, *"He can't find out."*

"But aren't you and me just friends?"

Say no, I had pleaded in my mind. *Say it's more.*

"It doesn't matter," she'd said. "If he even knows I *talk* to you, he'll ..."

She had never finished that sentence. She didn't have to. Last year Richie punched me twice, once in the stomach and once in the face, just

25

because he thought I had disrespected him. At Darkland he had a fear-some reputation. Now he was in high school, and except for being Cat's boyfriend I didn't know what he was up to. I just knew that on Monday, Wednesday and Friday he'd be waiting one hour and fifteen minutes after school ended, and after band practice Cat *had* to come out the big doors. Exactly then. And she had to be alone.

With Richie there was always an unspoken "or else."

"At the door," my mom said, and wheeled away.

I unfroze my jaw. "O ... kay ..."

Outside he stood in the shadows, hands jammed in the pockets of his black army jacket, just beyond the yellow glow our porchlight cast on the lawn. He'd worn that same jacket all the way through middle school. Back then it had been like his uniform — his armor. Now it was tired-looking, and frayed at the wrists.

Richie was looking at the ground. He didn't seem mad, he seemed different. I stepped outside, feeling more puzzled, suddenly, than scared. He motioned with his head to follow him.

It was chilly out, a damp night. I followed Richie into the shadows.

"How you doin'," he said.

"Okay."

"Been a while."

"Yeah. Everything all right?"

He shrugged. "I need a favor."

"From me?"

"Maybe."

"Okay ... "

He turned, toward our garage. "What's in there."

"In the garage? I don't know. Stuff."

"Yeah? A car?"

"No, just stuff. Boxes. That's our car," I said, pointing to our silver Honda, parked in the short driveway. Our garage was always too full for the car.

"Anybody go in there much?"

"Not really."

"Any blankets or anything in there?"

"Um ... I don't think so. Richie, what's this about?"

He shrugged. "If I crashed there, just one night. You wouldn't say anything."

"Well ... no ..."

"I'd be gone in the morning. No muss no fuss."

I looked at this shadow with eyes, and I understood: he couldn't be home right now. I didn't get why, and he wasn't going to tell me — but even so, I had some clue. I knew something wasn't totally okay at Richie's house.

One time last year, after we got to know each other a little, I said to Richie that he talked like a dad from hell, because sometimes he did — and then suddenly there was this rage. It came up from inside him like volcano lava. Even for Richie it was scary. He didn't want the rage, you could tell, but he had it. I figured it must have something to do with his family, but we never ever talked about it. We're guys.

"I'll bring some blankets out," I said. "No problem."

"Nobody can know." He glared at me. "I mean it."

"Don't worry. My mom'll start bugging me pretty soon about the garbage — I'm supposed to take it out before I go to bed. Then I can sneak some blankets out to you. No muss, no fuss," I added hopefully.

"Okay. Cool."

We walked over to the garage, to the side door. I quietly let him in.

7.

Wereghouls and Poisonbots

It was an unspoken thing between us that I never contacted her. Always she would call me, or text me. That way she could know I wouldn't pop up at the wrong time.

But this time I called her.

"He's in my garage," I said.

"Who is?"

"Richie."

Silence.

"Why?"

"I don't know. He's not big on explaining things."

"Things are weird here too," she said. "My yaya is plying me with food."

"Don't change the subject."

"I'm not! She thinks I'm hiding something."

"Well," I said, "you are."

"Yes, but why does she have to ... I mean ..."

"Your plan backfired," I said. "Didn't it?"

"What?"

"You know. Bring a boy home. Get her all worked up and worried — but about the wrong guy."

Long silence.

"Why do I have to have so much pressure from *everybody?*" she finally said. "I thought you were my friend."

"I am your friend. So why would you do that?"

Silence. I could hear her breath getting shaky.

"It's just ... I mean ... I've been so worried," she said. "He's been *so* stressed."

"But why? What's going on?"

For a while she didn't answer. Then she said, "Is he okay? How does he seem?"

"He seems fine."

"Is he hurt?"

"Why would he be hurt?"

"*Please*, Russell. Just tell me."

"Like I said, he seems fine. I brought him some blankets."

"What about a pillow?"

"A pillow?"

"Yes. Does he have a pillow?"

God. A *pillow*.

My call-waiting beeped. It was Janelle. I thought, *Good*.

"I have to go. 'Nother call."

Why was I taking care of the guy she really liked? What was wrong with me?

"Hello?"

"Whoa," Janelle said. "What's with you?"

"Sorry. Nothing."

"Listen," she said. "We got a situation."

"Tell me about it."

"You heard, right? Those boys are gonna post that film tomorrow."

"Oh. Yeah."

"Listen," she said — "those two have no idea. That girl has friends. She will *hurt* you. They're gonna post this on the *Internet*."

"That does tend to be where people post things," I said. "But so? It's a little prank."

"Maybe to you. But that girl cannot let them do this."

"No?"

"Oh no."

"Why not?"

"Because she's on top and they are nobodies. At the same time, she can't react."

"Why?"

Janelle sighed. "Okay, let's review. We are talkin' about *the* power figure. *The* girl."

"The Ice Queen."

"Right. If she reacts to our boys in public, she's stooping. She cannot do this."

"Okay ..."

"And I guarantee you, this girl thinks our boys are tryin' to bring her down. That's how she sees everything — it's all a power struggle. And she does *not* want that thing on YouTube. She can't be embarrassed by a couple of ... you know."

"Kids like us."

"Well. Like you. And this girl, who has to be perfect, can't let herself get famous for a stain. She's gonna *do* something about it."

"Okay."

"You think that girl would get someone to hurt our boys?"

"Hurt?"

"Like, I don't know, football players. Breaking bones or somethin'."

"Nah. Too old-school."

"I don't want those boys hurt."

Janelle was protective of our odd little group. Especially of Cam, for some reason.

"The White boy said he's posting his film tomorrow night," she said. "That leaves the girl one day."

"Okay."

"*One* day."

"Okay!"

"You hear *anything*, you tell me," she said. "All right?"

"Sure. Will do."

Janelle hung up, and before I could think about any of this, my cell buzzed three times. It was Elliot:

Big big big! I defeated two wereghouls and four poisonbots, and shattered an attack by FIVE slime trolls! I MADE LEVEL 50!!!

I had to smile. These were my friends.

They were out of their minds.

Later, I went quietly into the guest room and got a pillow. I figured I could put it back before my mom noticed, I could come home this afternoon and do that. After what happened yesterday at Cat's house, I was not going to be waiting for her after band practice.

Not this time.

When I went outside, light was showing on the lawn from the garage's back window. That made me nervous; I checked to make sure my mom couldn't see the light from her window. But her room was in front, so it seemed okay.

As I came up to the garage I could see Richie through the window. He was sitting hunched over on the floor, like he was working on something. His elbows were moving. The light glinted off something in his hand.

I couldn't see what he was doing. Then Richie shifted, and I saw that the thing was a knife.

I walked to the side door, set down the pillow, knocked once and walked away fast. I felt chilled.

8.

The Shunning

In the cafetorium the next day, Lauren got her lunch and swept past us. When Turner and Cam came rushing down the center aisle, I saw Serena glance our way from the top table.

The boys sat down fast, too wound-up even to get food. "You will not believe what happened," Turner said.

Janelle said, "The ice girl? What'd she try?"

"Not *her*," Cam said.

"You have to *see* it," said Turner. He pulled out his smartphone beneath the table. His finger flicked the touchpad as he talked.

"On the way to first block I'm walking along," he said, "and here comes our old friend."

"Who?"

Elliot and I leaned closer. Below the table, the phone's screen showed a paused video. It was shadowy, but you could see a girl with wavy blonde hair.

Elliot peered at it. "That looks like Bethany DeMere," he said.

"Yep," Turner said. "She came up and said I should meet her under the stairs between first and second block."

Elliot, eyes bulging: "Under the *stairs?*"

Turner: "I *know*."

Under the stairs was the private place where the sought-after kids — and only those kids — went to gossip, scheme, share beauty secrets, change their cyborg power cells, or whatever they did when no one else was watching. You could duck in there, but if you were not a top jock or on Lauren and Serena's A list, you would have known not to try.

I asked, "How did she say it?"

"Like, 'Come *meet* me,'" Turner said in a sort of purr. "'Under the stairs, after first block. I want you there.'"

Janelle's face scrunched up. "She said that?"

"I *know*," Turner said. "At first I didn't get it — but then I thought, Wait a minute. Bethany's with that group. She doesn't want me, she wants my video. From yesterday."

"Huh," I said. "Did you go?"

"Sure I went. And I brought backup." He nodded toward Cam, who gave us a little wave.

"You brought another *guy?*"

"Yeah — whatever happens, I want it on video. She says, 'What's *he* doing here?' I say, 'Oh, he's my friend. He just needs a place to text.' She looks at me like I'm pathetic, then she remembers she's supposed to like me or something. So she sidles up. I mean like close."

"You're making this up," Elliot said.

"I'm not! Cam's got my cell and he's pretending to text, right?"

Cam waggled his head and thumbs merrily over an imaginary phone.

"What he's really doing," Turner says, "is running my phone's video-cam."

Elliot said, "Huh. Isn't that kind of sneaky?"

Turner shrugged. I said, "It *is* Bethany." And we all knew what that meant.

Like Lauren Paine, Bethany DeMere did not care what she did to other people, so long as she got what she wanted. And what Bethany wanted was to be back on top, where Lauren was. I wondered how those girls could even stand each other.

"So," Elliot said. "This worked?"

"She says to me, 'We could do something,'" Turner said. "I go, 'Like what?' And she goes, 'If you do one little thing for me, I can do something nice for you.'"

Elliot was puzzled. "Do something?"

"Yeah."

"Like what?"

I said, "Elliot."

"What?"

Turner said, "She's like, 'If you just erase that video from yesterday, then' — and she came in really close, actually touching my arm with her ..."

He cupped his hands chest-high. Elliot's mouth fell open. Janelle rolled her eyes.

"Touching you?" I said. "*Touching?*"

"Yeah."

"And Cam is *filming* this?"

"Yes!"

"What'd you say?"

Instead of answering, Turner unpaused the video.

In dim light, Bethany's shape is up against Turner's shape. There's background noise. Bethany says, "So ..."

Turner steps away from her. "Uh," he says, "I'm, you know, honored and all. But I know what you're doing. And I'd really rather have my film."

Bethany jerks back, like she can't believe it. "Are you joking? What, are you gay?"

She turns toward the camera. "Are you ... are you filming*?"*

There's a sudden jerk. Now darkness.

Cam grinned. "Barbies goin' *down*," he said. "One by one."

Then, over his and Turner's shoulders, I saw something.

Bethany had gone up the center aisle with her tray, but when she came to the top table, she stopped. All the seats there were full. No one looked up at her. She kept standing there, like maybe she'd said something and no one had answered.

Then I saw Serena whisper to the Ice Queen. Lauren looked up, smiled, and said something to Bethany.

Bethany stumbled back a step. She looked around, then stooped over quickly to sit at the empty end of the theatricals' table. From the other end, Cat glanced at her. I slid to an aisle seat, so I could see better.

Bethany had her eyes down, a little too obviously staring at her phone. It looked like the girls had told her to check it, and now she was so rattled by what she saw that she couldn't remember to hide the thing. She sat very still. Cat sidled over next to her. No one else was watching, just me.

Cat leaned close and said something; Bethany moved her arm toward Cat under the table. Cat peered down, then looked up wide-eyed at Bethany. Then Cat must have felt me watching. She met my eyes and gave me a hand motion, like, *Come here.*

I pointed at myself: *Me?* Cat nodded.

"I'll be right back," I said. Our group was paying no attention. I walked up the aisle and sat down across from Bethany and Cat. When Bethany glanced up to see me and Cat there, her face crinkled like she didn't understand.

"It's not right," Cat said to her. "It's just ... not *nice*."

Bethany said, "But ... I don't want ..." Then she went silent, and very red.

"Show him," Cat said gently. "Show him what they said."

Like a little girl who'd been told what to do, Bethany handed her phone to Cat. Bending down, Cat held my eyes as she reached toward me under the table.

I looked around. No adults were watching. I took the phone, held it low and looked at the screen.

WE R THRU WITH U! U r pushy & conceited thinking yr so hot! We always knew u r slobby & gross & NOW we know yr a SLUT. Every1 knows what u tried to do under stairs! Never sit with us again never talk 2 us. Never even look at us! U r B& from the table. Y not go drown yrself? Except oh wait no1 would care.

I bent low and handed back the phone. Bethany took it, in a daze. Then I saw shiny warmups marching our way.

The Amplifier strode up and held out her hand. "You know the drill," Ms. Bender said to me. "You can get it back after school. In the office."

"It's ... uh ... not mine."

"Whose?"

I looked at Bethany.

"Ms. DeMere?"

"Huh?"

"Did you text?"

"No! I ..."

Ms. Bender held out her hand. "Please."

Like a red-faced robot, Bethany laid her phone on Ms. Bender's palm.

"In the office, after school," the Amplifier said, and she spun around and left. As she walked past the Royalty table, those kids whispered, giggled and snorted. And suddenly Bethany was mad.

"They think they can just *do* this to me?" she said. "Who do they think they are?"

"Well, basically," I said, "they think they are who you thought you were."

She gave me the popular person's disdainful squint. To Cat she said, "Do you believe those people?"

"I think you're better off," Cat said. "They're just mean."

"Mean people do suck," I pointed out.

"Oh, this is not over," Bethany said to Cat. "I know some things about them."

"Oh yes?"

The end-of-lunch bell rang. Bethany stood up.

"I swear," she said to Cat. "This is *not* over."

9.

The Whatever Class

After lunch our Language Arts class got moved to the computer lab. As we shuffled downstairs, I wondered if Ms. Corbin had finally decided she needed help with us.

We were the Whatever Class. "I don't *understand* you people," our teacher would say. "All my *other* classes are going so well."

Ms. Corbin was new to Darkland this year, and she seemed like a decent person — small and bright-eyed, with tightly curling hair and a way of peering at you like she really wanted to figure you out. But when any teacher is new, kids will test her, and some kids have to act like nothing will make them care. The Whatever Class had a lot of those kids.

I'm not saying we were all, you know, problematic. We had Bethany, who had to get an A and would do the work and suck up as necessary. We had Nicole Pearl, a friend of Bethany's from the top table who had a similar approach, along with Jon Blanchette the golden boy, for whom everything, including grades, came easily.

We also had Turner, who didn't start the drama but always enjoyed it; he kept saying he was going to sneak in his camera and record the Whatever Class in action. We had Emily, always self-conscious and shy, who in this class was absolutely mortified. She tried to disappear into her seat, and pretty much succeeded.

35

Those were the semi-normal kids. We also had the guy who, the first weeks of school, would get up and just walk around. He'd go sharpen his pencils, do whatever. Another kid would tilt his desk onto its back legs and keep scraping them back and forth, to see if the grating sound could make the new teacher crack. It almost did.

We had Otis Greeno, who would pull his sweatshirt hood over his face and lay his head on his arms the whole class. We had a heavy boy, Richard Sunshine, I swear that was his name, who whenever he was asked anything would just shrug. We had a girl who threw a book at another girl one day (that second girl had to leave school later, 'cause she got pregnant). And we had Baked Corrigan.

In class, Baked (his real name was Baker) would have one favorite weird word — for a long time, it was "potato" — and that's all he would say. Whenever he was called on. "Potato." After a while a rumor went around that he was a weed dealer and was constantly stoned. That was when people started calling him Baked.

We also had Amanda Burrell, a hard-attitude girl who'd smack Ms. Corbin with the f-word out of nowhere. She got other kids swearing, too. Once when Amanda got sent to the office, she whirled back at the door and yelled at us, *"I'll see you in therapy!"*

Those first weeks, the Whatever Class made Ms. Corbin cry at least once a week. One day she would come in with a new, positive attitude, then the next she'd be all tense and irritable. Sometimes she'd plead with us: "I don't *understand* you. Why are you *doing* these things?"

I don't think anyone knew, not really. I would wonder, *Why am I in this class? Is this where I belong?* But in time I realized there was no sense to it. Like a lot of life I guess, the Whatever Class was an unfortunate random accident.

It did get better. Ms. Corbin kept asking people why they would do the things they did, and little by little we discovered that if we answered, she would listen. She found out Amanda liked to play guitar, so she invited her to bring it into class. She'd let Amanda practice a little before class started. It settled her down. We also learned a little bit about her — for one thing, we found out she was getting married this summer. If we asked at the beginning of class how the wedding stuff was going, sometimes she'd start talking and that would be good for ten minutes.

Ms. Corbin also got tougher about consequences. After a while the rest of us mostly settled down. But our class was still excitable and full of characters — and now, going into the computer lab, we were entering the lair of Mr. Dallas, the technology teacher, an excitable individual himself.

As we took seats at the two facing rows of terminals, Ms. Corbin and Mr. D had a whispered confab. We all logged on and started opening up drawing software, batting out Chat messages ...

"I want everyone off SchoolStream," Mr. D announced. "Off *everything*."

Groans.

"Open Word, please. You'll be brainstorming. I want blank screens."

"Oh god," groaned Amanda Burrell, unhappily separated from her guitar.

"Could we darken the lights, please," Mr. D said — "Turner? Thanks. Now let me ... um, I'm not sure I've got ... Turner, could we have the lights back on? Uh ... thanks. Okay! Turner ... lights?"

The lights went down and a screen on the wall lit up. It was connected to Mr. D's computer, and we heard him tapping. Then a web page came up. It had two rows of kids' photos — kids our age from different places, with names like Jatu and Miryam and Jaquinto. Miryam had a dark red cloth wrapped around her face.

The page heading said:

Children of War

"Oh no," said Amanda.

"This is a web documentary," Mr. Dallas said. "It's got photos and videos of these kids and their lives, letters and pages from their journals, mp3s of their favorite songs, and news footage of the fighting and violence in their homelands. Sometimes in their neighborhoods."

The room got quieter. "Where are they?" I said.

"Pick one," Mr. D said.

"Miryam," said Bethany.

A video started. The girl sat on a chair in a plain room, in a dark dress and that red cloth. You could only see her eyes.

"My home is in eastern Afghanistan, near the city of Jalalabad," she says in accented English, "but I live now with my aunt and uncle in Kabul. I was going to a school for girls in my town, but in the night the Taliban came and burned it.

"I would like to tell you about my life," she says. "Actually Miryam is not my name. I have to be very careful. If some people found out I did this, they might try to kill me, or hurt my family. But I want to tell you."

Mr. D clicked back to the main menu. Kids said, "Hey!"

"Choose another one," he said. "I want you to get a feel for this."

So we had him pull up videos, pictures, a letter and some music — from a boy in Baghdad, a girl in Mexico where they were fighting a drug war, and a brother and sister in Africa who'd escaped some gruesome conflict and were living in a refugee camp.

We could have gone on and on. Then Mr. D did something, and the screen went blank.

"The web documentary is a new form," he said. "We're seeing some projects by adults, artists, organizations, some college efforts, a few high schools. I haven't seen any so far by middle schoolers."

A dorkily excited quiver crept into his voice. "We," he said, "are going to be among the first."

Silence in the dark.

"Us?"

"Yes! You're going to create some of the first-ever middle-school web documentaries. They'll be creative multimedia — video, audio, text, PowerPoint, whatever. Today you're going to brainstorm topics and form teams."

"If your work makes the grade, we'll post it on TeacherTube," Ms. Corbin said.

"What's *Teacher*Tube?"

"It's like YouTube only it's not blocked in schools," she said. "We want you doing topics that relate to life in this school. What do you want people to know about? Some aspect of your lives here."

The silence now was kind of vibrating. We looked at each other in the dark. Creative multimedia was something we liked.

"What could you do?" Ms. Corbin asked.

"Music."

"Amanda? Yes?"

"Yeah — music. There's some really good musicians in this school. All kinds."

Next to me, Emily sat up straighter.

"We could record kids playing," Amanda said. "Some kids write songs; we could put up their lyrics. Maybe have a kid give a lesson in playing an instrument."

"I want to learn how to do GarageBand," said a round shape. Richard Sunshine.

"I could show you," Amanda said. "Make a video."

Now there was buzzing. Good buzzing. On the big screen in big blue letters, Mr. D typed:

MUSIC

Under that he typed:

videos — performance
audio files
lyrics
lessons
instruments
GarageBand

Then he said, "What else? We're brainstorming. What could you do?"

"Sports," said Jon Blanchette.

In blue letters: SPORTS

"We could film games," Jon said. "Put up schedules and scores, interview kids who played well. Have our own SportsCenter."

"Guess who'd be the anchor," somebody said.

"SportsCenter! Right now," Jon said, grinning because he *would* be the one.

Nicole Pearl suggested dating. Some guy said, "I want to do bathrooms."

Ms. Corbin said, politely, "James? Bathrooms?"

"Yeah. We could film with hidden cameras. In the girls' room. What are they *doing* in there?"

"You will never know," said a girl.

"Uh ... well ... we're brainstorming," Ms. Corbin said. But Mr. D didn't type that one in blue letters.

After a while the screen was covered and the lights went back up. Ms. Corbin said, "Now you'll pick your teams. Groups of four. Questions?

"Yeah. Why us?"

Ms. Corbin shrugged. "You're a different group, so we're giving you a different kind of chance," she said. "What have you got to say? We'll give you the tools. What will you do with them?"

"We want leaders — team leaders," Mr. D. said. "It's a big job. You'll have a team of four ..."

"And by next class, by Friday," Ms. Corbin interrupted, "I'm going to want each leader to have written up a brief proposal for your topic. You'll then have two weeks to do your project."

Massive groans. "Two *weeks?*"

She smiled. "Nothing inspires creativity like a deadline."

"I want leaders," Mr. D said. "Who?"

Amanda Burrell's hand went right up, which was amazing. She had never even volunteered to answer a question.

"I want to do music," she said.

Jon volunteered with sports, of course. So did Nicole with the dating idea — and Bethany. She hadn't even suggested a topic. I figured she just had to be a leader.

When we had five leaders — 20 kids, five teams — Mr. D said, "All right. Each leader choose one team member. Ms. DeMere, you go first."

"I want him," Bethany said, and she pointed at Turner. He looked startled, but I could tell she was already scheming. She needed a cameraman.

"All right," Mr. D said. "Amanda, music team?"

Amanda pointed to a skinny alternative kid, Gabriel. "I heard you play bass," she said.

"Yeah ..."

"Electric?"

"Yeah. "

"I want you in my band. I pick him," she said to Mr. D.

Nicole picked for dating, Jon picked for sports and so on. When it came back around to Bethany, Ms. Corbin said, "Each person picked in the last round makes the next selection for their team. Mr. White, who's your choice?"

"Emily," Turner said. "We'll need music."

Emily looked crushed. On a team with *Bethany*? But she said nothing, of course.

When it all came around again, Ms. Corbin said, gently now, "Emily? Can you pick your final team member?"

Emily turned to me. "Russell."

Bethany looked appalled. I said, "No *way!* Uh, not you, Em, I just ..."

"All right," said Mr. D. "Let's keep going."

And that's how Bethany DeMere found herself teamed with the Out Crowd.

10.
Cookie Dough

After school ended, I was drifting along wondering what to do. I would not be waiting for Cat. Not today. She'd probably wonder, too. *Where's Russell? He's always here.*

Not this time.

When I'd started for school in the morning, I stopped by the garage and opened the side door. Richie was gone. Beside the door, on the floor, the blankets and pillow were folded neatly. Strange. I'd never thought of Richie as being neat.

Right now everything seemed strange. Kids flowed by laughing and chattering. I kept stopping, looking at nothing, then wandering on.

"Yo — what planet are *you* on?"

"Oh. Hey."

Janelle shut her locker door and caught up. She said, "What you thinkin' so hard about?"

"Nothing."

"Oh right. If there was an edge to the earth you'd fall off. Now tell."

"Um ... well, this thing happened in Language Arts," I said. "It's a situation."

"Oh yeah? What?"

Janelle's head snapped back when I told her.

"You're on a project with *her?*"

"Yeah — and she's up to something," I said. "I think she wants to get back at the Royalties."

"For what?"

I told her how Bethany got shunned.

"Those girls did that?"

"Yeah — it was nasty. I saw it all."

Janelle smiled. "You saw it 'cause you were watching that Latino girl."

"She's Filipino. And I was not."

"Oh, right. And now you're all red for nothin'."

"They, um, told us to brainstorm topics for the project," I said quickly. "Kids were saying things like, like, music and, um, food and sports.

41

But Bethany didn't say a thing."

"Uh huh."

"Then when they asked for leaders her hand went right up."

"Russell."

"What?"

"You need to let it go."

"What?"

"You *need* to let it *go*."

"Um ... well ..."

Janelle swung herself in front of me and stopped. "That girl is never gonna give you what you want," she said. "She just doesn't like you that way. She oughta be proud to walk with you, talk with you. But she makes you hide it. Doesn't she?"

"Well ... I mean ..."

But I had never said anything about it. Not to anyone. "You don't understand," I said.

"Oh no? I see you watching that girl all the time when you think nobody else is lookin'. You think nobody sees that? You think *she* doesn't see that?"

I shrugged.

"She just don't *feel* it," Janelle said. "She could treat you like you deserve to be treated — and she *doesn't*."

That's not the whole situation, I thought — but you know what? It was true.

"I'm just speakin' as your friend," she said.

"I know. But listen — I also have to figure out about Bethany."

"Yeah." She grinned. "Good luck with that."

We were outside the library. I stopped.

"One thing I don't get," I said. "Why would Lauren do that to Bethany? In front of all their friends. What was the point?"

"That was the point," she said. "You don't get that?"

"I definitely don't get that."

"Okay, I'm gonna explain this once," Janelle said. "The White boy told everyone he was posting that video, right?"

"Right."

"And like I told you, the ice girl can't let that happen. But she also can't be seen to react."

"No. 'Cause that'd be stooping," I said.

"Right. But now that girl's got something on Bethany, because

Bethany did that little tug-of-war with the Powerade yesterday, then she yelled and made everybody notice. Bethany messed up, right? So Bethany owed her."

"Okay ..."

"So she sends the girl out to get that video. 'Go rub your little ... assets on that boy. Do whatever — just get that thing deleted.'"

"Oh, come on," I said. "Do girls really think guys are that easily played?"

Janelle just looked at me. I said, "What?"

"Do we need to go back over what we were just talking about? You and that girl?"

My face got hot. "But what Bethany tried with Turner and Cam didn't work!"

"No, because our boys are crazy. They are not *normal*. So what's the ice girl gonna do? She can't block YouTube, but she has to do something — and fast. People are watching."

"So she throws Bethany out of the group," I said. "In front of everyone."

"That's right. 'Cause the girl failed."

"I get that. And now ..."

"Now you're on the girl's *team*," Janelle said, and she grinned. "You got all that?"

"What I don't get is why girls have to make everything so incredibly complex."

"Everything *is* complex," Janelle said. "Just because boys have no clue, just because all you want to do is shoot hoops and punch each other, does not mean stuff is not goin' on."

I started into the library. "I think I'd rather be clueless," I said.

Janelle shrugged. "Can't help you with that. I'm just wonderin' what those girls are gonna do next."

"You think there's more?"

"Has to be," she said. "That video's still going up on YouTube."

"What do you think they'll do?"

"I have *no* idea."

Janelle turned and swayed off in her purple hoodie down the hall.

Now — how did this happen? — here I was standing in the library, where I had always waited for Cat.

I had no idea what I was doing. I slumped at a table. Then I remembered something, and sat up straight. It was the glint of light on a blade. Suddenly I knew what I had to do.

When she came out of the band room, I walked right up to her. No more pretending.

"Don't go with him," I said. "Not today."

"What?"

No one else was around. But I leaned close, and whispered. *"He's got a knife."*

She exhaled, and just looked at me.

"I saw it last night," I said. "I went to bring him a pillow, like you wanted, and I looked in the window and saw it."

She shook her head. "It's not what you think."

"Oh, so you know?"

"It's not what you think."

"What, it's not a knife?"

"Well ... it is, but ..."

"Does he bring it to school? You can get *expelled*."

"No! That's what you don't get. It's only ..."

With a burst of static, the PA broke in.

"Please excuse the interruption. The cookie dough is here. Thank you."

We just looked at each other. Random PA announcements erupted at Darkland all the time. I said, "Only what?"

"Huh?"

"You said, 'It's only.' Only what?"

She looked unsure. Didn't say anything. I said, "It's a *knife*."

"It's only at home."

"But he had it in my garage."

"He ... uses it," she said. "He needs it."

"Oh. Right. And you're *going* with him?"

"You don't understand! Oh, this is great," she said, red-faced now. She rummaged in her locker. "This is all I need — for *you* to start acting like this."

"Like what? Like this is something dangerous? Are you crazy?"

"No! Yes! *Maybe I am.*" She slammed the door. "Maybe everybody is making me crazy, because nobody understands and nobody wants to. It's all judging and jumping to conclusions, and the one person I thought I could trust was you. And now you're all like *'he's dangerous,'* and you don't know *anything!*"

"I do," I said. "I know him. You know I do."

"You don't! You have no idea what he has to deal with," she said. "That thing is a good thing, and you have no idea. You just want to judge him like everybody else."

"Well ..."

"You know what it's like for him? He goes into a store and the manager follows him. Up and down the aisles. He walks in the streets, and a police car shows up and cruises by. Just because he looks scruffy and he walks a lot, they think he's a bad person. And now *you?*"

"What? I was just ..."

"Jumping to conclusions. I *know.*"

"It ... was ... a knife."

"I know what it is, but you *don't!* Just don't come with me. *Don't!*" She grabbed her sax case and stalked away.

I followed her, hoping she'd look back, but she never did. In the main hall she shoved open the doors. As they swung closed, I came up and peered through the glass.

Outside it was a gloomy afternoon, and he was leaning against his tree. She walked down the steps and over to him like he had a tractor beam, pulling her in. He took her hand and they walked away. She never once looked back.

They were out of sight when a red Audi pulled up in front of the steps, and stopped. I stepped back from the door so I couldn't be seen. I didn't leave the building until the red car had gone.

As if this wasn't enough for one day, we had to have a team conference call with Bethany before dinner. She'd texted each of us, giving us the number and the time — five o'clock, calling into her dad's business phone because it could have four people on at once.

The whole thing annoyed me. This was how it went:

Bethany: "I have our theme."

Me: "*You* have our theme?"

Bethany: "Yes."

Turner: "What is it?"

Bethany: "Social Meanness."

Me: "Social *Meanness?*"

Bethany: "Yes."

Turner: "Okay ... How would we do that?"

45

Bethany (after a pause): "I would like ... interview kids."

Me: "You could interview yourself. 'I'm here with the *former* Meanness Queen ...'"

Bethany: "And you could film it. I mean Turner. We could interview popular kids about, like, what they've done to be in a certain group. To improve their popularity."

Me: "Look, this has to be something we agree on, and I don't agree with this. You just want to get back at people, or some other weird thing. Basically it's all about you."

Bethany: "Well, that's ridiculous. Anyway we have to have a theme. Anyone have a better idea?"

Silence.

Bethany: "I didn't think so."

Emily: "I ... I wish ..."

Me: "What? It's okay, Em. Just say it."

Emily: "Could we maybe do music too? I mean, I know it's not original 'cause Amanda's doing it, but ... well ... "

Bethany: "You *can* do the music. For Social Meanness. Like theme music."

Emily: "Okay."

Me: "Look, we need to agree on this. And I don't."

Bethany: "Hey, did you volunteer to be leader? No. And now we have a proposal due Friday, and I have to write it and *unless* there's a better idea, I am proposing Social Meanness."

Silence.

Me (sigh): "Whatever."

Bethany: "Okay. This'll be great. We'll have the *best* project."

Me: "Riiiiiiight."

11.

The Pull of the Stars

All day it had been gray and cloudy out, but that night the sky cleared.

I was sitting on my bed, looking out my window, when around nine o'clock there were suddenly stars. I had used up my two hours online. My mom was strict about this: after I'd been on for too long, she would materialize and emit loud threatening noises. I could stall by pretending not to hear, then by saying "Right, right, I'm getting off," then "I'm getting *off*, okay?" — but eventually I had to get off.

So I was stuck in my room. I could have been texting; I had my phone, and the messages were still coming in over Turner's film. The video, once he'd posted it, turned out to be fairly herky-jerky. After all, the camera had been duct-taped inside Turner's sweatshirt. But you could definitely see the prank unfold: the stain starting, then Bethany reaching for the bottle and Lauren jerking it toward herself. As they struggled you saw the blue zigzag widen on Lauren's sweater, or top or whatever you call it.

I had to agree with Janelle: it *was* a lame prank. Blue Powerade? Who cares? It was also, let's face it, kind of mean. But as I watched I couldn't help feeling some kind of, I don't know, pleasure or quiet satisfaction. Lauren and her friends doled out cruelty whenever and however they wanted to. They destroyed people's reputations just because they could. It wasn't so awful to watch something happen to one of them for a change.

But then, in the part where Ms. Bender came up and spoke to Lauren, I spotted something. I paused it and went back. Right there, when the Amplifier bent to talk to Lauren like a royal guard conferring with the queen, with the stain so obvious on Lauren's chest — right there I saw something in the Ice Queen's eyes. Something ... like fear.

Yes. Yes. The more I looked, drawing the Play icon back to review that bit again and again, the more I was sure. *She's petrified! She doesn't know what to do.*

It reminded me of something I had glimpsed once in Richie, that day

47

when I said he talked like the dad from hell and his rage came roaring up. After he'd smashed something of mine and settled down, what I saw in his eyes was like a deep, sad fear.

I wondered: *Is Lauren Paine scared, too? Lauren **Paine**?*

Just like with Richie, I figured I would never find out. But it got me thinking and wondering, and that's how I came to be sitting on my bed looking out when the sky cleared.

My cell buzzed three times. It was Elliot.

This is bad. This is really really bad!

I thumbed back: What?

The Scourge has launched an assault on a major Coalition city. I have to join the defense. We might be up all night!!

I didn't answer. I opened my window, breathed in the air and looked out. In the next yard, the top of a tall pine tree looked like a cone of darkness all surrounded by stars. I sat there, looking up at those stars.

I wanted to *be* somebody. It seemed like my friends, some of them at least, already knew who they were. Turner had his films, Emily had her music, even Elliot was happily battling dark forces in his alternate universe. Plus he had Emily. And whatever Cat felt about Richie, whatever that tractor beam was that pulled her out to him today, I had to face the truth. She didn't feel that way about me.

How do you get someone to feel that way about you? I had no clue, and I was stuck on that. I was stuck on the ground, in myself — stuck in a kid's bedroom, looking out at stars.

Kids our age feel everything. We feel the pull of everything. And we can't *be* kids any more; if you show that kind of open-hearted, flying energy you get laughed at by kids like Jon Blanchette, or brutalized by people like Lauren. But what can we be? We're not even in high school yet. We have to wait. At the same time we feel too much. Every day is like life and death: we're on the edge of everything, on the edge of our lives, and we don't even know who we are.

Turner was going to be somebody for sure. After tonight, in our school at least, he already was. Janelle ... well, she got to be Janelle, a big girl who said what was true and didn't care what anyone thought. In middle school, that's a *power*.

Myself, all I could see were shapes in the dark. And faraway stars.

My cell buzzed three times. I sighed, and shut the window. This text was from someone whose cell number I didn't recognize.

Every1 knows whos in love with Cat Aarons! That pathetic RussT person. He is totally obvious about it & she is SO out of his league. Every1 knows it but him. LOL he is SUCH a loser!

I just sat there. RussT was my screen name on SchoolStream, our school computer network. (My last name is Trainor.)

But ... what?

And *why*?

Another text came in, from Janelle.

This is getting passed around 2nite. Sorry thought you'd want 2 know.

Below that, she had forwarded the same "every1 knows" message.

It was just ... I felt shaky and naked, like the world was looking at me and laughing.

How many kids had seen this?

Every kid has forwarded a text. We do it all the time. Most of us keep an address book on our phone, and when you want to pass a message on because it's funny or weird or some spicy rumor — for whatever reason — you can choose up to ten people from your address book to send it to. A lot of times, kids will just select ten people at random. So in a few hours, even a few minutes, a message can go fanning out farther and farther. And farther.

I had no idea how many people had seen this — that was part of what felt so exposed. You can't see on your phone who started a forwarded message; you can't even tell for sure that it was forwarded. You can only read the number of the person who passed it to you.

I texted Janelle: Who sent this to you?

She wrote back: Just some kid forwarding. Its another dumb rumor. Don't worry 2 much.

I tried to tell myself that. It's just regular meanness. Kids won't care.

But Cat would. And would Richie find out? And why — this question kept going around in my head — *why* did everyone have to know?

49

This was something personal, just our friendship. Why couldn't it stay that way?

Don't worry 2 much.

How much is too much to worry?

12.
Every1 Knows

When I came up to school in the morning, it seemed like everyone outside was texting or showing other kids something on their phone. It felt like that dream where you're walking along a crowded hall and suddenly realize you're not wearing pants.

When the doors opened, I'd just come through when someone grabbed my elbow. It was Cam; he spun me around and walked me back out. I said, "What are you *doing?*" — but he kept me going, gripping my elbow hard, until we were around a corner and no one else could see.

Cam had on a brown soldier's t-shirt and desert-camouflage cargo pants. He yanked out his cell and flipped it open.

He said, "You see this? I got it a few minutes ago."

"What?"

He held his phone up, showing me the screen. His eyes were on fire.

OMG did u hear this?? Yesterday a kid went behind the stairs & he saw Turner White & that black kid who wears camo they were making out! With each other!! It was DISGUSTING!!! The kid got out of there but he saw it. Now every1 knows about the 2 lover boys they need to take it somewhere ELSE its GROSS!!

I said, "Holy crap."

"And this one," Cam said. He jabbed at the phone, then held it too close to my face:

Its true about the grade 8 gay boys! Ick ick ICK!! I know the kid who saw them he's totally freaked. Video kid and camo boy the Parkland homos its

50

Something hit me. *Every1 knows*. The text about me had said that, just that way. Just like both of these.

"This is bullshit," Cam said.

"Yeah."

"No, I mean it's *total* bullshit. It isn't *true*."

"Okay."

"It *isn't!*"

"I believe you, Cam," I said. "I'm your friend, okay?"

"Yeah, so who isn't? Whose number is this?" He held up his phone; you could see the number of the person who'd sent him the last text. He said, "You know it?"

"No."

Cam dialed the number. He put the phone on speaker. We heard a couple of buzzes, then:

"Hey, it's Jon. Cool that you called. Leave a message. Peace."

Cam said, "You know who that is, right? I can tell you know."

"How does Jon Blanchette have your cell number?"

"Blonde kid? Sports guy?"

"That's him."

"We were supposed to play ball one time." Cam shoved his phone in his pocket. "That's all I need to know."

"But wait," I said — "I don't think Jon wrote that text, it doesn't sound like him. He just forwarded ... hey wait, okay?"

"Yeah, no I don't *think* so."

And he was gone. He was around the corner and then — I ran to catch up — he was striding very fast through the front door.

Some people afterwards called it a fight, but it wasn't a fight. Just because you have great hair and a smooth coolness doesn't mean you can do anything but smile, at first mockingly but then a little confusedly, the way Jon did when Cam came up to him on a fast, bent-forward walk.

Jon was talking and laughing with a couple of other guys at their lockers. His smile changed into a puzzled look just before Cam punched him — *bam* — in the face.

The back of Jon's head smacked against the edge of his open locker door and he fell forward. As he came down, Cam kneed him — *wham* — in the side of the head.

Now Jon was half in the locker and half splayed on the floor, one leg bent back underneath him. Blood spurted from his nose and started puddling on the floor as he looked up with a hurt, perplexed expression. His friends backed away and stared. Jon curled around himself as the gleaming dark puddle widened beneath him on the floor.

It was silent. We heard only Jon's breathing, ragged and jerky, mingled with something like sobs.

Cam glared at Jon's friends. "Anybody got anything to say now?" he said. "Anyone got stories to tell *now?*"

Everyone stared. Cam turned and stalked down the hall, down the stairs, and out the big doors.

The hall was still silent. Then a girl started to scream. The first adults came running.

Jon was taken away in an ambulance. We heard his nose and jaw were both broken. (That turned out not to be true.)

We also heard — somebody heard it in the office — that Cam was arrested that morning, at his house.

PART TWO

Casualties

13.
In the Dust

At lunch we were in shock. Everyone was. People talked in low voices, if they talked at all. A lot of kids just sat and stared.

Bethany sat by herself at the end of the theatricals' table, apart from Cat and Allison and their friends. I didn't want to look at Cat — but when I saw Bethany's wavy blonde hair, something hit me. I remembered something. Then I was walking fast up the aisle.

Bethany looked up started when I set my tray down across from her. I said, "It was you. Wasn't it?"

Her head drew back; she gave the squint. "What?"

"You started that rumor. About those guys. It was *you*."

She glanced around, then leaned over and whispered, "What are you *talking* about?"

"You called them gay yesterday."

"I did not."

"Yes you did, I saw it on video. Under the stairs. You said it, then last night you made up this crap story about my friends being under the stairs with each other when they were really there goofing on you. You couldn't stand that, so you made up a story and started texting it around, and that's why that thing happened today. And now you're *lying* about it."

I sat back and glared at her. I mean, I was mad.

"That's ridiculous!" Bethany said. "Everyone knows who started that rumor."

That did it. "*You* started it," I said. "You wanted to get back with that group, so you did this. It's your fault what happened."

Tears came into Bethany's blue-green eyes. They were, of course, tears for herself. "That's so *mean*," she said.

"Oh yeah, *that's* mean." I stood up. "You know what? I'm going to make sure every single person in this school knows you started this. And I'm not doing any stupid project on some stupid team with you, either."

"Wait! Just wait." She glanced around, then pulled out her cell. "You can see my call log. I didn't send a single thing out yesterday."

"Did you get those texts?"

"I got 'em. A lot of people got 'em — but I didn't send anything. I'm not doing what those girls want any more."

"What do you mean, what those girls want?"

Bethany shrugged. "They create these rumors, then they expect everyone to forward them — and people do. Most kids are scared not to. Nobody wants to be the next target." She waved at her phone. "I mean, look what they can do."

She handed me her cell, right out in the open. "But I'm not scared of them," she said — "they already slimed me. So go ahead, start some new rumor. That's what *they* do. Or you can check my log. See if I sent anything."

I could tell she meant it. "Put that away before you lose it again," I said, pushing her phone back.

She took it. I sat back, and thought.

"Okay," I said, "so you go back to your so-called friends. Lauren says, 'Did you get the video erased? You did, right?'"

The way Bethany's eyes flickered, I knew this time I had it. So I kept going. "You said, 'I couldn't! I tried but ... I think they might be gay or something.'"

She stared at the table.

"Then *this* happened," I said.

Cat slid over. "What are you two talking about?"

I didn't answer. I couldn't look at Cat. Bethany wasn't looking at either of us.

Cat said, "Is this about what happened this morning? That was horrible. Isn't that boy your friend? The one who did that?"

"Yeah," I said.

"And that poor kid he did it to," she said to Bethany. "He's *your* friend."

Bethany shrugged. "I don't know who's my friend any more."

"Allison said there were some messages?" Cat said. "That started this?"

I said, "You didn't get any?"

"No. What happened?"

"Some things got forwarded around," Bethany said in a flat voice. "Last night and this morning."

"What about?"

"The ones today were about that boy Cam," Bethany said. "And ...

55

another guy. They were stupid."

"Stupid?"

I sighed. "People made up a rumor that they're gay."

Cat was puzzled. "Are they?"

"No!"

Bethany said, "The one last night was about you two."

Cat said, "Who two?"

"It was ... more about me," I said.

"What?" Cat was alarmed now. "Like what?"

Bethany thumbed her cell, then showed it under the table. Cat looked down, reading; then her eyes got big. She asked me, "Who *sent* this?" I shrugged, but now she was glaring. She got up and stalked out of the cafetorium.

Bethany was interested. "She seems mad," she said. "Like at you."

"Yeah, well I don't care what she thinks."

"Oh no?"

"No I don't, all right?"

And actually, I didn't. I knew Cat would now obsess about what this meant for her and her precious secret relationship. Meanwhile I had other things to worry about. One kid was hurt really bad, and my friend was under arrest.

"Well, anyway," Bethany said, "you can see why Lauren did that. It sure changed the subject."

"Meaning what?"

She looked around the cafetorium. "You think anyone is talking about a prank video any more?"

"Huh." I hated to admit it, but she had a point.

"I noticed something about those texts," I said.

"What?"

So I told her about *every1 knows.*

She said, "See? I'm telling you, those girls did all of this. They had to get revenge. And they did."

"But why me? I didn't have anything to do with that prank, or the film or anything."

"But you're the leader."

"What?"

"You're the leader," she said. "Of your ..." She made quote marks with her fingers: "Your 'group.'"

"Are you out of your mind?"

"You don't even *know* that? God." Bethany looked around, like she was searching for someone cooler to talk to. I got up and left.

Between afternoon classes I went searching for Janelle. She hadn't come to lunch for some reason. At her locker, she looked at me like she didn't want to be found. She said, "What?"

I let people flow by till it was just us.

"We should do something," I said.

She shut her locker door. "Like what?"

"I don't know," I said, because I didn't. "Is Cam ... is he in jail?"

"Is that what you want? To know if he's in jail?"

"No, Janelle, I just want to do something. I mean we're still his friends, right?"

For a few seconds she studied me. Then she said, "After school. I'm going where he lives."

"You are?"

"Yeah."

"Could I come?"

She eyed me. "You sure?"

"Yes. Can I?"

She nodded once. "All right."

So that's how after school Janelle was leading me to a trim little house, a block behind the downtown stores. It was a pale-yellow home with a white porch, and even the yard looked clean.

In the north where we live, by April the snow has mostly melted and people's yards and houses tend to look tired and dirty, especially the edges of their lawns by the sidewalk or the street. Whatever the snow has covered all winter, now it's exposed — cigarette butts, crushed Dunkin Donuts cups, McDonald's bags, unfreezing dog poop. It's all there.

But not here. Right to the street, this yard was neat.

The front door opened as we came up the steps. The dark-skinned lady who stood there was one of the skinniest adults I had ever seen — her short hair was cut tightly around her narrow face, and her bright eyes were intense. She stepped out on the porch and stood there like she was vibrating.

"Hello, Ms. Avery," Janelle said, going up the steps.

"Hello, Janelle." They hugged quickly. I stayed two steps down.

"This is my friend Russell," Janelle said. "He wanted to come."

The lady probed me with laser eyes. Then she held out her hand.

"I'm Denise Avery," she said. "I'm Cameron's aunt."

"Uh, hi. I'm Russell Trainor," I said, stepping up to shake. I felt a little nervous.

Ms. Avery held open the door. "I'm grateful you've come by," she said. "Both of you."

"I'm way sorry," I said, with typical dorkiness, as we went in. "About what happened."

She nodded, and closed the door.

All around the neat little living room were family pictures, mostly of older black people, everyone dressed up like for church. The only kid in the photos was Cam. There was little Cam in church clothes, somewhat bigger Cam in a soccer uniform, and Cam in pajamas under a Christmas tree with a pile of presents. Even when he was little, he was bright-eyed like his aunt.

Ms. Avery saw me looking. "You can tell it's him, can't you?" She smiled.

"Oh yeah."

"Cameron is my brother's son." She glanced at a framed photo, on the mantel above the fireplace. It was Cam with a big, stocky man in camouflage fatigues and dark beret.

I thought, *Huh!* — because now I got it. His dad was in the Army. That's why Cam wore camouflage. His name just happened to be Cameron.

In the picture with his dad, Cam looked softer-faced and younger. Also really proud. He wasn't wearing camouflage, then.

Janelle said, "Have you talked to him?"

She nodded. "I've been down there all afternoon. He'll be coming home soon."

I said, "Is his dad with him?"

They looked at each other. Ms. Avery shook her head once, then she took a deep breath. "He was doing *so well*," she said to Janelle.

It got quiet.

"It wasn't all his fault," I blurted. "There was a stupid rumor. It wasn't true or anything."

Ms. Avery's eyes locked on mine. "What kind of rumor?"

"I ..."

"He has a friend," Janelle said carefully. "A guy he makes movies with."

"Oh, he loves those movies! He's always talking about them," Ms.

58

Avery said. "He's very proud of that."

Janelle gave me a sharp look, like *Don't go there*.

"That boy has so much inside," Ms. Avery said. "Those videos gave him one little way, just the start of a way, to do something ... with all that." Her phone rang. "Excuse me," she said, and hurried out.

"Don't talk about that," Janelle said. "Not right now."

"Why not? Shouldn't they know?"

She shook her head. "It's too sensitive. Maybe later."

Then Ms. Avery came back. "They're ready to release him," she said. "I'm so grateful I can tell him you came by."

Janelle said, "Can we wait?"

"You know ... he's very upset right now. Tonight I think it's best for him to just be with family."

"Okay."

"The reverend is coming by, too."

"Good," Janelle said. "Good."

"Yes." Ms. Avery stood up. "Thank you, Janelle," she said. "I know this is difficult for you, too. It's been a long day."

She sighed, and glanced at the photo on the mantel.

"Such a long day," she said.

As Janelle and I walked up the street, I said, "So, are his parents down there with him?"

"Huh?"

"I just wondered — are his mom and dad there?"

She shook her head no. Then she was walking fast, gone up ahead.

"Hey," I said — "stop, okay?"

She stopped. I caught up. I said, "That's his dad in the picture, right? On the mantel."

She nodded.

"So ... is he like overseas? Fighting, or whatever?"

Suddenly Janelle was fierce. "Why do you have to ask so many questions? He's *got* family, all right?"

"Um ... yeah, okay."

"He *does*."

"Okay," I said. "All right."

She let out a long breath. "Damn," she said. "And you're the one wanted to come."

"What?"

"I mean, you're the one that wanted to be here, and I gotta be harsh with you." She looked down. "My bad."

I had never once heard Janelle apologize. For anything. "It's all right," I said.

"I don't know where his mom is, exactly," she said. "Before he moved here he was staying with his grandparents. But he got in some kind of fight there. He had to leave that school."

"Oh."

We stood on the edge of the street, by people's tossed-out butts and fast-food wrappers. I waited. There was more, I could feel it.

"His dad was in Iraq," she said — "a truck driver, in the Army. He did two tours, like two whole years over there. Then he came home, everything was cool. Him and Cam got to be together. But after a couple months they called him back."

"Back?"

"Yeah. You're done with your duty, but they say, 'You got to go back.'"

"Why?"

"'Cause they said so, I don't know! This time they sent him to Afghanistan. Couple weeks later, he's out driving a truck in a supply convoy in the desert. I guess it was really dusty, nobody could see. And the road blows up."

"The road?"

"Yeah. Someone buried a bomb. Went off underneath him. Just, boom. They couldn't even find pieces of him."

"Oh." It was like the air was going out of me.

"He was just gone in the dust," Janelle said. "They couldn't send a body home or anything."

"God."

"His mom was having some troubles, then after that happened, what I heard is she got pretty bad. His grandparents had to take him in, but ... he got mad. In school. He hurt somebody."

I sort of groaned. "Oh."

"When he came here, I know his aunt from church — she asked me to look after him. 'He's a good boy,' she said, 'he's just got so much to deal with.' That's what she kept saying. 'He's got so much.' I thought he was doing okay."

Janelle was still looking at the street.

"This wasn't all his fault," I said.

"Yeah, well. Not one other person will see it that way."

We stood there. Finally Janelle said, "What about the kid he hit? How's he?"

"Jon? I heard he's pretty hurt."

She shook her head. "This is bad. This is really bad."

I didn't know what to say. We started walking again.

After a bit I said, "So you go to church?"

"Yes, I go to church. You got a problem with that?"

"No! No. Does Cam go?"

"He didn't *want* to, but his aunt said he had to. No point arguing with her."

"I can see that. So when you said he's got family ..."

"I meant her."

"Huh."

"So," she said. "Now you see the situation."

14.

In the Cave

This was a moment for the Man Cave.

The Cave was a pine-paneled room in Elliot Gekewicz's basement. It had a bar that his granddad built for Elliot's dad, who never used it. The bar was still decorated with old metal beer signs that his grandpa put up; in another corner, a bumper-pool table was covered in dust like the bar. Elliot called these things "rec room archeology." You know, guy stuff from the past.

I liked it here.

The modern-day center of the cave was a 58-inch flat-screen TV, hung on the wall across from the bar, with a brown couch set in front of it. But when I got there, the TV was off. Elliot was sprawled on the couch, playing Dominion Quest on his laptop.

"Don't *ever* mess with me," he said into his headset mike. "Oh, you are so dead."

I stooped over to see two grotesque, body-armored mutations bashing each other on his screen. One of them went down.

"Whoa — you suck!" Elliot said. "Oh, hey. I didn't mean you."

I shrugged. He paused the screen. "Absolutely no way that guy defeats me again."

"What guy?"

He shrugged. "Some loser in Lithuania. You *distracted* me."

"Yeah, that's the problem," I said, flopping on the couch. "If only you didn't have distractions. Then you could focus."

"I'd be like Level 92. I would rule." He grinned. "I would *devastate.*"

"Everyone needs a dream," I said, staring at the ceiling.

"That is so true. Hey, want to play Zombie Massacre?"

"You know — that'd be good."

For a long time, until partway through seventh grade when he finally got friends — at first, me and Cat — Elliot was generally considered to be the weirdest kid in our grade. He was definitely the most picked-on. For years he'd been obsessed with dinosaurs; he got so deeply into them that prehistoric reptiles, for a while, were all he would ever talk about. He didn't like real life at all. And the way kids treated him back then, I couldn't really blame him.

Then, after he made some human friends, Elliot left his dinosaurs behind. Now he was totally into his Dominion Quest and video games. These weren't exactly reality, but they were at least more interactive.

He powered up the big screen and for an hour or so we shot, machine-gunned, machete-hacked and bazooka-blasted a plague of zombies that were attacking abandoned shopping malls and drizzly city streets. If we didn't kill enough of them quick enough, they ate our intestines. Then we had to restart.

It was just what I needed.

"Weird day," Elliot said as we thumbed our controls. "Watch it — that one!"

"Got him. Every day is weirder," I said. *Zam zam zam.*

"Yeah?"

"Seems like." I had a flame thrower. *FaWOOOM.*

"Nice," he said. "That text about you. From last night."

"Yeah?"

"Well, that sucked."

I thought, *Great. Even Elliot knows.*

"Tell me about it," I said.

"So what're you gonna do? Whoa!" *Ratta tatta tatta bam!*

"I have no idea," I said — "but I did notice something. Those messages about Cam and Turner ..."

"Yeah?"

"Well, they had one thing similar to the text about me."

Onslaughting zombies filled the screen. Elliot thumbed up more firepower. Undead body parts flew all over. He said, "What thing?"

"Well, each one said, 'Everyone knows.' With the 'one' written like a number, right?"

"Okay."

"So ..."

The zombies, undeterred — you can't deter zombies — were almost on us. I said, "Could we pause this? We're gonna die anyway."

"Nevah surrendah! But okay." Zombies, rearing up to gut us, froze in mid-rear.

"I figure the same people wrote all three messages," I said. "I talked to Bethany. She's sure it was the Royalty."

"Makes sense," Elliot said. "It's what they do."

"Yeah. Also, Bethany didn't mean to, but she basically gave Lauren the idea for the rumor about Turner and Cam."

"You mean like saying, 'Those guys didn't give me the video, they must be gay?'"

I looked at him. Elliot could surprise you.

"That's right," I said. "So those girls made that up, everyone passed it around, and bang."

"Yeah. Horrible."

"Bethany says they did it for revenge on Turner and Cam. And I mean, it was terrible what Cam did," I said — "but he's still our friend. Right?"

"Yes. Sure."

"So I just ... I feel like we should do something," I said. "I just have no idea what."

I flopped backward on the couch. I heard Elliot say, "It's like the Coalition resisting the Scourge."

"Elliot ..."

"No, it is! Listen, okay?"

Elliot still held the controller; the zombies were all frozen behind him. "In the game," he said, "the Coalition, that's my side, is a motley bunch of princeships and republics. Nobody wants to rule the world, we just want to be left in peace to do our thing. You know, have battles and quests, trade gold and gems. Build cities and everything."

"Oh. Right."

"But the Scourge is united, because its rulers have no scruples — they'll seek to destroy anyone who dares resist their dark authority. We know in the Coalition that if we don't band together, they'll overrun us. Then their power will be total."

"Okay ..."

"So don't you see it? In school," he said, "everyone knows those girls will spread a rumor about anyone. If you say, 'Hey, this is really warped,' you're putting yourself at risk. You could be next."

"Exactly."

"But that rumor today, and what happened — this is big time," Elliot said. "If something like this happens and nobody fights back, then that group has total power, and everyone knows it. Then Parkland is Darkland *all* the way."

"It's not a video game, Elliot."

"But the game is based in reality! If those girls can just decide who they want to destroy and everyone else is too scared to do anything, then what power don't they have? Nobody's safe. Everyone tries to protect themselves, even if that means you have to pass along a rumor you know is a lie."

I was starting to see it. "Okay ..."

"That's how this works," he said. "The forces of light become fragmented and ruled by fear, and then the dark swarm takes over. It happened under the Nazis. It's happening here."

"So ..."

"So we're the last line," Elliot said. "We have to band together."

"Us?"

"Yeah. If we push back, we'll get allies. That's how this works."

I lay there looking at him, this bright geeky gamer in his basement, a screen full of zombies frozen behind him. I said, "You know what, Elliot? Either you're totally lost in fantasy or you're the only one who really sees it."

"We could *do* it," he said. He grabbed his laptop and started tapping keys. "What do we know about the Scourge?"

"You mean the Royalty?"

"Yeah. Them."

"I don't know. Wait — Bethany said, 'I know some things.'"

"Things? More than one?"

"I'm pretty sure that's what she said."

"Can you find out more?"

"Well ... we have to work together tomorrow, in Language Arts," I said. "I'll see what I can get out of her."

Elliot nodded, and peered at his screen. "Welcome to the Coalition," he said. I wasn't sure if he was talking to me or his laptop.

That night, Cat called. "I am very upset," she said. "About that text."

"Okay ..."

"Don't I have enough problems right now? Don't I have enough stress?"

"Uh ... what?"

"Would you believe my yaya is *spying* on me?"

"I know."

"You *know?*"

"I saw her pull up on School Street yesterday," I said. "After you left

65

with Richie. After you turned your back on me."

"Why didn't you tell me?"

"I wasn't really in the mood."

"So? She was driving around town *looking* for us."

"Did she find you?"

"No, but ... I really don't need *this* happening right now," she said. "Did everyone see that text?"

"I don't know. Not everyone."

"But what if somebody says something to him? He'd be so mad at me. This is so unfair!"

I said, "It's unfair."

"Yes."

"Because it could cause problems for you."

"Yes!"

"Do you ... Cat, do you realize that message was actually aimed at me?"

"Huh?"

"It was meant to humiliate me," I said. "To make everyone laugh at me — not you. Has that even occurred to you?"

For a moment she was quiet. Then she said, "Oh, so this is something *else* I'm supposed to be stressed about? Do you realize how much *pressure* is on me right now? Why did you have to let this happen?"

There, that right there. That was it.

"You know what? I'm done with this," I said. "I'm done keeping your secrets. I did everything just the way you wanted — and now when this happens, it's all about you. I'm sorry, but I'm done."

"Russell ..."

"No, I mean it. Call somebody else from now on. Tell someone else about your pressures. You know what? Maybe tell your *boyfriend*."

I hung up.

All right, I probably could have thought of lots better things to say. In fact, I did. For hours that night, when I was lying on my bed staring up at the ceiling, then sitting at the window looking at the stars, then back on the bed seeing nothing but red numbers on the clock, I thought of many sharper, cleverer, more cutting things I could have said.

But I said what I said.

And I wasn't sorry.

15.
Life Particles

"Oh, look. It's the lovesick loser!"

That was Lauren Paine, first thing Friday. Her cluster of suckups and imitators rippled with soft laughter as Lauren struck a pose, hand on her hip. Serena Sunderland hung toward the back, watching. I started to go around them.

"You and your friends are the biggest losers in this school," said one of the suckups. "Everyone knows it."

I stopped. "Interesting you should say that," I said.

"Why? Didn't you know?"

The girl looked around for approval. In back, Serena's eyes danced.

"No, I mean how you said it."

Lauren shrugged. "She said you're losers. Duh."

"She said, '*Everyone knows.*'"

Serena's eyes focused on me sharply. I thought: *She's the smart one. Remember that.*

"Everyone does know," the suckup said, a little unsurely.

"First of all," I said, "you people *should* be ashamed of yourselves. What happened yesterday was your fault. And you have no idea what the real situation is."

The suckup acted surprised. "Oh, you mean the *lovers*," she said. The others laughed.

I said to Lauren, "You think you can put out anything you want and get away with it. But this time you won't. I promise you."

"Oh, really," she said. "And *you're* going to do something about it?"

I didn't have an instant comeback. "We'll see," I said, defensively. Lauren rolled her eyes, like this was too easy.

"See what you can do," said Serena behind her. Her voice was soft; but when she spoke, the followers parted.

Serena was very good-looking, with her full body and her long, flowing dark hair — but it was her eyes that caught you. They sort of danced, like she knew something. Her entourage laughed, then flowed past. Serena gave me a little half-smile. Then she went too.

Farther along, some guys by their lockers were talking about Jon

Blanchette.

"His face is pretty technicolored," said Big Chris Kuppel, a friend of Jon's who was also a friend of mine. "But he's gonna be okay."

"So his nose isn't broken? I heard his nose was broken."

"I heard it was his jaw," said another guy.

"Nah," said Chris. "He just has to rest a couple days."

"If you break your jaw, they wire it shut and you have to drink milkshakes for like eight weeks," said a boy with superior medical knowledge.

Someone said, "Cool."

"Idiot. You can't even chew."

"But milkshakes." When I walked away the guys were discussing what flavors they'd have.

A little cluster of girls stood with Allison Kukovna, Cat's red-headed friend in the theatricals. Allison caught my eye, then glanced dramatically at the girls. I slowed down to listen.

"This whole time he was *that dangerous*," one of them said.

"Why couldn't he stay where he belongs?" said another.

"In *gangsta land*," a girl whispered, and they all, except Allison, quickly laughed.

The girls drifted away. Allison said to me, "Can you believe that? 'Why couldn't he stay where he *belongs*?'"

I said, "Where's he supposed to belong?"

Allison gave a dramatic shrug. "Nobody says what they mean. But everyone knows."

"Why, because they said he's gay? He's not gay."

"Russell. When kids say *gangsta land*, they are not talking about gay people."

"Oh." Then I got it. "You mean 'cause he's black?"

She just shrugged, like wasn't it obvious?

"Well, that's ridiculous," I said. I wanted to say what had happened to Cam's dad, and his family — but I couldn't. Allison was a talker. She would tell everyone.

She said, "Have you seen Cat?"

"No."

"You're blushing!"

"I am not."

"You are! So ... you haven't seen her?"

"No!"

"Okay. Okay." She gave me an odd look as she turned to head for class. As she did the PA came on.

"Please excuse the interruption. We are working on the alarm system in the building. If an alarm should sound this afternoon, please do not evacuate. Repeat: if you hear an alarm, do not evacuate. Thank you."

At lunch, Bethany was doing her first interviews for the Language Arts project. It was not starting well.

She was wearing an *outfit* — a dark-blue pantsuit, I swear — and she was leading Turner around accosting people at tables. Turner wore his usual black and had the minicam. The Royals were watching and, you could tell, snarkily commenting. I found myself looking at Serena. She had this sort of aura. She didn't look back.

I watched Bethany zoom in on the skateboarder/alternative table. The boys there were scrawny, had unusual hair. Bethany said, "Um ... can I ask you guys some questions?"

They squinted at her. A couple of the guys nodded at Turner. He looked a lot like them, actually.

"What questions?" said a skinny kid named Isaac in a black-and-silver hoodie.

"Well ..." Bethany gave her hair a little shake, to make it ripple down her back. That had always been always one of her power moves, but now it just looked odd. She said, "Have you ever been the targets of social meanness?"

The guys looked at each other. One snorted. "Social *meanness?*"

She nodded, less surely. "Yes."

"That is a kind of awkward question," said Isaac. "I mean, coming from you."

Bethany sighed. "Well? Have you?"

"Oh, nooo."

"No?"

"Or maybe yes."

"What?"

"Well, I mean," Isaac said, looking around the table, "sometimes we can be targets of negative peer-group behaviors. But whose fault is that really? After all, we could dress and act more like the other children."

Earnestly, the guys murmured agreement. Bethany peered at Isaac clench-browed, like she wasn't sure if she was being mocked or what. Turner, filming, tried not to smile.

"Well," she said gamely, "why don't you?"

"It's hard to say," Isaac said. "We seem to have quirky priorities."

"Um ... could you give me an example?" Bethany asked.

Isaac said, "An example of having quirky priorities?"

"Yes. I mean ..."

A guy piped up who was wearing a purple t-shirt, with two eyes on it and a sort of question-mark nose. "I myself," he said, "am working on concentrating my subatomic life particles."

The others nodded, earnestly. Bethany said, "*What?*"

"It's an astral-body thing," he said. "You probably wouldn't understand."

Bethany started backing or stumbling away. Turner rolled his eyes at the guys, stopped filming and followed. I went and got into the food line.

Janelle was sitting alone at our table, and for maybe the first time all year she wasn't wearing her hoodie. I sat down across the table. "Where's your purple?"

She shrugged. "I was gettin' enough weird looks."

"Why? You've been wearing that thing all year."

Janelle poked at her food. "It's not the clothes," she said.

"Did you talk to Cam?"

"Yeah."

"How is he?"

She shrugged again. "How would you be?"

"I don't know." Honestly, I didn't.

"They're probably gonna expel him," she said.

"They are? How do you know?"

"Well, he's suspended 'until further notice.' They're gonna have some meeting. You *know* what they'll decide."

"I do?"

"If it was two white boys had a fight," she said, "people would just say, 'Oh, that's what guys do.' But this time they say, 'Oh, he's *dangerous.*'"

"I heard some of that," I said.

"Yeah."

"But, I mean, it was *scary*. What he did."

"Yes, and he should be in trouble and he is," she said. "But why'd it happen? You and I both know about that rumor — but nobody's gonna talk about that. They'll just say he's ghetto."

She sat back. "And they *will* kick him out," she said. "You watch."

"We can't let those girls get away with this," I said. "We're the only

70

ones who know the whole situation."

"It doesn't make any difference," Janelle said. "When something like this happens, you find out how people really see you."

Janelle prodded the taco she wasn't eating. She sighed. "You just wouldn't understand."

Walking toward Language Arts after lunch, I saw Big Chris's blonde flattop up ahead, and I had an idea.

I caught up to him. "Chris."

"Russ Ell. Wassup?"

"I need to tell you something."

Kids flowed around us as we stopped. He said, "What?"

I started to tell you, then wondered if I should. This was Cam's private business. *Yeah,* I thought — *but they might kick him out.*

"His dad," I said. "He got blown up."

"Whose dad?"

"Cam's. He was in the Army."

"Where?"

"Afghanistan."

"IED?"

"What?"

"Improvised explosive device," Chris said. "My uncle's over there. It's what everyone's scared of."

"It was a bomb. Buried in the road," I said. "He was in Iraq, then he got done and he went home. But they made him go to Afghanistan, and he got blown up."

Chris shook his head. "Jeez."

We started walking together. We had to get to class.

"The thing is, Cam's my friend," I said. "I know what he did was wrong, but ..."

"I know about those messages," Chris said. "I got 'em, but I didn't forward 'em. Not the one about you, either."

"Huh. Thanks. But ... Jon did."

Chris frowned. "Yeah. With those friends of his, it's not okay to say no."

The door to Ms. Corbin's class was coming up. In a rush I said, "That rumor about Cam was a total lie. I mean total. And now people are saying he did what he did 'cause he's black."

Chris's forehead wrinkled. "They are?"

"Yeah — and he might get expelled. But the thing is, no one else knows about his dad. And that's part of it, right? That and the lie — they're part of what happened."

Chris nodded. Then he said, "Russell, I gotta get to class."

I said, "What if Jon knew?"

"Jon?"

"Yeah. What if he knew about Cam? About what happened to his family?"

"Huh." Chris nodded. "Yeah, I get it. Let me talk to him, okay? I'll get back to you."

He hurried off down the hall.

"Thanks," I called after him.

Without turning around, Chris waved.

16.

Conferencing

In Language Arts, Amanda Burrell sat strumming her guitar in the front row. Mr. Dallas sat on a table to one side and watched as Ms. Corbin clapped her hands.

"All right! You'll be breaking into your teams today," she said. "We'd like you to brainstorm the kinds of multimedia you'll be generating for your web documentaries. What elements do you want — photos, video, audio, text? Who's going to get those pieces, and how?

"To give you an idea of the possibilities," she said, "Mr. Dallas has brought in some equipment from the computer lab."

Mr. D grinned lopsidedly and held up both hands. In one he had a Flip cam, in the other a blue plastic thing with a bulbous round handle. It looked like a little kid's atomic space blaster.

"This is an audio recorder," he said, holding up the blaster. "I know it looks a bit silly, but it is digital and it does work. You can capture interviews, conversations, background sound, whatever you need. Then plug the recorder into your USB port to download your audio. Of course the minicam works the same way, but with video too."

He waved a silver camera at us. "We've got five audio recorders and four Flips. You just need to sign them out with me, okay?"

Ms. Corbin clapped again. "All right, people, let's move desks! Make clusters of four."

As we made ours, Bethany sat down first. "Okay. I submitted our proposal."

"You mean your proposal," I said.

"I emailed it to Ms. Corbin last night."

"Did you even think of showing it to us?"

Bethany shrugged. "We're doing Social Meanness. We talked about it."

"*You* talked about it," I said.

"Dude," Turner said to me. "It's okay."

"Yeah, well, I got news for you," I said to Bethany. "Nobody is going to say anything real to you, on *camera*, about stuff like social meanness."

"Why not?"

"Because you're you, Bethany."

"What's that supposed to mean?"

"It means you treated other kids like they were lower life forms for a long time," I said. "People remember. They're not going to suddenly see you differently just because you put on some blue suit like you're on the nightly news."

Bethany looked down at her clothes, and actually blushed. Turner sat watching us. Emily was silent, as always.

Bethany looked up defiantly. "I can't believe you," she said.

"Oh no?" This was fine, I wanted to fight. There'd been too much stress floating around everywhere. Too much cruelty, too much crap.

"No — I can't," she said. "Look, I know you blame me for that rumor, and I feel really bad, okay? But kids say stuff like that all the time. Guys say, 'You are *such* a homo,' 'That is *so* gay,' and it doesn't lead to somebody nearly killing someone."

"Yeah, well this time this did," I said. "You *should* feel bad."

Then Emily said, "But I don't understand. What would be so wrong with being gay?"

We just looked at her. "If it was me," she said, looking really puzzled — "I mean if I was gay, wouldn't I still be the same person?"

"Of course you would. I totally agree with that," said Bethany, and she spun to me. "Why can't you be more open-minded?"

"Hah!" I laughed like a gunshot; people turned to look. Then I realized I didn't have an instant comeback. As I tried to think, Bethany got smug. That infuriated me — and then I did have a comeback.

"It's not about whether somebody is or isn't gay," I said — "it's about encouraging the haters. A lot of people, especially guys our age, do think being gay is something ... weird. I mean, let's face it. Maybe they don't understand it, maybe they're scared of it, I don't know. But those girls *know* that. And they used it."

Turner had been quiet. Now he said, "You should see how people are looking at me now, since that rumor. It's like a lot of kids don't want me to get too close, or something. It's ..." He looked down. "It's just weird."

"And you *did* that," I said to Bethany. "You gave those girls that idea."

"But I didn't mean to," she said. She had lost her advantage and she knew it. "Anyway we all got hurt by those girls." Her chin went up stubbornly. "You might not remember or care, but I got a text too. It was nasty."

I nodded. I did remember.

Bethany said, "The only one on this team who didn't get hurt was ... was ..."

"Emily," I said. "Her name is Emily."

"Right. Hi," Bethany said. Emily blushed, and looked down. I did, too. Her sneakers were orange today.

"So," Bethany said, "now we can show people what really happens in this school. You talk about haters — I agree with you. That's why I want to do Social Meanness."

"But you were *one* of them," I said. "This whole project is just some power game for you. All you want is to get back with that group."

"How do you know what I want? Look, Russell, I can't help it if I'm not your dream partner. I mean, everyone knows you'd rather be paired with someone *else* ..."

"All right," I said — "you know what? That's it." Heat flooded my face. "Just *forget* it." I yanked my desk away with a raw scrape.

I sat there staring at the wall. Was this how it had to be? Just because I had cared about somebody, maybe I used to care, did I have to be teased and taunted about it for the rest of my freaking life?

The tables around us were buzzing on their projects — but not ours. Then I heard Emily's voice.

"If you poke at someone where you know they're sensitive," she said, "we'll know we can't trust you. We'll know you're still one of them."

"What?" Bethany said. "What'd I say?"

Then Ms. Corbin called out, "Bethany? Russell? Are you conferencing?"

"No," I said.

"I'm *trying*," said Bethany.

"Well ... keep trying."

"Russell ... look," Bethany finally said. "I didn't mean anything about you — I just meant people know you and I haven't totally gotten along. Honestly. I'm ... I'm sorry, okay?"

I sat there. Another person I never thought I'd hear apologize.

"Come on, man," Turner said. "It's okay. Come on back."

I did feel kind of stupid, staring at the wall. Very slowly, I turned back around.

"Okay," Turner said — "so let's get busy, all right? We got a project to do."

Bethany nodded. She said, "Can I say something that really bothers me? Just by looking at Lauren and Serena and that group, I can tell they aren't even affected by what happened yesterday. I think they actually *liked* that their rumor could lead to something so horrible. Can you believe that?"

I nodded. "You said you knew some things about them," I said.

"I did?"

"Yeah. After you got that text, you said it."

"Well ... I know they find things out about people," she said. "I know they're *organized*. There's an inner circle, a really tight group. But they never let me into that."

"Come on," I said.

"No, it's true! I mean I tried, but ... they never really accepted me. Like they never totally trusted me."

"Imagine that," I said.

"For God's sake, Russell, I *said* I'm sorry."

"Yeah. But you're still you."

"And you're still *you*," she said. "Stubborn as a dog."

Now Bethany and I were staring each other down.

"Are dogs really stubborn?" Turner asked Emily.

"We have a golden retriever," she murmured. "He's so sweet."

The PA crackled.

"Please excuse the interruption.
The robots are in the basement after school. Thank you."

Nobody else seemed to hear it, but Turner started to sputter, then Bethany and I watched each other's face dissolve. There'd been so much pressure; now we were trying to stifle the laughter that to me felt like an earthquake, rumbling up from inside. Emily, confused, said, "What? They mean the Robotics Club. Elliot's in it."

That did it — we cracked up. I had no idea Bethany had a sense of humor, but now she was slumped in her chair, shaking and hiding her face in her hands. Turner's head was on his desk, and I was having a hard time breathing. I went, "*Hreek! Hreek!*"

People looked at us like we were crazy. Ms. Corbin said, "Russell? *Bethany?*"

Bethany nodded and waved a hand, like *I'm okay — just give me a second*. And slowly we pulled ourselves together. Bethany wiped her eyes, pushed her fingers through her famous hair.

"Okay," I said. "So seriously — I mean seriously, okay? I do want

76

to do something. But why should people tell us anything on camera? I watched those guys goof on you today."

"Yeah," Turner said — "and some people will do that, but so? If you just walk up and ask a question, you never know what you'll get. We can say, 'Are you aware of social meanness in this school? Do you think it's random, or is it organized?'"

"You would ask that?"

"Why not?"

"But I don't want to do it randomly," Bethany said — "I want to ask people to talk who've been targets of that group. People who know what they do. We can try, Russell. Why not try?"

I nodded. "Yeah. I want to."

"Okay! So," Bethany said to me and Emily. "What could you guys do?"

Emily said, "What if we collected the texts? It's what they use." She looked at Bethany. "Isn't it?"

"Well, sure," Bethany said. "That way, when other people start forwarding a rumor, nobody can trace it back to them. They're very clever."

I said, "Can I ask you something? Honestly?"

"All right."

"What did you mean, saying those girls never really trusted you?"

"Well, they're incredibly careful about who they let into their inner group. That thing they asked me to do, with you," she said to Turner — "I think that was a test. If I ... did something with you to get that video erased, then they'd have this *hold* over me — because I would have done something I wouldn't want anyone to know about.

"But if I couldn't do it," she said, "then they'd have a reason to throw me out. Which they did."

"But," I said, "why would they want to throw you out?"

"I think I might have been ... I don't know ... not needy enough," she said. "They like to find your weakness. Then you're more likely to go along with ... whatever. You know."

"Which brings us back to the texts," Turner said. "What if you put something on KidNet? *'We're collecting nasty text messages. If you've ever received one ...'*"

"Or sent one," Bethany said. "Ask people to send them to us."

"But even if they did," I said, "what would that prove?"

Turner shrugged. "If you're doing multimedia, you want to collect all the stuff you can. Then you figure out how to put it all together. Maybe we can make people look at what really happens."

I remembered Janelle saying, "You and I both know about that rumor, but nobody's gonna talk about that."

Emily was nodding at me. "Let's do it," she said.

"Okay," I said. "Let's try."

17.

In the Kitchen

That Friday afternoon, things started getting interesting.

Also strange.

First, I was definitely, absolutely no longer waiting for Cat after school. Those days were done.

Second, Bethany — I had to give her credit — was doing what she said she would. After the last class was over and the end-of-school rush had crowded out through the big doors, I saw her in the hall having an earnest conversation with some other eighth-grade girls.

Turner was standing to one side, watching. I joined him.

"What's she up to?"

He shrugged. "Talking with other kids who've been targets."

"Of the rumor machine?"

"Uh huh."

I heard one of the girls say, "They did that?"

Folding her arms, a second girl nodded. "*Oh* yeah."

I said, "How come you're not filming?"

"She says not yet. She has to develop her sources."

Bethany turned and gave Turner a look, like *Why are you still here?*

"We should go," he said to me.

We started moving down the hall. I said, "What does she mean, develop sources?"

"Well, people have to feel you're on their side, right? Before they'll talk on camera. I think she figured that out after Emily said that thing about people needing to be able to trust her."

That made me think of something. "What'd you do with the cell-phone video you and Cam made? The one under the stairs?"

"I still have it. She knows I do."

"Has she asked about it?"

"Nope."

"Hmm ... So if she's two-faced — if she uses us ..."

"You know," Turner said, "I don't think she wants to. I've been talking to her, and I mean, it's still pretty much about her, but I don't think she's the same exact person she was. Being bounced from that group, then seeing what happened with that rumor ... I think it kind of woke her up."

"Huh."

"I mean, look what she's doing now," he said. "Before, she'd have tried to manipulate or intimidate people. Now she's building trust. Or trying to." He glanced back at her. "She's good on camera, too."

"Oh, she's cute."

"Well ... she films well."

"So you're working with her now," I said. "But what about Cam?"

He winced. "I feel bad — I haven't called him or anything. Do you know if he's okay?"

"Not really," I said. "Janelle thinks they're gonna expel him."

"Oh, man." Turner looked down. "That would be *terrible*."

I could hear the band practicing; I had to get out of there. I said so long to Turner and pushed open the outside doors.

Out here it was softly warm. I glanced across the street. Richie wasn't there, not yet, but the red Audi was parked a little ways up the road. The second I saw it, Cecelia popped out. She was coming my way. There was no escape.

I walked down the steps. "Hi."

"Hello Russell, how are you?"

"I'm okay."

"Where is my girl? Is she coming?"

I shrugged. "I think she has band."

She looked past me, scanning. "She really does," I said.

"Yes. I am looking for him."

"Um ... who?"

"I think he comes here, and they go somewhere," she said. "I don't think he is in this school. Also I think you know who he is."

She held my eyes. *The trouble with females,* I thought, *is they're too damn smart.*

"Catalina comes from a good family — and they are concerned for her," CC said. "It is so easy for a girl this age to make a terrible mistake and ruin her future. Please tell me what is happening."

I looked at CC. She was right; Cat could really mess up her life. I didn't want that. I only had to tell CC what I knew. Maybe she could stop it, then.

But I couldn't. I just couldn't. Instead I said, "If she knows you're waiting, if she sees you out here, you won't see a thing."

"So tell me. You are her true friend, I know it. *Tell* me."

I just looked at her. I shook my head. This was Cat's drama. I was done with it.

"I'm sorry," I said. I felt her eyes on me as I walked away.

It was cool in the Man Cave. Emily said hi when I came down, but Elliot didn't look up from his laptop.

"No public groups," he said. "It's all friends-only."

"What is?"

"Lauren's Facebook. Serena's too," he said. "Same with everybody who sits with them."

"What are you trying to find out?"

"If they do stuff through Facebook, they could have a group there," he said. "It might be where they hatch their plots. Or something."

I opened my laptop. My Facebook page had a friend request. I tapped on that icon and this came up:

Serena Sunderland has sent you a friend request.

I said, "Whoa." The buttons said "Confirm" and "Not Now," like this was something normal.

Elliot and Emily came around, to look. "Well, well," he said — "the Scourge reaches out."

"Maybe she *likes* you," Emily said.

Elliot and I looked at each other, then shook our heads. That wasn't it.

"Just accept," Elliot said. "We're in the game." So I did.

While we were digesting this, I got a text from Big Chris.

What u doin?

At Elliot's, I wrote back. Wassup?

Come 2 Jons? He wants talk 2 u. House not far 14 Laughlin. Nok on side door. OK?

Elliot was puzzled. "How come Jon Blanchette wants to talk to you? Isn't he hurt?"

"Not that bad. Listen, I better go."

I was at the stairs when Emily said, "Just ... be a little careful. Jon is Lauren's boyfriend, you know."

Elliot and I both said, "He *is?*" Em nodded.

Elliot said to me, "See? There are many alliances."

You might assume that an ultra-cool kid would live in some futuristic dwelling that hovers above the ground, maybe rotates — but Jon's house was regular. A little kid's bike lay sprawled by the driveway. I knocked on the side door. It was an ordinary metal storm door, with a battered dent where kids, going out, would kick it open.

Big Chris answered. He said, "Hey."

In the dim kitchen, Jon sat at a narrow table. He didn't look at me. His mouth was a little puffy and his face was pale. I guess the bruising had faded — he wasn't totally back to normal, but he didn't look that bad. On the table before him was a large plastic cup with a tiger family on top.

It was a mother tiger, with two cubs — I looked at this because the situation felt awkward — in a green plastic nest on top of the cup. A straw poked up through the mother tiger's head.

"Want some juice?" Chris said, "There's apple or cranberry. Or mixed."

"He could have some of my Sprite," Jon said. "It's okay."

It was funny, how Jon said that to Chris — like I was in another room. But it wasn't like he was mad, or snobby. He was just ... different.

Chris was standing at the fridge, waiting.

"Um, cranberry would be fine," I said. "Or maybe cranberry mixed with Sprite?"

"That doesn't sound bad," Chris said.

"I could try that too," said Jon's voice.

I turned. He was looking at me.

"I never thought of that," he said.

"It might be good."

"Yeah."

81

Chris filled a glass from the Sprite bottle and a juice carton and gave it to me, red and bubbly. Then he filled Jon's tiger thing.

"Nice cup," I said to him.

"Well, it was easier to drink from when my mouth was swole up."

"So you're, like ... better?"

He shrugged. It was like he was only partly there.

Chris sat down. "Tell what you know," he said to me.

I took a breath. Then I told about visiting Cam's aunt's house, about the picture of Cam and his dad. I told how Cam's dad came home to his family, but then they made him go to Afghanistan and he got blown to pieces in the dust. I told how there was nothing left of him to ship home, and how his mom got messed up from that. I said how, since then, Cam had been going from home to home.

When I got done, I just sat there. I sipped my drink. Nobody said anything. I looked over and saw that tears were flowing down Jon's face.

"It's okay," Chris said to him — but Jon stood up, shoved a door open and left the kitchen. The door swung closed behind him. He left his tiger cup behind.

"He's been having a rough time. With emotions and stuff," Chris said, like to explain. "Since the thing happened. I'll be back, okay?"

"Yeah, okay."

Then I was alone in Jon's kitchen. On the fridge were magnets and photos and scraps of paper. A round white magnet had a clip that said, "TO DO," but nothing was clipped to it. I looked at Jon's cup. Below the tiger family it said "San Diego Zoo's Wild Animal Park."

The door creaked open and Chris came back. He sat down.

I said, "Is he okay?"

"Yeah." He shrugged. "He ... kind of wants you to go now. I think he's embarrassed. But, like, he heard you. He heard what you said."

I nodded. Then Chris said, "Are people really saying this happened because that kid's black?"

"Some people anyway. They say he's ghetto."

"Jeez. But nobody else knows what happened to his dad, right?"

"No. Just us. And one other kid."

Chris shook his head. With his flattop haircut and his jock friends, you could assume a lot about Chris — but I knew one thing. He was a good guy.

"I hate this crap," he said. "Rumors and gossip and crap. I hate what it does to people."

"Yeah."

He slapped the table. "We should bring these guys together."

"What guys?"

"Our guys. Jon and Cam."

I gaped at him. "What?"

"I'm *serious*, man. Look, Jon heard what you said. He's not a bad guy, honestly. He just happens to have, you know, natural gifts."

"Okay."

"But, see," Chris said, "because he's like that, people *look* to him. They listen to him. If we could get him and your guy together, get them to work this out or whatever — I mean, what if Jon comes back to school and he's okay with Cam? What if he tells people, 'Look, this guy's been through some stuff, he lost his dad in the service of this country — we need to cut him a break, okay?' If he said that, people would *hear* it."

"Especially since Jon was the one who got hit," I said.

"Absolutely. So we need to do that."

"Okay. How?"

He sagged. "Oh. Huh." Then he popped back up. "Hoops!"

"Um ... hoops?"

"Yes! Your boy plays," Chris said. "I saw him at the court on School Street once, working all by himself. He's got skills. If he'd come here sooner he could have played on the team with Jon and me."

"Huh. I had no clue." The truth was, I really didn't know Cam that well.

"So what if tomorrow," Chris said, "you tell your guy Jon wants to shoot some hoops with him at the park? Just, you know, to make things cool."

"What if he won't come?"

"Tell him it's important. Tell him Jon gets it, and he wants things to be cool. I'll tell Jon he needs to get out of the house and we're going to go shoot baskets. If you guys happen to show up at the same time, I tell Jon, 'Hey man, stick around. Nothing bad's gonna happen.'"

"But how do we know that? It could get ugly."

"We don't let it," Chris said. "You and me. We don't."

I thought about it. "Okay," I said. "What time?"

"We'll text about that," he said. Then he glanced upstairs. "You better get going."

Well, I thought as I headed home, *It's a start. If it works.*

18.
Social Pressures

Bethany resumed annoying me almost immediately. Before I even got home, I had a text from her.

Evybody needs to get on MidStream rite away!!! HUGE disaster!!!!

MidStream was our school network's version of Instant Messaging. You could have several people in the same conversation, but we were limited to these lame screen names by Mr. Dallas.

I got home and obediently signed on.

RUSST: what?
BDEMURE: Tell him. I can't stand it.
TURNVID: we need to change our idea.
BDEMURE: They rejected me! Can you BELIEVE this??
RUSST: huh?
TURNVID: we just have to change the topic.
BDEMURE: They rejected me! Them TOO!
RUSST: what are you talking about?
TURNVID: they say we can't do social meanness. "It would show Parkland
    School in a negative light."
RUSST: who said?
TURNVID: corbin and mr d
BDEMURE: I'm SO TIRED of people rejecting me!!
RUSST: maybe if we'd thought up the topic as a team in the first place ...
BDEMURE: Oh, that's great. Second-guess me NOW.
RUSST: hey, I been second-guessing you all along.
BDEMURE: Yes it's SO helpful.
TURNVID: will you two please?
EMMUSIK: But isn't it only that word meanness they don't like?
TURNVID: I think so
BDEMURE: We could give it a new title. Social PRESSURES
TURNVID: that could work

BDEMURE: Excellent. Thanks Emily!
RUSST: hey you learned her name nice
BDEMURE: Did you two send out the request for nasty messages?
RUSST: not yet been kind of busy
BDEMURE: Do it tonight! Important!!
RUSST: yes our leader
BDEMURE: I mean please send it. OK?

But first, I called Janelle. I took a breath and told her my and Chris's idea. I expected to hear, "That is the *stupidest* ... This is his *private* ...."

But she said, "You guys want to do that?"

"Yeah," I said. "And we'd be there to make sure nothing, you know, bad happens. I mean, Chris is a big guy. And he's okay. I know him."

"Really?"

"Yes. Really."

"Well ... okay," she said — "but Ms. Avery's not gonna let him go anywhere unless she says he can. We're gonna have to be completely straight with her."

"We are, aren't we."

"Oh yes. I'll talk to her. When do you want to do this?"

"Tomorrow morning."

"How early?"

"Not that early," I said. "We're guys."

"Yeah." She sighed. "I know. I'll talk to her."

I was plugged in before dinner when my cell buzzed three times. It was Cat.

We were downtown and CC almost saw us. She was driving around again — we had to hide in an ALLEY. This is NOT good.

Yeah, well that was her problem. I went back to ohnoyoufail's new YouTube video.

Elliot called. "If they do have a group on Facebook, maybe that's where they cook stuff up," he said. "Like, 'Now we're going to trash this person. Here's what you need to do.'"

"Could be."

"There are lots of private groups on Facebook," he said. "You can only pull one up if you've been invited to join. Even if you're in the group, its name won't show on your list of groups. You have to know the name, and type it in."

"So, basically, we can't find out anything," I said.

"Em said you're supposed to put out a message, asking for nasty texts," he said. "Maybe that'll bring in a clue."

"What kind of clue?"

"Basically," Elliot said, "I have no idea."

"It's really great to have you on our side."

"Oh, I know."

Friday evening before dinner, I broadcast this message, as a School-Stream email to the whole eighth grade:

Hey Darklanders,

There's a lot of nasty texting going on. Rumors spread fast because people get pressured to pass them along. I'm part of a project on Social Pressures at our school. We want to show what happens.

So I'm asking you:

1. Have you ever received what you would call a nasty or mean or evil text message? Do you still have it? If so, send it to me, RussT on KidNet.

2. Have you ever been part of forwarding an ugly rumor by text? If so, what was the rumor? Were you pressured to forward it? How?

After I sent the message I watched this amazing video. Somebody filmed a mountain biker from behind as he went straight downhill in this incredibly steep slum in Rio de Janeiro in Brazil. He shot down ramps they'd built and bumped along old crumbling stairs, straight down from narrow alleys. The guy was in a Red Bull racing suit, and slum kids in torn t-shirts watched him plunge down those stairs. It was *crazy*.

I paused the video and flicked to Facebook, to see what was happening. Turner was watching some movie. Somebody I didn't think I knew had beaten his own top score in Crystal Golf Solitaire. Someone I was sure I didn't know was going it all alone and was scared; there was a quiz somebody wanted me to take to find out which swear word best described my personality ... sigh ... and suddenly a Chat window popped up in the lower right and there was the name Serena Sunderland. The tiny photo by the name showed her looking sultry against a dark background.

Hiiii. What u doing?

I was starting to feel like my life was being lived by somebody else. I wrote back: messing around before dinner. why?

Serena
Just wondering. U don't have too many fb friends, y not?

Russell
I'm not that into it

Serena
R u happy to have 1 more?

Russell
What?

Serena
R u happy to have me?

Russell
Whyd you want to friend me?

Serena
Maybe I want to get to know u.

Russell
yeah. maybe

Serena
I saw that email u sent every1. Think any1 will give u anything?

Russell
what do you think?

Serena
I guess u will find out. Y isn't Cat Aarons on your friends list?

Russell
why you want to know that?

Serena
FB is all about friends. I have lots. Y isn't she on your list?

Russell
Cat's not into this. She studies mostly

Serena
That's not what I heard

I thought, *What?* I closed the Chat window. If I could have slammed it shut I would have.

My cell buzzed three times. It was Cat. She was the only person I knew who punctuated her messages perfectly, like she was being graded:

Today he got SO mad at me about CC, like it was my fault she was looking for us! I promised him I haven't told her anything but he doesn't believe me. He said I am two-faced, and he doesn't know what I am doing when he's not with me. He said these things!

Russell, he is scaring me. When he gets angry it's like another person comes out. I try so hard to be who he wants but he always finds a reason to get mad! And he says it's MY fault when he gets upset. I don't think I can please him any more and I don't know what to do!!

Are you there?

This one was harder to ignore — but it was always about Richie, with her. I was just the friend she complained to about him.

Well, I didn't care any more. I went back to Youtube, hit Play, and went back to bumping down the stairs of a hillside slum in Brazil.

19.
How It's Done

"How can you be sure?"

"I am sure," I said.

"That doesn't answer my question," said Ms. Avery.

"Doesn't matter," Cam said from the couch.

"Of course it matters," Ms. Avery said.

Janelle and I were sitting on chairs at her dining room table. The dining and living rooms were really the same space in this little house, separated by the red couch Cam was lying on. The back of the couch faced us, and his feet stuck out from the end. Ms. Avery had brought us lemonade, then she started in grilling me.

"How can you be sure this isn't a setup?"

"Because Chris is my friend and I know him," I said. "We texted this morning. He said Jon and him'll be there around eleven, and we should just come."

"This friend of yours," Ms. Avery said, looking into my eyes. "He promises no fighting."

"Yeah. I mean yes. And he's a good guy. He got me to go to Jon's house yesterday after school, to tell Jon what happened to ..."

Now both females were staring at me. My mouth was open but nothing was coming out.

Ms. Avery said, slowly, "What happened to whom?"

"Well ... um ..." I took a breath. "Janelle told me about Cam's dad. I'm really, really sorry," I said to the back of the couch. Cam's feet didn't move.

"People were starting to say stuff at school," I said to his aunt, "like there's something wrong with Cam, or that he did that because he's ... I mean ..."

"Because he's black," Ms. Avery said. "Just say it."

"But people don't know the truth," I said. "They don't know the whole story."

I looked at Janelle and then Ms. Avery. I felt *so* awkward. I said, "So ... I mean, when people don't know the whole thing, they sort of fill in the blanks, you know?"

Ms. Avery nodded. "Yes," she said. "I do know."

"So I talked to my friend Chris and I sort of blurted out about Cam's dad. Then Chris said I should come over to Jon's after school, and, um, maybe tell him, too."

This didn't sound so good coming out, but I just stumbled on. "We weren't trying to invade you guys' privacy or anything — we just felt like if Jon knew, maybe him and Cam could work it out. If we could get them together with a basketball, I mean, maybe ..."

Cam sat up. "So, what, he thinks he can play?"

"Well ... he was top scorer this year, and the team was pretty good. I guess he's decent."

Cam heaved himself off the couch and walked down the hall. A few seconds later he came back, a ball under his arm and a pair of black Nike mid-rises dangling from his hand.

"Let's go see how good," he said.

I wanted to say, "We weren't talking about a *game*, just shooting hoops" — but Ms. Avery had fixed her laser look on Cam.

"You want to do this," she said. He shrugged. She crossed her arms. "If there is any trouble," she said — "any trouble at *all* — you understand what that would mean for you. Yes?"

He nodded.

"Let me hear you say it," she said.

"Yes ma'am. I know."

"If there's any problem, if you get there and things are not what you expect in any way, I want a call from you *immediately*."

"I know."

"Do you promise?"

"I do."

"*What* are you promising?"

"I'm just goin' to play — nothing else. If they've got something else in mind, I don't get into it. I call."

"Right away."

"Right away."

"All right." She studied him some more. Then she smiled. "Go show that young man how it's done. And, Cameron."

"Yes?"

"Do it right."

Cam put his hand on the door, then turned back to me.

"You comin'?"

I was going down their steps when my cell buzzed three times. It was Elliot.

Where you?
Going to Schl St court
Cam going?
Yes
Jon 2?
So I hear

It was sunny out, but it had rained last night and there were puddles on the basketball court. Chris and Jon were kicking at them, trying to push the water away, when Chris looked up and spotted us coming up the street. He said something to Jon, who looked up and stopped kicking puddles.

Cam walked a little faster. Jon watched us come with a blank expression. I wondered if it was okay, what we were doing. Was Jon ready for something like this, physically? Emotionally?

I stopped at the edge of the court as Cam strode onto it. He held the ball clamped to his side, Nikes hanging from his fingers. With the other hand he scooped out the ball and pushed down a pass that bounced up into Jon's hands. Jon, of course, caught it.

"Game to eleven?" Cam said. "Win by two?"

Jon looked unsure. He glanced at me, then at Chris. "What," he said, "two on two?"

Cam shook his head. "Just you and me. You cool with that?"

For a second, Jon didn't answer. He looked at the ball in his hands. Then he bounce-passed it to Cam.

"Okay," he said. "But you're gonna need your good shoes."

At first Jon played a little shaky. Cam faked just by glancing up and then he was past him, laying it in. Beside me, Chris raised an eyebrow.

When Jon put up a weak shot and it fell short, Cam snatched the ball, dribbled up top, and this time worked his way into the lane, backing Jon down; then he turned to pop off a jumper that swished. Mixing his game up like that to keep Jon off balance — driving for a running hook in the lane, then pulling up for a jump shot — Cam got up 5-1 and I thought this wouldn't be close, but then Jon came to life. It seemed like he got some balance, and Jon with his balance was nice to watch.

I liked basketball. I wasn't so good at it but I watched a lot of games, and now it was like I heard an announcer's voice in my head. Cam was laying back on defense, but Jon lifted up a shot from outside and it slipped in — so the next time Jon got it, Cam covered him tighter. Jon got him going down the side of the lane, then he whirled back, rose in the air, raised the ball and spun it from his fingers. It feathered through the net.

When Cam tried to muscle in close on his possession, Jon ducked under and knocked the ball free. He dribbled up top, took Cam down to the baseline with long, high-dribbling strides, then rose up smoothly with a jumper that went in. When Cam missed a long shot he shouldn't have taken — he was rushing a little, now — Jon drove him back and again lifted up a smooth jumper that slipped through the net.

Cam had the ball and Jon was crouching to defend, both guys breathing hard, when a silver SUV came up School Street and pulled to a stop. The front passenger door opened and Bethany got out.

She was wearing a scoop-neck blue top that showed off her cascading hair. The back door opened and Turner unfolded himself. He had his black minicam in his hand. I thought, *What in the world?*

The guys ignored them. It was 5-4 Cam now, and when Cam tried to force up a close shot Jon flicked it away, then beat him to the loose ball. Bethany said, "Hey guys?" But Jon swooped into the lane, rocking Cam back and forth. Now he was rising up, getting off a tough shot with Cam in close and straining as Bethany called out, louder, "*Guys?*"

The ball clanked off. Cam grabbed it.

"Hey." Jon held his hands out for the ball. "No shot. Distraction."

"Yeah, right," Cam said, dribbling.

Suddenly there was tension. Jon stood his ground, holding his hands out for the ball. Cam stopped dribbling, made a disgusted face. He shook his head ... but he bounced it to him. No trouble. He had promised.

"Hel ... *lo?*"

Both heads jerked around to Bethany. "What?" said Jon.

"Do you guys mind if we film this?"

"For what?"

"For the Morning News."

Cam said, "Say what?"

We have a morning news show that's new this year. Kids do it; it goes on a SchoolStream video feed to all the homerooms. I thought, *Oh god.*

Jon said, "Why would you want to film a playground game for the Morning News?"

"Then I want to interview you guys after," Bethany said. "Because of, you know. What you're doing."

Jon looked at Cam. "What are we doing?"

"I am wearing you out. Beatin' you down."

"Ah, but I got *skills*," Jon said. His smile was back. Cam snorted.

Bethany said, "So it's okay?" They shrugged, and bent to start again. She nodded to Turner, who raised his camera.

Cam got even more physical, sweating through his gray Georgetown t-shirt (no camouflage today) and powering the ball in close when he had it, but he couldn't knock Jon off his game. There was more banging and bumping now, but neither guy called fouls.

Jon was up 9-8 when Cam missed a shot, snatched his rebound, went up with a hard smack against Jon and banked it in. The contact made me tense up; I saw Chris flinch. Jon took the ball to the top of the key, drove Cam down the right side and put up a jumper that clanked off.

Cam grabbed the rebound, dribbled up top and started working Jon into the lane, backing him down with a jolt here, a jostle there. It felt close to some kind of edge. Cam jammed up a shot in close; it smacked off the backboard and went in. Turner was hopping all around, crouching and moving to get *his* shots.

Now it was game point, 10-9 Cam, but Jon had the ball. He faked a charge forward; Cam's weight shifted back, then Jon rose up and swished a sweet jumper to tie it. When Cam got the ball back, he lowered his shoulder and bulled into Blanchette.

"Foul," Jon said.

"You can't call that," said Cam.

"Why not? You can't just bang into people."

"How about you play your game and I'll play mine?"

"How about you play it right?"

Cam cocked his head. He said, slowly, "Are you tellin' me how to play?"

Jon shrugged. "I don't know what you call that. It's not *basketball*."

"You just don't want to lose," Cam said.

"Not that way I don't."

"Oh no?" They were nose to nose, now. "Why don't you tell me how you want to lose," Cam said. "I can take care of it."

Jon grinned, and shook his head. Cam stepped back and looked at

Jon's face.

"You okay or what? You don't look that bad."

"I'm all right," Jon said. "But you don't need to go around hittin' people."

Cam shrugged. "People say stupid crap about me," he said, "I'm gonna come at 'em."

Turner, crouching and shooting, moved in closer.

"That stuff wasn't right," Cam said. "Wasn't true, either."

Jon nodded. "It was stupid," he agreed. "I shoulda left it alone."

"Yeah. And, you know," Cam said, "I went in too hard. I know it."

"That was freaky. I didn't know *what* happened."

"That stuff made me crazy," Cam said. "But I get that you didn't start it."

"Naw," Jon said.

"So that was stupid too," Cam said. "What I did. No doubt."

Jon shrugged.

"So we cool?" Cam asked.

"Yeah."

"Check?"

Jon's head bobbed yes, and that was it. Cam bounced the ball to him; Jon caught it, flipped it back, and bent low to defend.

They struggled back and forth to 13-13. The guys were tired, their shirts soaked. Jon, dribbling up top after Cam had banked in a runner to tie it, stopped and spun up a high-arcing shot. Cam turned and watched it go in. Then he took the ball and started pounding his way inside, but the ball shot off his foot out of bounds.

Jon got it back. It was game point now, and this time Cam was on him.

Jon jerked like he was going to his right, Cam stumbled a tiny bit reacting, and Jon was past him. Cam scrambled after, and he'd almost caught up when Jon took one last, long, graceful stride and went up. Cam leapt up after him — clean, no contact, both guys reaching high. The ball spun off Jon's fingers, just beyond the tips of Cam's, and it just ... barely ... slipped in.

"Nice," Chris said, and he clapped. "Nice *game*."

It was, too.

Jon offered his water bottle to Cam, who drank some and then Jon did. Turner was filming up close, then Bethany moved in.

"So," she said. "How did you decide to do this?"

Cam looked at her funny. "Decide what? We played a game."

"I came with my buddy," Jon said. "He came with his."

"But ... so ... are you *friends* now?"

They looked down. "I don't know," Jon said.

"Whatever," said Cam. "I get you next time," he said to Jon.

Jon grinned. "Any time you want."

Bethany said to Jon, "Why did you want to do this after he hurt you?"

Jon stopped smiling. He looked at Chris. "My friend said we were just gonna shoot baskets," he said. "I didn't know anyone else was coming."

Bethany turned to Chris. "So you planned this?"

"Well ... kinda sorta," Chris said. "We figured if we could get these two together — I mean, we're guys, right? Something happens, we deal with it and it's over."

"Yeah," Jon said. "Also ... you know. I heard about his dad."

Bethany's head tilted. "What?"

"His dad. He got killed. A little while ago. In Iraq."

"Afghanistan," Cam said softly.

Bethany just looked at them.

"Sorry," Jon said to him.

"Helmand Province," Cam said. "Hell ... man."

Bethany said, "Was he ... in a battle?"

"He was driving a damn truck."

"Oh." For once, I think Bethany had no idea what to do or say.

"It's harsh," Chris said. "Way harsh."

Cam, not looking at anyone, shrugged.

Jon said, "He did it for you and me — you know? Like, for all of us. Going over there."

"I don't *think* so," Cam said, and his eyes caught fire. "He wanted to be *home*, all right? He did two damn tours, then they made him go to that place." He was almost shouting now. "That *place*. He didn't *belong* there, 'cause he did his duty, all right? He *did* it!"

"Okay," Jon said.

Cam's eyes were hot and wet. "They did it — *they* made him go. He wanted to be *home!*"

"Yeah," Jon said. "Yeah."

Cam turned away, shaking his head; then he stalked off the court.

When he looked back at us, his eyes were brimming over. In a shaky voice he said, "Don't you ever say he went there for me. Don't *ever*."

He turned and walked away. He left his old sneakers and his ball behind.

"Nice," I said to Bethany. "Really nice."

She shrugged and turned to Turner. He looked at his camera, nodded and shut it off. Bethany started walking back to the SUV. Its windows were tinted; I guessed her mom or dad was in there. I didn't care. I followed her.

"What do you think you're doing?"

She squinted at me. "What?"

"What are you *doing?*"

"A very good story. For the Morning News."

"Since when are you on the Morning News?"

"I emailed Mr. Dallas this morning. He advises the program."

"I know that."

"He said we could go ahead, and the news team will look at it Monday morning."

"Did you see what you just did? Do you even care?"

"What? I asked a few questions."

"Everything was going fine," I said, "till you showed up with this stupid ... How'd you hear about this anyway?"

"From my cameraman."

"From your ... oh for God's sake. How'd *you* hear about it?" I said to Turner.

"From Elliot," Turner said. "You texted him."

Bethany got into the SUV and shut the door. "You know she's using us, right?" I said to Turner. "She thinks this is her new path to power."

"Yeah, well, that thing we just shot? That was *great*," Turner said. "I got incredible stuff."

Bethany's tinted window came humming down. "Tuuurner," she purred.

"Later," he said to me. He got in the vehicle and it pulled away.

20.
Just About Found

I rang the doorbell at Ms. Avery's. I had Cam's stuff. She stepped out on the porch and closed the door.

"What happened?"

"Well ... is he okay?"

"It's hard to tell," she said. "He went in his room and he won't tell us anything. So." She crossed her arms. "Tell me. Please."

"Well ... him and Jon played a really good game. Jon won, but it was close. It was good. They were fine. Then after, Jon said he was sorry about Cam's dad."

She nodded. "All right."

"Cam kind of got upset about that."

She nodded. "Well ... okay. But you and your friend tried."

"It was going really well," I said. I didn't mention the filming. It was just too outrageous. Instead I held out the ball, and the sneakers. "He left these."

"Thank you."

"I'm really sorry."

"Don't be," she said. "There's just ... there's no good way to manage a grief like that boy has."

She started to go back inside. Then she turned back. "Thank you for trying," she said.

"Is Janelle here?"

"No. She went home. Maybe you should, too, Russell."

"All right."

I got home checking my cell — no messages from Janelle. Nothing from Catalina either, not that I cared. When I came in the back door, my mom was waiting.

"You had a visitor," she said.

"I did?"

"Yes. It was quite interesting."

She went to the kitchen counter and picked up a square metal pan covered in foil. She lifted the foil; cut in squares inside was something

97

that looked like Rice Krispie Treats, with a brown gooey top.

"Apparently this is called *bibingka*," she said, pronouncing the odd word carefully. "It's a kind of rice dessert."

"Huh."

"A young Asian woman brought it by. Very polite. Pretty."

"Oh."

"Oh? That's all you're going to say?"

"Can I try 'em?" I went for the pan but she pulled it back.

"Do you *know* this woman?"

"Well, possibly."

"I'll take that as a yes. How do you know this woman?"

"She's Cat's, I don't know, housekeeper. She likes to cook."

"Are you having a fight with Catalina?"

I gave her a look. "Why would you ask that?"

"Because when this woman — does she have a name, by the way?"

"Yes."

"Okay. What would her name be?"

"It would be Cecelia. That's all I know."

"Well, when Cecelia brought this, she said, 'It's a peace offering. From my girl.'"

"She said that?"

"Yes. Russell, why do I have to do this tap dance with you to get the slightest whiff of information?"

"Because you're on the no-information plan. Haven't we gone over that?"

She rolled her eyes. "But why a *peace* offering?"

"I don't know. Can I have some of that?"

She handed over the pan. "Be kind to that girl," she said. "She counts on you."

I shrugged, and sidled past her.

I was eating the rice thingies with one hand — they were delicious; I think they had coconut — and checking Facebook with the other, and was about to go on SchoolStream to see if anyone had submitted any nasty texts when a Chat window popped open.

Serena
Hellooooo

Russell
hey

Serena
Where u been?

Russell
why?

Serena
I missed u here.

Russell
oh I'm sure

Serena
No I did! I was waiting for u. 2 come.

Russell
really?

Serena
Didn't u feel it?

I felt it then — like a twinge, or a flicker up my spine. It may have been interest, may have been evil. Hard to tell.

Russell
I don't know

Serena
Get any mean texts?

Russell
I don't know wait

I popped over to SchoolStream and logged on. Checked for messages.

There was nothing.

My Inbox was completely empty. I stared at it. How was this possible? I'd sent my message to the *whole eighth grade*.

Serena
So?

Russell
why do you care?

Serena
did u get even 1?

Russell
there's time.

Serena
Oh sure. How's your friend?

Russell
what?

Serena
I hear she's with some1 older.

Russell
you are evil aren't you

Serena
So r u 2 still friends at all?

Russell
bye

Serena
Whoa your not! your not are u?

Russell
it's none of your business, you know that?

Serena
Whoa that must HURT

I needed food. I gobbled more of the rice thing, and when my cell buzzed three times I couldn't grab it because my fingers were sticky. I washed up and it was from Cat.

Russell I really need you right now! I have a bad problem. He says I have to come be with him, he says I have to but it's Saturday! I can't go out on Saturday! I would have to tell her where I'm going and I can't do that!!

He doesn't care he says I HAVE to. He says he'll walk to my house and I have to go with him. When I say I can't he says I'm letting him down and I'm not a true friend. He says I'm not a true friend Russell! And my mom is texting me ALL the time. She and CC are suspicious and I'm caught in the middle with all this PRESSURE and nobody trusting me it's like being squeezed to death.

She went on for page after page on the cell. I really didn't want to read it.

I hope you got the snack OK. CC and I made it together. We get along in a lot of ways, but Russell if she finds out about him and tells my mom they might send me back home and cut me off from everyone. I'm serious! At home if they think you've gone too far with a boy it can be BAD. They treat you like a non-person forever. You can lose your family lose your future lose everything!!
Are you there Russell? Please are you there??

I was finishing the rice thing when the cell buzzed with a call. I washed my hands fast, and caught it.
"What happened on that playground?"
"Hey, Janelle."
"Hey yourself. Why is Cameron saying he doesn't want to live here any more?"
"*What?*"
"He's called his mom. She said he can go be with her again. He's packing."
All I could say was, "Whoa."
"I am asking you," she said. "What happened?"
I took a deep breath. I told her about Bethany and Turner showing up and filming.
"They said it's for the Morning News?"
"Yeah," I said. "They filmed them playing. It was a really good game. And right in the middle of it, Cam and Blanchette kind of like worked things out. It was pretty cool, actually."

"So why would he come home and shut himself in his room? And tell his mom he wants to leave here?"

"I ... don't know."

"Yes you do," Janelle said. "I can tell you do."

"Well ..."

"Don't you mess with me, Russell. What happened?"

"Well, Jon said he was sorry about Cam's dad. And then ... Cam got kind of upset."

Silence.

"How upset?"

"I don't know — he didn't want to show it. He said some stuff, then he walked away."

"Were those kids still filming?"

"Yeah."

"How upset was he?"

"Well ..."

"Did he cry?"

"Well ..."

"Russell. *Tell* me."

"It was hard to tell, okay? But maybe sort of almost."

"Could you *see* this 'almost'?"

"Yeah ..."

"Oh, no," she said.

"You think that's bad?"

"Is that bad? Is that *bad*? First there's a rumor that he's gay, which does not feel good to a young black man, okay? There's a lot of prejudice around that. Then there's what happened in the hall, so everyone's saying he's a psycho young black man, right? And now everyone's got to know his private business about losing his daddy — and everyone's got to see him cry? Are you serious? Is that *bad*?"

I didn't know what to say. All I'd wanted was for him and Jon to work it out, and maybe for people to understand. I never meant for Cam to be humiliated or anything.

I asked, "Is he really gonna go?"

"He wants his aunt to drive him there. Today."

"Will she?"

"Well, she says it's not a good situation. His mom's not in a good place, but she's still his mom, right? If he wants to be with her and she wants to be with him, his aunt has to say okay."

"But she's good for him — his aunt is. Right?"

"Ms. Avery? She's real good for him. But she's tough on him, too. He's in there packing and she says to me, 'He was so lost when he came here. You and me and the church and those friends of yours, all of us together had him just about found. Now he's going to have nobody to watch over him, and I fear to God what's going to happen to that boy. The hole inside him is so deep, I just fear to God.'"

I didn't say anything.

"That's what she said," Janelle said.

"What about the police? Doesn't Cam have to go to court or something?"

"Probably not," she said. "Ms. A. says because the boy turned out not to be hurt bad, and they're juveniles, Cam probably won't face charges. She knows people in the justice system."

"She does? How?"

"Never mind."

I thought about it. "I could tell Bethany and Turner they can't show that video," I said.

"It doesn't matter. Not any more."

I didn't know what to say. "I'm sorry, Janelle."

"Yeah."

"I'll call you later," I said. "Okay?"

"Don't bother. Nothing to say."

She hung up.

I was confused. I wanted to go back on Facebook. I was wondering about Serena when Turner called.

"We got *incredible* footage," he said. "And listen — we're going to make this work for us. For the project, okay?"

"Um ... what?"

"Bethany's doing a standup. That's the intro to a news video. She's going to tell about the rumor, and how it got spread around by text, and that's why Cam got so mad ..."

"Wait. Why?"

"What do you mean, why?"

"Why do you want to do this? Why not just let it go?"

"Let it *go*? Are you nuts? This stuff is great!"

"Isn't it kind of ... I don't know, personal? The stuff about Cam's dad? And, I mean, that gay thing?"

"That rumor was about me too," Turner said. "It caused all this trouble and I am not letting those girls get away with it, all right? I thought that's what you wanted, too."

"Well ... I don't know." It just felt really complicated, now.

"So Bethany does the intro, then we edit together a really good piece out of what I shot on the playground. We show the game, all that tension and how they almost fought again but instead they worked it out, right? Then the guys tell what happened to his dad, how they're sorry and all. It'll be *great*. People will see it on the Morning News — then maybe things will be different. Things could change, Russell."

I wasn't sure what to think.

"We can *do* it," he said.

"Yeah, okay. Well, good job."

When I got off I was hungry again. I looked for something else to eat.

I never did answer Cat.

21.
Losing Yourself

The cool thing about the Cave was that down here, you could lose yourself. On Saturday afternoon I was totally into doing that.

Elliot and I played video games — Hoop Jam and Storm of Battle, this time — for two hours at least. I lost track of time. After a while I just sat and watched while he played Dominion Quest. My phone was turned off. Unfortunately, Elliot's wasn't.

The ringtone on his cell was, I swear, the theme from *Star Wars*. He looked at the message.

"Em says your team needs you. Are you here?"

"*I* don't know," I said, sinking farther into the couch. "What do they want?"

He texted, and waited. "Team commander babe wants everyone on KidChat for urgent confab."

"Urgent?"

He nodded. "Says urgent."

"Does it say why?"

He shook his head. I sighed, heavily. "Can I use your laptop?"

BDEMURE: Everyone here? Russell finally?
RUSST: yeh
EMMUSIK: Hi, Russell
RUSST: hey
TURNVID: sup
RUSST: yo
BDEMURE: Russell, how many texts have come in so far? From your
    message?
RUSST: dunno haven't checked lately
BDEMURE: Well can you please?
RUSST: k

I checked my KidNet message center. What I found was what I'd found before.

RUSST: uh ... sure you want to know

BDEMURE: Why? 2 many?

RUSST: no

BDEMURE: How many?

RUSST: 0

BDEMURE: You have NONE?

RUSST: you got it

TURNVID: well that fits

EMMUSIK: What do you mean?

TURNVID: tell em B

BDEMURE: I asked a few girls to tell us, on camera, how that group does things, what they've done to people. Yesterday some girls said they might ... but today they shut down. Totally. People won't talk to me at all.

RUSST: why?

BDEMURE: Some kind of word has been put out. Everyone is scared. You don't realize how much power that group has. If you cross them or don't do what they say, they WILL destroy you.

RUSST: so that's why she was asking

BDEMURE: Who?

RUSST: serena

BDEMURE: What was Serena asking? Where?

RUSST: on fb. She wanted to know if we got any texts.

BDEMURE: You were on Facebook with SERENA?

RUSST: so?

BDEMURE: Did that girl friend you?

RUSST: maybe

BDEMURE: Russell, you are kind of naive so I need to tell you. Serena Sunderland is not a nice person, ok? She's online all the time and she finds out what you really want or you are scaredest of. Lauren is all about image but Serena is the black widow spider. If you get in her web she will OWN you.

RUSST: don't sugarcoat it tell it to me straight

TURNVID: Hey the girl wants to bite you sounds kinky!

BDEMURE: Will you 2 PLEASE? Look, our project is due in 2 WEEKS. Some-body who sees our TV report might give us something.

RUSST: who? someone with a death wish?

TURNVID: Emily's doing theme music. For the video.

EMMUSIK: I have some good ideas

BDEMURE: Russell?
RUSST: sup?
BDEMURE: What will you do?
RUSST: with what?
BDEMURE: Oh never mind.
TURNVID: dude see what you can find out from Serena now she's your
     FRIEND
BDEMURE: Oh please. I am signing OFF!!!

When I finally turned my cell back on, walking home from Elliot's, I had three texts.
From Big Chris:

Yo Russ L, Jon sez he owes u. He sez game got him back in the zone. C-man

From Janelle:

He left. Ms A took him. She said it takes six hours.

I texted back:

Did he say anything? Goodbye?

No

And I had this from Serena, who I had no idea how she got my cell number:

Hiii Russell guess what ... Cat and I r friends now! I got her to go on FB and I am her first friend. She's real sad and worried says u turned your back on her. She needs some1 to talk to and u didn't even answer her. So do u hate her now??

I stopped walking and stared at that. What?

I shouldn't have been surprised about her friending Cat. Everyone knew Serena and Lauren collected the best-looking girls for their group, and Cat was beautiful in a similar way to Serena: dark hair, dark eyes, a deeper kind of good-looking. I could see Serena trying to rope her in.

But why would Serena want to know if I hated Cat? Why would she even think that?

Trying to think like a popular girl gave me a headache. I came in the back door of my house, and there was my mom again.

"That boy who came to visit you the other night," she said.

"Huh?"

"That boy. He was at the door. Remember?"

"Oh. Richie."

"He's in the living room," she said.

"*What?*"

She nodded, and started to go in there. I stood frozen. She turned back.

"We need to be a little careful," she said softly. "I don't know what's going on, but that boy is *upset*."

She went into the living room. *Oh great,* I thought as I started to follow. *I gave up the stupid crush. Now I'm about to be killed for it.*

22.

Richie's Secret

In our living room Richie was pacing back and forth. He didn't stop when my mom went in. I figured I was done for.

Maybe today, when she'd been so stressed and upset, Cat had broken down and confessed to Richie the horrible secret that she and I used to be friends. Now he was going to beat me to a pulp in my own living room while my mom (could anything be worse than this?) would try, screaming, to pull him off. She might try but he was strong. So he would mostly kill me first.

All this flew through my mind in an instant. And then it didn't happen.

I went in, but Richie kept pacing. He jammed his hands in his pockets, then balled them into fists as he stopped to stare out the window. He jerked a cell phone from his pocket and peered at it, then shoved it back in his pocket and started pacing again. His hands kept working, clenching, changing. Then he saw me.

His eyes were jumping around and they lit on me — this was when I should have been dead — but his eyes kept going. It was like he was looking for something or someone that wasn't here. I took a breath and figured, *Okay. He's crazy upset, but not about me.*

Then it hit me.

It's Cat.

He had ordered her to hang out with him today, but she wouldn't, right? She couldn't. So he'd gone over some edge.

My mom looked at me and raised her eyebrows, like, *Say something.*

I cleared my throat. Richie, pacing, didn't look over. I said, "Uh, yo, Richie? Hey, man — what's up?"

He shook his head. Didn't answer. Then my mom said *"Richie"* in that sharp-crack voice she uses to get my attention. He stopped and looked at us, but his eyes still flickered around.

"Young man, *something* is going on," my mom said to him. "We're here. You're all right. *Are* you all right?"

Richie looked down at himself. He didn't look all right, but it was hard to say how. He was his usual scruffy self — not quite the scornful

109

tough guy he'd been last year, but worn thinner, like his jacket. That's when I noticed that one of the big pockets on his jacket was ripped. It was hanging half off.

"I'm all right," Richie said, like he had just figured this out.

"Well then what's going on?"

He started to pace again. My mom said, "Stop. Please. You're going to wear a path in my carpet."

To my amazement, Richie looked at the carpet and then at my mom like he was worried. "I didn't mean to," he said.

She gave a quick laugh. "It was a joke. Not a good joke, but a joke. Why don't you sit down? Let's all sit down."

But Richie shook his head. He was looking at my mom in a sort of pleading worried way, like he was scared the carpet wasn't okay, or that she wasn't okay — but he couldn't sit. He stood with his hands moving around like they were separate, nervous little creatures.

"Russell, let's you and I sit down," my mom said. We did, her on a chair and me on the couch. Richie kept looking all around, mostly out the window, never anywhere for long.

"Please," my mom said. "Tell us what's going on."

He said, "I ..." Shook his head.

"It's okay," she said.

"I told her what I was gonna do," he said. "I *told* her."

"Told who?" my mom said. "What did you do?"

I thought, *Oh no. Oh **no**.*

He's done something to her.

"I told her ..." He shook his head hard. "It was gonna be bad this time — just ... it was gonna be really bad. She begged me not to do anything, but I said I had to. I had to. I *told* her!"

He stalked to the window and stared out; flicked out his cell, glanced at it, shoved it back. I thought, *He hit her! She said no to him and he went crazy and hurt her. He knows what he's done. That's why he's freaked.*

I thought: *I have to find out if she's okay.*

I stood up. "Um," I said, pulling out my phone. "I need to ..."

My mom's hand shot up, palm out. "No. Put that away."

"But I have to check with somebody."

"It can wait."

"But maybe it can't."

She gave me a look. I sat back down.

But what if she's hurt?

"What was going to be bad?" my mom said to Richie in her calming tone.

He didn't answer.

"You said something was going to be bad," she said. "Can you say what it was?"

He shook his head.

"Why can't you tell us?"

Because he did something terrible, I thought. *I have to **call** her!*

"Is somebody hurt?" my mom asked.

My head snapped around. How did *she* know?

Richie started pacing again.

"You don't know if someone's hurt," my mom said, guessing now. "Someone might be."

He kept pacing.

"Richie," my mom said. "Why is your jacket torn?"

He looked down at his jacket, then back at us. I thought, *What did you **do***?

I knew he had rage because I had seen it. And I knew Cat wasn't strong — not in that way. She was trusting and kind.

I said to him, "What did you do?" My mom looked at me sharply, but I had to know. I said, "What did you *do?*"

"What I said I would," he answered. "I *had* to. Then when the anger went crazy ..." He looked at us almost desperately. "I never should have left. She said '*Please* go' — but I never should have!"

I said, "Why did you do it?"

"She made me. She *made* me. She said, 'Please. You have to go *now.*'"

I said, "How bad is she hurt?"

"Maybe bad. I don't know, I'm not there. I never should have *left!*"

I stood up. "I have to call someone," I said to my mom.

"No you don't."

"Yes. I *do*. Two seconds."

She puffed her cheeks out at me, but I didn't care — I rushed out into the kitchen. No messages on my phone. I called her cell. It rang and rang. Nobody answered. I pictured her lying there.

When I finally got her voice mail, I said, "Are you okay? *Are you okay?* Listen — I'm sorry I didn't get back to you today. I should have, I know — there's been a lot going on. You need to — I just need you to call me. I *need to know if you're okay*. Please *call* me."

111

I looked around. What else could I do? I could call her house phone — but I didn't know the number. I yanked open drawers until I found the phone book. I leafed through, found her dad's name, dialed the number.

Nobody answered. When the deep voice of Cat's dad came on the answering machine, I tried to sound calm.

"Hi. This is Russell. Catalina's friend. I just want to know ... could someone please call me? I just want to know if Cat's, I mean, if she could call me or if someone else could if she can't. That'd be great."

I hung up without leaving my phone number. With cells you never have to. I was going to call again, leave my number, when my mom shoved open the kitchen door.

She hissed, "Will you get back in here? This is your friend."

"Not exactly."

She closed the door. "I don't know what that means and right now I don't care," she said. "This boy's got trouble. He came to you for a reason."

"He has no friends."

"What?"

"He doesn't. Just Cat. I'm afraid ..."

"Well, he came to *you* and we need to find out what's going on," she said. She pushed the door open, then stopped. She looked around the living room, then turned back.

"He's gone," she said. "He's not here."

"Okay. We need to ..."

"Where would he have gone?"

"I don't know. I need you to drive me to Catalina's house."

"What? Why?"

"Mom, *please*. I'll explain on the way."

But my sense of where Cat's house was turned out to be kind of vague.

"Well," my mom said, "which way should I turn? And why are we doing this?"

"Um ... I think maybe this — no *that* way. Try that way." I was looking for landmarks, trying to remember. We had to *find* her.

"Is this right?"

"Um ... yeah I think so." My mind was whirling. How bad was she hurt? Would Richie go back there? Was this the way?

"No, wait," I said.

"Wait what?" She pulled to the side. "Russell. You really don't know, do you?"

"Um ..." I was looking around, getting desperate.

"I just don't think this is the time to go visiting," she said. "Shouldn't you try to reach your friend? He's very upset."

"He's not my *friend*, Mom. Can we just turn around? If we try that other way ..."

"Russell, no. Something bad has happened. Where does that boy live?"

"Mom, I don't *know!* And we have to find ..."

My cell buzzed. I grabbed it. It was Cat.

I said, "Hello? Are you all right?"

"I don't know why I should call you back," she said. "You didn't call *me* back."

"Are you okay?"

"Well ... in what way?"

"You're all right. You're not hurt or anything."

"I *am* hurt. I was very hurt that I needed to talk with you when things were really hard and you're supposed to be my friend and you didn't even *answer* me. All last night and today too. You didn't even say thank you for the present."

"Yeah, but listen ..."

"Serena's right. Boys don't understand friendship at all."

"What? Hang on a sec." I said to my mom, "What?"

"Is that your friend?"

"Which friend?"

My mom rolled her eyes. "Who is it, Russell?"

"It's Cat."

She nodded. "Ask her where he lives."

"Huh?"

"*Ask* her where he *lives.*"

"Why?"

She rolled her eyes and held out a palm. "Give me the phone."

"What? No."

"Give me the *phone.*"

"It's my phone."

She puffed up into Warrior Princess mode. "I *pay* for that phone. Hand it over, please."

I sighed. This was so wrong. But I gave it to her.

At least Cat was okay.

Richie's house — as my mom got the directions, it gave me a twinge to know that Cat knew right where it was — turned out to be in back of downtown, in the same neighborhood where Cam's aunt lived, though not on the same street.

"This is ridiculous," I said.

"I'll be very happy if you're right."

She pulled over.

"This isn't it," I said. "It's number 511. This is ... 522. It's up there, see?

"I know. Let's just sit here a minute."

I didn't get that, but anyway there was nothing to see. Richie's house was sort of small like the others in this neighborhood, and worn-looking compared to Ms. Avery's neat little package. It had a white porch, like hers — only hers had chairs to sit on. This porch had nothing.

I said, "See? There's nothing there."

My mom said, "Hmm." But she didn't move. I was thinking I should call Cat back and tell her she might be in danger when Richie came out, almost running, from between two houses up the street.

He zipped across the street, rushed up to his front door, opened it and stood there a second like he was listening for sounds inside. Then he stepped in and pulled the door closed, slowly, like he didn't want to make any noise.

We sat there.

"Well, that's it," I said. "We better go."

"Let's just stay a minute," my mom said.

"Why?"

She sighed like a compressed-air blast. "Russell, that boy was very upset about something. Did you not get that?"

"Well, yeah, but she's okay."

"Who's okay? Catalina?"

"Yeah."

"Is that who you thought this was about?"

"Mom. Who else could it be about?"

She didn't answer. She sat there looking at Richie's house, like the front door was about to open up and tell us something. But it didn't. Nothing happened. This was the biggest non-drama I ever sat through.

I finally said, "Look, if you want to stay here and play Harriet the Spy all day, okay. I'm gonna walk home."

"Well ... all right. I guess we should go."

She shifted into gear, and started to pull out.

That's when we heard the siren.

23.
The Waiting Room

We were at the Emergency Room, in the waiting area. When we came in and sat down I saw Richie, standing over by the desk where you'd check in. He didn't see us; he was talking with the lady behind the desk, and he didn't look happy. It looked like he wanted to go back where the patients were, but the lady wouldn't let him. He wasn't giving up — he kept trying. He was still standing at her desk when the police came in.

The first two cops who'd come to Richie's house now walked up and spoke to him. One put a hand on his shoulder, like he was trying to calm Richie down before he arrested him. Then Richie looked over and noticed us.

Back in his neighborhood, the siren had come closer and closer, then an ambulance pulled up. They turned off the siren but the ambulance just sat there, a white-and-green box with its lights flashing redly on the houses all around. Then a police car pulled up and the two cops got out. One walked up to the house, while the other went to the driver's window of the ambulance and talked to someone inside. They hadn't noticed us yet.

The first cop was on the porch when the front door opened. I could see Richie standing there. The cop talked to him, then turned back and nodded. Now the ambulance lights went off and two people in white shirts got out. They went up the steps while the first cop said something into the radio on his chest. Then he went in, too.

A second cop car came wheeling up. Two more officers got out and stood by the car, looking up and down the street. One of them spotted us. He came up and bent to my mom's window.

"Can I help you?"

"The boy who lives there is a friend of my son," my mom said. The cop looked at me, then back at her. She said, "He came to our house a little while ago, and he was very agitated and upset. We were trying to find out what was wrong when he ran out. We were worried, so we came here. We were just waiting to see if things were okay."

"Did he say anything to you, give you any sense of what happened?"

"Not really," my mom said. "I mean ..."

"He said it was gonna be bad," I said. "He said the anger went crazy."

"That's *right*," my mom said.

The cop nodded. "Just hang tight for now. Stay in your car, okay?" He went back to stand by his car.

My mom gazed at the house. "I was afraid of something like this," she said.

"But ... she's okay," I said. "I talked to her. You talked to her, too."

"Russell. Do you still think we're talking about your friend?"

"You mean we're not?"

She looked at the house. "I don't think so," she said.

The ambulance people got out a stretcher, on folding legs and wheels, and brought it into the house. A few minutes later they brought someone out. It looked like a woman. Richie came out next, between the two cops.

So he had done something terrible. Just ... it just wasn't to Cat.

But they didn't put Richie in a cop car. Instead, the two officers walked with him to the back of the ambulance. One of the ambulance people climbed in back with the stretcher, then Richie got in, too.

And now, in the ER, when Richie walked over to us, the cops just watched.

"How did you get here?" he asked.

"We drove," my mom said. "We were worried about you. How is she?"

"I don't know." Richie looked down the hall, where they took people. "She was out when I found her. I thought she was dead at first."

We didn't say anything. I was just staring at him. "You must have been terrified," my mom said.

"She was all crumpled up! They say she might have hit her head.

When she fell, or something. You can't usually ... see ..."

His voice trailed off. "I never should have left," he said to the floor. "She begged me and begged me not to do anything — she said it'd only make it worse. I said I *had* to. But then if I hadn't left ... She said '*Please* go.' But if I'd only *stayed* ..."

"It's not your fault," my mom said.

"It *is*." He looked at her fiercely. "I told him *no more* — and that's when he ... when we ..." He looked down at his torn pocket.

"This isn't your fault," my mom said again.

"She was saying, 'Please go. Just for a little while.' But I should have *stayed*. I said *no more*. And now ..."

It almost hurt to look in his eyes.

Now Richie went back to the cops, and spoke to them urgently. They talked with the lady at the desk; then they walked him down the hall into the patient area. A few seconds later, the outside doors wheezed open and Catalina came running in.

She saw us and hurried over. "Is Ellen ... is she all right?"

"We don't really know anything," my mom said to her. "They're looking at her now."

"Where's Richard?"

"He's in there too."

I said, "Who's Ellen?" Nothing made sense — it was like my brain wouldn't work. Cat's mouth opened, then stopped. She seemed flustered, like she wasn't sure what to do.

"Russell," my mom said. "Maybe you and Catalina should go have a talk."

Cat looked around. A few other people were sitting on the plastic chairs. She said, "Will you come get me if they say anything? If he comes out?"

"Of course," my mom said.

She nodded and I followed her, out into the short, wide entryway between the waiting room and the sliding-glass outer doors. Cat leaned against the wall, like she was suddenly really tired.

"I thought you were hurt," I said.

She looked startled. "Why would I be hurt?"

"Well ... I thought he came to your house or something, like really mad."

She looked at me in a searching way. Then she nodded.

"He does get angry," she said. "He's under *so* much stress. But he has

117

never hurt me, never touched me in anger in any way. It's really, really important for you to understand that."

"Okay. But why?"

"Because of what happens." She looked toward the ER. "Because of this."

"What is this? Who's Ellen?"

She opened her mouth, but didn't say anything. A hospital guy in scrubs came out.

"I'm sorry — we have to keep this area clear," he said. "For incoming patients."

We shuffled outside. It was cold out here, damp and gray. Cat looked agonized.

"Please," she said. "This has to be absolutely between you and me."

"Okay. Sure."

She took a breath. "Ellen is Richard's mom," she said.

Something warm flowed through me, like recognition. *Oh.*

"And she's hurt," I said.

"Yes."

"But Richie didn't hurt her."

"Of course not."

"He told us he went in and she was, like, crumpled up."

Cat winced.

I said, "And it wasn't ... a burglar?"

She shook her head. Now the feeling I got was prickly, and strange. I whispered, "His dad."

She nodded.

I said, "His *dad?*"

She nodded.

"Richie said he knew it'd be bad," I said. "He said he had to do something this time — then he said the anger went crazy and she begged him to go. Now he keeps saying he never should have left."

Cat breathed, "Oh ... Richard."

"Did he know his dad was going to hurt her? Is that what he tried to stop?"

She got a very grim look. "I ... yes. I'm afraid so."

"So when he said the anger got crazy," I said, "he didn't mean *his.*"

"Oh, no."

"So, I mean ... has this been going on for a long time?"

Nod.

"And Richie — is he the only kid?"

Cat shook her head. "He has a sister. She's older. She left home the minute she could."

"So ... hey, wait," I said, getting it now. "His dad beats him up too, right?" Sure, that was it! "That's why he always had to pick out some littler kid and terrorize him. Right?"

She was shaking her head no, but I didn't stop. "That's why he *did* that stuff — because his dad did it to him!"

"That's not it," Cat said. "That's not it *at all*."

"It's not?"

"No!"

"Then what?"

Cat just looked so sad. Then it came over me, another feeling of getting it. I didn't like this feeling at all.

"He's been there," I whispered. "If his dad's been like hurting his mom for a long time, if it happened in his house ... then he was just a kid. He couldn't do anything."

From the sadness in Cat's eyes, I knew this was it. I said, "But ..."

"But Richard has never hurt *me*," she said. "Even when he got so stressed and upset and so ... torn to pieces inside. He would tell me how things had to be with us, where I had to be and just what time — but that was okay. I understood. Our relationship was the only thing he could control. But he never hit me."

I nodded.

"You *have* to *understand*," she said.

"Okay."

She started whispering, even though nobody else could hear. "His dad would always do it behind closed doors. In their bedroom. Richard would hear it. He couldn't stop it."

"But why not? That's what I don't get. I mean, Richie's a strong guy." I thought of the times he got mad at me. He was scary.

"Because if he ever tried, he could put his dad in a rage and then later his mom would get hurt much worse," Cat said. "I'm so afraid that's what happened this time. His father lost his job this week."

"Oh. Uh oh."

"The economy's bad, you know? That night, his mom asked Richard to go stay somewhere, because his dad was really ... ashamed. She wanted to take care of him. She tries her best, she really does. That's why he came to your house that time. But this time ..."

119

"This time he knew it'd be bad," I said. "He kept saying that."

She nodded. "It was building and building, the way it always does — and Richard said this time he would stop it. He had to try. It had built up in him, too. So bad. All these years, not being able to do anything — inside himself, he was fighting it so hard. That's why it's so important to understand that he's never hit me. He has the anger, but he fights it. "

I nodded. "Okay."

"She's never had to come *here* before," Cat said, glancing at the ER entrance. "Richard's dad is really good at doing it so nobody can see. They both hid it. They never talked about it."

"They never *talked* about it?"

"No. Not a word. Not ever."

"Wow."

I thought about it. "So," I said ... "when it started this time, he confronted his dad. That's when the anger went crazy. He said she begged him to leave."

She nodded, sadly. "After he left, his dad must have gone out of control." She glanced in the window again.

I said, "Richie said when he got back home, at first he thought she was dead."

Cat's breath caught. She looked back at me almost desperately. She shook her head.

"I couldn't talk with you about this at all," she said. "But I've been *so* scared."

24.
The Mask

It was night, now.

And what a day.

Richie's mom was still in the hospital — they were observing her to see if she had internal injuries. She'd been hit really hard in the midsection area, then she'd fallen and hit her head. That was how Richie found her, unconscious on the floor.

Richie's dad would be under arrest, if they could find him. Richie didn't know where he'd gone and didn't seem to care. He talked with the cops for a while, then he waited with us. He and Cat held hands.

I understood better, now, why they'd hung in so tight together. As they sat by each other on the waiting-room seats, I thought how she was right there for him. He was lucky for that. My friend Cat was tough. If she was your friend, she was your friend for real.

"I'm sorry I didn't answer your messages," I said to her. Richie was in his own world, staring down the hall.

"It's okay," she said.

"No — you were in a rough place and I didn't even text you back. It was ... there's kind of been a lot of stuff going on. I got distracted. But, you know, I really did like that rice thing."

She sat up and beamed. "Bibingka! Isn't it *delicious?*"

The eager way she said that made me ache for her, suddenly and so bad.

Cat said, "I told CC you were mad at me. She said, 'Let's make him a treat. He'll forget everything!' We had so much fun. For a little while, it was me who forgot things."

As I looked at her I melted inside, one more time. But she was looking at him.

Now it was night, and I was in my room and there were new things that mattered. I thought about that picture of Cam and his dad. Cam would be back with his mom by now. How was that? What did it mean that his mom wasn't in a good place? Did they *have* a place? Did Cam have a bed?

I thought about Cat — about how, when her parents got divorced, her dad had taken her away from her mom and everything she knew and brought her here to cope with a kids' culture that, at first especially, had seemed cold and mean to her. Then she grew into a beautiful girl, living in an empty house. She was studying so hard, talking online with her mom, and all the time trying to save a boy who was secretly in hell.

I thought about Janelle. Cam had meant something to her in some way I hadn't realized. None of us had. If you're a big girl like Janelle, nobody thinks you have feelings. What had that been like? What had she lost this weekend?

People think kids my age are obsessed with superficial things, like what people think of us and if we look right and where we are in the popularity order, and we do think about that — we sort of have to — but we also care about this deeper stuff. There's just nothing we can *do* about it.

For example, if you were really worried about your dad who might get blown up in Afghanistan, or your mom who couldn't cope right now — or if you were concerned about your friend who might not have a bed to sleep in tonight, or your friend's parent who was being held for observation for internal injuries, and if you couldn't do a single thing about any of those things because you were still a kid, what would you do?

Would you obsess about clothes or image, so nobody would give you that squinty look tomorrow and say, "You're wearing *that?*" Or would you go all strange alternative, putting on an off-putting look like a suit of armor? Would you start getting high all the time so you might not have to feel anything?

And what if you felt like everyone was always watching? What if it felt like every single person was judging every single thing you did, everything you said, every mistake you made?

That's how it is for us. It can feel like you're walking on the edge of a cliff in the dark, and any step could plunge you into falling where no one will hear. Any step you take. That could be the one.

I went down the hall to the guest room. I knocked. Richie opened the door, then stood blocking it.

"Hey," I said. He nodded. I said, "I was wondering if you want to watch a video. Or something, I don't know."

He had on a brown t-shirt and jeans. My mom had taken his jacket to fix the pocket. Without it, Richie almost looked like a regular kid. He had a regular kid's challenging, defensive eyes.

"I'm kind of doing something here," he said. He turned a little bit and I saw, past him on the carpet, some wood shavings. Thin curled bits.

"Are you ... carving something?"

He hesitated. "Yeah."

"Really? What?"

"It doesn't matter."

"You're not carving up the furniture or anything, right? I mean, no offense, but ..."

"You think I would do that?"

"No, but ..."

"All right, okay." He sighed. "Come in."

He went in and sat on the bed. Reaching under it, he pulled out a rough, partly carved piece of wood. It was pale and wide, the size of a thick book. There was sort of a face coming through it.

"I'm doing like a mask," Richie said. "At least I think that's what it is." He turned the wood this way and that. The pale rough surface was developing a wide nose, slit eyes like an alien's, and a broad, simple mouth.

"It's really rough," he said. "I don't know what I'm doing. I've only done a few things."

I reached out to touch it. He held it up so I could. "It's pine," he said. "Cheap wood, but soft. Easy to work with."

"How do you ... I mean, how do you do it?"

He reached under the bed and brought out the knife.

It was a regular old pocketknife — a simple one, with a nubbly brown handle. Its long blade was out, the smaller one folded in. Richie gripped the handle, dipped the side of its blade into the wood and peeled off a shaving. I watched the pale curl hit the carpet and bounce, once.

"There's all kinds of tools you can get," he said in a new, brighter way. "There are these different-sized little knives that all fit into the same handle. You can get gouges" — he made a motion with his hand, like he was gouging somebody's eye out — "that can take away a lot of wood when you're just starting something and finding its shape, you know? But so far I just have this knife. I got it after my grandfather died. It was his."

"I thought it looked old-fashioned."

"Yeah, but it's good. I'm real careful with it."

"Sure."

"You have to keep it sharp."

"I guess."

123

He looked at the wood. "If I was going to make a real mask, I'd need a gouge to scoop out the wood back here. I can use the knife to scrape it smooth in front, when it's ready — then I can get some sandpaper to make it smooth. Or if I want it to stay rough, I can just use this."

He balanced the knife on a single straight finger. Then he folded it up, and put it away.

"I probably shouldn't do this," he said. "Your mother might freak."

"I can get a broom and dustpan," I said. "Remove the evidence." I meant to make him laugh but he didn't.

"You think it should be an alien? Or just a strange person?"

"I don't know," I said. "How do you figure that out?"

"I don't know. I guess you just kind of work at it until something comes through."

We both looked at the mask for a while. Then Richie said, quietly, "It was decent of her."

"Who?"

"Your mom. Giving me a place to stay tonight. She's all right."

"Are you worried? I mean, if your dad comes home or whatever?"

He looked up with hot eyes. Then he went back to his mask. Held it up. "What I like about it is, it's totally chill," he said. "Not showin' you one single thing."

He was turning the mask this way and that, to catch the light, when my pocket vibrated. One, two, three. I pulled it out.

Private caller.

"Uh, I better go take this," I said.

"Cool," Richie said, still inspecting his mask.

"Hell*oooo*." The girl's voice was soft and flirty.

I didn't answer. I was back in my room, now.

"No way should I be calling you," she said. "My friends would be *shocked*."

"So what do you want?"

"I just feel bad for you," Serena said. "I've been talking with Cat — we're friends now, you know? And I've been thinking how hard it must have been for you, when you wanted her *so* bad and she just wanted ... that other boy. Isn't that the worst thing in the world, for a guy?"

"You think I'm stupid? Like I'm going to talk with you about anything personal?"

"Why not? Cat tells me lots of things."

"Oh, I bet." But I thought: *Does she?*

"She does," Serena said. "She said you liked her, and she felt so bad for you but she just likes him. I thought, whoa. That must have been *so* hard."

"Serena, what do you want?"

"What do you mean?"

"You friended Cat, and you've been trying to get stuff out of me. Normally you wouldn't talk to me if the moon turned purple, but now you're being all 'ooh, I feel so *bad* for you.' What are you trying to get?"

"Maybe I'm just ... interested."

"Oh, I get that. But in what?"

"Maybe it's you," she said. "Maybe I want to find out about you. Would that be so terrible?"

"Look, you tried to embarrass me in front of everyone in school, and I'm thinking you just want to do it again. But I'm not telling you anything, all right? Find someone else and go suck *their* blood."

"That is so cruel! Cat's right about you. I didn't believe it, but she's *right*."

"About what?"

"She said ... well ..." Serena took a breath, like this was really hard. "She said you're not trustworthy. She said she counted on you, but when she needed you to be there, you turned your back. She says she can't trust you any more, and I can see why. You're not even *nice*."

"You're lying."

"I am not! You're not a good friend at *all*."

"Are you kidding me? I was a much better friend than you'll ever be, all right? I listened to her and kept her secret and everything. I don't care what she says — and I don't care what *you* say, either."

I was about to slam the phone down when Serena said, "Stop, okay? See, this is why I wanted to hear your side of it. So ... maybe *she's* not the most trustworthy friend? I mean you really cared about her, and now she's trashing you? I mean, whoa. Maybe I'm wrong about her."

"I don't want to talk about this, okay?"

"I know — you were loyal! You kept her secret and *everything*. Now she's saying things about you. Maybe she's not the person I thought she was?"

"She's a good person," I said. "She's just under a lot of stress right now."

"Oh, I know — you can tell." Her voice went low with concern.

"She doesn't talk about her boyfriend at all. He's not like hurting her, is he?"

"No!"

"Oh, good — because that would be really bad. I mean, sometimes there are secrets you shouldn't keep. If someone's getting hurt."

"No. It's her culture, that's all."

"Well ... I know she's Filipino. But why can't she talk to me about him? We're friends now."

"But she's not stupid, Serena. You're the last person she should tell."

"Why? What would I do?"

"You'd *tell* people. If this got out, it could get back to her family, and ..."

I stopped dead.

"Uh *huh*," Serena said. "Her dad is American ... her mom is Filipino. She told me that. So ... it's probably not her dad she's worried about. It's probably ... well, okay! Hey, thank you very much, you've been *so* helpful. Bye now!"

There was a click, and I sat there staring at the phone.

A voice in my head said, *What did you just do?*

25.

Brown Boots

"I have no idea what you're talking about," I said.

"Of course you don't!" Bethany said. "Boys never notice anything about girls that does not involve ..." She leaned over our cluster of desks, and cupped her hands.

"Oh," Turner said. "Those."

"Not just those," I said.

Bethany said, "Oh yeah? What else?"

"Hair. We notice hair."

"If it's blonde," Emily said, then looked down bashfully. Her hair was brown. Her sneakers were green, today.

Bethany toyed with a length of her wavy blonde cascade. "I hate my hair," she said, looking at it sadly.

"What? Why?"

"It's horrible."

"Okay, that's just weird," I said, because it was. Last year when she was the queen, Bethany's hair was *the* hair. She would shake it off her shoulders in this smug, superior way. Now she looked at her same hair like it was breaking her heart.

"It's kinky and horrifying," she murmured. "You don't understand."

Turner and I looked at Emily, who said, very softly, "It's not like *hers.*"

"Ah."

Yes. Sometimes it seemed like every girl who hoped to be somebody in our grade had to find a way to look like Lauren Paine. The slender body, the particular clothes and shoes, and the long, very straight hair.

"But the point is," Bethany said, snapping back to life, "every girl in that group showed up this morning wearing the same boots. You just look — high brown boots. They've all got 'em. That means over the weekend, Lauren said so. Now in one day, *maybe* two, every girl in this school who wants to have any status at all will be wearing the same style. Especially the ones who want to be the next one in."

She sat back, crossed her arms. "Two days at most. You watch."

The other teams in Language Arts were buzzing around us, or were off in the computer lab. We were supposed to be working on our project, and in a way we were. Ms. Corbin had told us Social Pressures had been accepted as a topic, and social pressures were definitely what we were talking about.

I said, "What do you mean, *the next one in?*"

Bethany shrugged. "When they push someone out, someone new gets in."

"The group is that tight?"

"Well, *yeah*," she said, giving me the look that says, *Everyone but **you** knows that*. After the weekend I'd had, that just ticked me off.

"Hey — believe it or not," I said, "everyone in the world is not obsessed with the top frickin' clique of eighth-grade girls at Darkland Middle School. And who cares if they want to wear boots? Why do *you* care?"

Bethany blushed and said nothing. Then it hit me why.

For Lauren the image dictator, making sure all the top girls came to school today wearing the same new thing was a way of showing who was inner circle and who was not. Everyone — all the girls, anyway — would see, and know.

I looked under the desks. Bethany was wearing soft little dancer shoes. These used to be, I had the vague idea, what the cool girls wore. So all day she'd been stuck in those limp shoes while the ones who'd gotten the secret fashion directive from the Ice Queen were strutting around in new, high leather boots. Bethany would have gotten the look. *You're wearing **those**?*

"Maybe we could film the boot-wearers," I said. "Ask them why, or whatever. We've got to get something for the project. Everybody else is interviewing kids, filming games, getting people to give music lessons — all this stuff. Far as I can tell, we've got nothing."

Over the weekend Lauren and Serena had totally blocked my campaign for nasty texts. I still had no responses.

"*I'm* not interviewing anybody about any boots," Bethany declared. "And we don't have nothing. We have the whole film about the boys playing basketball."

"How is that about social pressures?"

"Be*cause*, that whole trouble started with the top girls spreading a rumor. And our film, we worked on it all weekend — it shows what happened. When we put it out on the Morning News, it will change everything."

She looked around the room, then back at us. "You watch," she said.

Oh sure, I thought. *And if that happens, who'll be the star? Why ... that would be you.*

"Serena called me," I said.

Bethany's eyes popped. "When?"

"Saturday night."

"Serena called you *herself?*"

"Yes."

"Did she try to get any information out of you?"

"Ahm ... I don't know."

Bethany scrutinized me. "She got something, didn't she." She sighed. "Russell, did you not listen to me? About that girl?"

"Yes. She's evil. Check."

"So what did you tell her? What did she want to know?"

I didn't answer. I'd been pretty bothered about it, actually.

Bethany kept peering at me. "For her to call and manipulate you in person ... you must be a serious target. I wonder why."

"I thought you said I was a leader."

She shook her head. "That can't be it. I wonder what she's ..."

While we were talking, Mr. Dallas came into the room. He went over to Ms. Corbin, who was talking with another team. Mr. D whispered something to her. She glanced at us and nodded.

Mr. D. came over. "Bethany? Turner? Could I see you a minute?"

When those two came back, Bethany was beet red. She plopped down. "I can't believe it. This is *criminal.*"

"What?"

"Tell them," she said to Turner. "I can't talk."

Turner sat down slowly. He was staring at nothing. "They ... said no," he said.

"No what?"

"They won't show our report."

"Who won't? Who's they?"

"It's *them,*" Bethany said. "They control everything."

"I don't understand," I said. "Mr. D said you can't show your thing on the Morning News?"

Bethany nodded. "He said the committee looked at it and decided no."

"Why?"

"Oh, they *said* it's because it has profanity. And because we filmed it off school grounds. And he said it's too personal. I mean he was just babbling. The real reason is, it's *them*."

Emily said, "But how?"

"Who's on the Morning News committee?" Bethany said, "Kids. Who are the anchors? Kids on the committee. And who in this school tells kids what they'd better do or else?"

Emily said, "Right now the anchors are Cayenne Sheffield and Michelle Boone."

"Cayenne's in the group and Michelle's a hyperventilating wannabe," Bethany said. "*They* made this happen. They're making *all* this happen." She whirled to me. "How many texts did you get so far?"

"Uh ... none?"

"Still?"

"Yep. Still none."

She looked at each of us. "See? It's *them*."

I said, "What about Mr. Dallas? He's a teacher."

"He's *clueless*," Bethany said. "They all are."

"He said, 'It's a student-run program,'" Turner said, imitating Mr. D. "'I'm just the messenger.'"

"We can't let them stop us like this," Bethany said. "I don't care what the power ladder is in this stupid school. This is *America*."

"But you don't have to let them stop you," Emily said. She'd been looking at the rest of us in a puzzled way. When we looked back, she blushed.

"Well," she said, "I mean ... can't you put this on YouTube? On your site," she said to Turner. "We could put up Facebook links and everything."

Turner's face opened. "God," he said. He grinned.

"But," I said, "what about the project?"

"This *is* the project," Turner said. "From now on we record everything. We go back to Mr. Dallas right now, and get him to tell us on camera why we can't be on the Morning News."

"Will he do that?"

"How can he say no? He's got kids interviewing people all over school. Then, after we put the film on YouTube, we interview kids about whether they saw it, and if they did what they think. If we get any messages, any texts — if there are any new rumors — we record those. We collect everything, put it all in the project. We show those little fascists they can't stop *us.*"

Looking around at each of us, Turner broke into a wicked grin. "Basically," he said, "we kick their skinny little butts."

We were starting to nod at each other when Ms. Corbin came over, looking concerned. She bent low so only we could hear.

"I heard about the news committee," she said. "I hope you guys aren't too let down."

"Oh," I said, "we'll manage."

"Yeah," Turner said. "We'll cope."

"If you're *creative*," Ms. Corbin said, "I know you can still make your project succeed. Creativity is all about trying and trying again. Not everything's going to work — but if you keep at it, things *will* fall into place."

She stood up. "They say when one door closes, another one opens. You just have to try to find that door."

Bethany nodded very sincerely. "That is so wise," she said, and looked at the rest of us. "We can really work with that."

"Oh, yeah," we murmured. "For sure."

Ms. Corbin looked pleased. "I had a feeling about this group," she said. "I thought, if you can just come together as a team, you might surprise everyone."

"Oh, don't worry," Bethany said. "We're planning to."

When classes changed, in the hall I passed three girls strutting in soft, high brown boots. *Looks expensive*, I thought. I didn't see the Ice Queen, but I did spot Serena. Her boots were black suede. They had turned-over cuffs that rose up above her knees. They looked *really* expensive.

Serena saw me looking and delivered the appalled expression of the ultra-hot when confronted with a lesser species. She spun and stalked away, her suede boots scissoring down the hall. As I watched, I heard the PA come on again.

"Please excuse the interruption."

That was all it said.

After school I waited in the library. I just needed to talk to Cat. Stuff was going on and we needed to talk.

As soon as band practice was over, Cat came hurrying into the library. She looked around, saw me and strode over. It hit me that all year she'd known I hung out in here, waiting till the moment when I could go position myself at my locker just before she emerged from the band room. All along, she knew.

"How is he?" she asked, sitting at my table. "How did he seem?"

"I guess he's okay. I don't really know. He mostly keeps to himself."

I didn't say anything about the mask, which Richie had worked on intently Sunday night after being out all day walking around by himself. At least, that's what he said he'd been doing. At dinner Sunday he hardly said two words to my mom and me. He was surprisingly polite, though. To my mom he was always polite.

"What was it like?" I asked Cat. "I mean, for him."

"When the bad things happened?"

"Yeah."

"I can't even imagine," Cat whispered. "He would hear it. His room is just down the hall."

I did not want to hear that she knew where his bedroom was.

"His dad's voice would get very low," she said. "His mom would start to cry. Sometimes she'd be like pleading. Then there would be these ... sounds. Like thuds. Then a different kind of crying."

I waited. There was nothing I could say.

"Then his dad would leave," she said.

"Leave?"

"Yes — leave the house. He'd go to a bar or something. And Richard would go in there."

"In ..."

"To their room. He'd try to comfort her. Ever since he was a little boy. Things would build and build, and his mom would try and try to make things nice but his dad would get all touchy and suspicious, like nothing could ever be okay — and then before long it would start happening again. Richard would be in his room and he'd hear the sounds. Then after the front door slammed and his dad was gone he'd go in there, and his mom would be crying. And hurt, in places you couldn't see. Richard would try to comfort her. And you know, he never really could."

Cat looked at me with her deep eyes. "That's how he grew up. That's why he is the way he is."

We sat for a while. Then I said, "What's going to happen?"

She shrugged. "They discharged his mom. From the hospital."

"When?"

"This morning."

"So she's okay?"

133

"Well, there are no major internal injuries. Richard doesn't want her home alone. He didn't go to school today — he went to the hospital, to help her get home. I guess a policeman brought them."

"So, like, where's his dad?"

"Nobody knows. Richard won't leave his mom alone."

"What's he doing all day?"

"I don't know — sitting? Going crazy?"

He's carving, I thought. *He's got the knife.*

"Are you going over there?"

"Oh no," she said — "he would never let me. CC is coming to pick me up. She's probably out there now. I have to go home, have merienda and pretend nothing is happening."

She stood up. I had an idea. I said, "Why don't you talk to her?"

"Who?"

"CC. Tell her what happened. Say you're his friend and that's why you've been so worried. Say that's why you've been, you know, so secret. She might just get it. Imagine the relief."

She sat, thinking. Then she said, "I'd need you."

"Me?"

"Yes. Please, Russell — come have merienda again. If you come, I can do it."

"Well ... what's she making today?"

She smiled. "Ah, boys and food. We will have wonderful things. We always have wonderful things. That is what is fabulous about Cecilia."

When we got to the front door she said, "Can you wait here just a second? Let me make sure it's okay."

I watched her go out, then through the glass I saw Serena Sunderland stride up to Cat on the steps, smiling like she was surprised to run into her. Cat nodded as Serena talked, but she also glanced at the red Audi.

When Cat said something, Serena stepped back and smiled. She looked my tall, dark, beautiful friend up and down, almost like she was picturing her in a pair of new leather boots.

26.

Soundtrack

"So this boy," CC said. "Are you in love with him?"

The kitchen table was packed with fruits and Filipino dishes. My new favorite was *kutsinta*, little rice muffins topped with grated coconut. They were sweet but the moment was tense.

"I ... care about him," she finally said. "And he cares about me. And that's not a bad thing," she added warmly.

"No," CC said — "it's a dangerous thing. That is different."

Cat gave me a bug-eyed look. Oh, this was starting well.

But then Cat just told her. She laid it all out, about Richie's home life and what happened on Saturday. I'd been wondering how she had gotten herself to the hospital without CC finding out. It turned out she had said she was going for a walk, then used her cell to call a taxi. When she got back an hour later, CC was busy making merienda.

Now CC just listened and nodded. She didn't seem upset or shocked. When Cat finished, she said, "Where is his mother now?"

"Home," Cat said. "She's cleaning."

"She is ..."

"Cleaning. The house," Cat said. "It's what she does when things get bad. She's making it nice for him."

I said, "For his dad? To come *home?*"

Mournfully, Cat nodded.

"But," I said, "the cops are after him!"

"Richard says ... she told the police ..." Cat sat looking at her lap.

CC said, "What?"

"She told the police she won't testify. If she has to, she will say she fell down stairs. Nobody else saw what happened, so ..."

I said, "So they can't do anything?"

"Not if she won't tell the truth."

"I don't get it," I said. "Why doesn't she just leave? Pack up and get away?"

"Well, she tells Richard she doesn't have the money. But he says she's really scared that if she tried to leave, her husband would find her, and ... he's told her ..."

135

"What?"

Cat flushed. She didn't answer.

CC said, "Perhaps her husband has told her that if she tries to leave, he will kill her."

Cat's eyes went wide. She nodded. I said to CC, "How did *you* know that?"

"There are men like this everywhere," she said. "Everywhere. Sometimes I think it is we women who are the fools."

Cat's head shot up. "What? Why? We don't do these things!"

"No — but we forgive the ones who do. We make everything nice for them, no matter what. We pretend it is all okay."

Cat looked puzzled. "What do you mean, we pretend?"

"Maybe we try too hard to understand," CC said. "We think we are caring for a man, when really we are only making an excuse."

"You mean *me*, don't you? You're talking about me!"

"No," CC said — but Cat was on her feet. She stalked out of the kitchen. We heard her stomp upstairs.

CC looked at me, sighed, and reached for the car keys.

She was driving me home when I got a call from Janelle. I said, "Yello."

"Hey." She sounded flat. Not like her at all.

I said, "You okay?"

"Yeah."

I waited, but that was it. Usually when Janelle called, she had something to *tell* you. This time, nothing.

"You don't sound okay," I said.

She didn't even answer. I said, "Have you talked to Cam?"

"A little. He's there."

"With his mom?"

"Yeah."

I waited. Just dead air.

"I'm really sorry," I said. "About what happened."

"Wasn't your fault." She sighed. "Wasn't anybody's, I guess."

"Well, I can think of a few people."

"It doesn't matter," she said. "Life's a pit and you fall in. Big news."

"Ah ... well," I said. "So ... what's up?"

Long silence.

"I just ... I don't know," she finally said. "Nothing."

It was like she was calling from some dark empty room. She finally said, "I gotta go" — but without any energy. The words just fell down and lay there.

"I'll call you later," I said. "All right?"

"You don't have to."

"I know," I said. "I want to."

"Whatever."

I sat there for a while, listening for more. Then my screen said: Disconnected.

My mom and I were eating dinner. I asked her, "How come it seemed like you knew what was going on, with Richie and stuff, even before we found out?"

"Well, I didn't. But from what we were seeing and hearing, I was afraid this was what made sense."

"Huh."

"Lots of families have secrets," she said — "and domestic violence is a lot more common than you'd expect. Now I'm wondering about Richard. Does he do this? To your friend?"

"No — she said he fights it," I told her. "The anger about it. Cat says he's never hurt her. She got all emotional, telling me that, like it's really important."

My mom nodded. "Well, it is. He's trying to break the chain."

"The what?"

"The chain. Unless someone breaks the secrecy and changes the pattern, stuff like this just gets passed down. From generation to generation. What Richard is trying to do — it's a really hard thing *to* do."

"You mean it's hard for him *not* to hurt her?"

"Very possibly."

I could hardly grasp that. "Weird."

"Imagine how this is for him, Russell. I wonder how he's feeling right now."

"I don't know." I shook my head. "I'm not even sure he knows."

My phone buzzed four times. It was Elliot.

"They're posting the video tonight," he said. "They've been working like crazy on it."

"They have?" I had no idea. I'd been totally left out.

"Yeah, to get it ready for the world," he said. "Emily's really proud of her music. She says even the B word is good in it. She's like a natural."

"Huh."

On Turner's YouTube site, the new film was titled *Darkland*. I thought, if I'd helped — not that anyone had asked me — but I *could* have come up with a more creative title.

Then the movie started.

Darkland
A film by Turner White

It opened with two shiny puddles on the court, seen up so close that at first you weren't sure what they were. They just looked like liquid mirrors, with dull gray all around.

While you peered at this, slowly realizing you were seeing gray clouds reflected in water, Emily's music started. At first it was quiet: a beat, a pulse far away. Then it was stronger, intense bass and electronic percussion coming up louder and closer and pulling you in as the camera drew back from the puddles, and you were looking at the basketball court at the School Street park.

It was empty, a dreary day. They must have come back Sunday morning. Everything looked wet and lonely. But the music was enveloping now, pounding and dangerous — then it stopped, and Bethany stepped out from where she'd been unseen on the sideline. She was wearing the same blue top and black pants she'd had on Saturday. They had worked carefully.

Bethany held a microphone. It was wireless. I didn't know Turner had a wireless mike, but why not? This was what he loved. You could feel Turner in this film already: his eye, his way of making you see things from some new point of view.

Bethany pushed her wavy cascade off her forehead — she did look good, I had to admit it — and said, "The story you are about to hear, and see, is true. It's about two eighth-grade boys in a regular middle school. It's also about an ugly rumor that neither one started. It's about how this rumor nearly wrecked their lives" — I thought that was a bit much, but oh well — "and about how the two of them came together here, on this basketball court" — Bethany stepped aside and held out her arm — "to work it out and tell the truth. Face to face. Boy to boy."

She waited a beat.

"Man to man."

Oh please, I thought — but I couldn't look away. Emily's music surged up again, this time an electronic orchestra; and we were in a tight shot of the two boys, one black and the other blonde, going at each other one on one. Cam had the ball and Jon was in his defensive crouch, hands flicking at the ball as Cam worked it and his body this way, then that. Cam backed in closer and jostled Jon, bumped him, then he spun and lifted off a shot —

And the scene froze.

Now Bethany was standing on the steps of Parkland School. She said, "The rumor was that one of these boys, the one you just saw dribbling the ball, was gay. That rumor was spread using text messaging, by a group of popular kids at this school who maintain their power by spreading rumors like this, and by keeping everyone afraid they'll be the next target."

Bethany paused for one beat. "It's a powerful tactic," she said — "but in this case it caused a violent response. Various kids forwarded the messages, as they usually do. When the boy who was the target received one of the texts, and figured out who had passed it on to him, he found that guy and attacked him.

"Those two boys are the ones you just saw," Bethany said as the camera drew in on her face. "The boy with blonde hair was left on the floor of this school" — the camera drew back as she held her arm out at Darkland. "He was almost unconscious. The other boy, the one who attacked him, was suspended from school and might be expelled."

Turner's tight editing shot us back to the two players surging back and forth on the court. It was jarring but cool, a series of quick cuts: Jon lifting a layup, Cam grabbing a rebound, their bodies banging as they chased a loose ball, then a darting steal by Jon, a hard foul by Cam. Emily's music was hopping now, banging drums and bass and guitars, rock with a metal edge — then it stopped.

"Why?" Bethany stood on the empty court. "And which was more violent — a lie like that or a physical attack? Also, once both these things had happened, what could anyone do? The damage was done, right?"

She paused, looking straight into the camera. "Luckily," she said, pausing for drama, "each of these boys ... had a friend."

The shot cut to Chris and me, standing on the sidelines watching. Then back to Bethany.

"These two friends knew each other. And one of them knew that the boy who was the attacker ... had a tragic secret. It was something no one else knew."

I thought, *Hey, Janelle knew it. See, if they'd checked with me ...*

"The two friends talked about this," Bethany said to the camera. Her voice was warm. "They thought that maybe these boys, who are both ballplayers, could be brought together away from everyone else. If that could happen, then maybe ..." Dramatic pause. "Maybe they could work this out."

Now the film gave the game, highlight by highlight, with Bethany letting you know the score as the action jumped from one smooth fake to the next banging basket. Turner had been everywhere, ducking in for angles, zooming to catch an expression at a critical moment, drawing back to get the whole drama of a hard shot that tied it. It was like watching a really good game, except with jump-cutting to keep the tension up, and with a *story*.

Then it showed the confrontation.

"That stuff made me crazy," Cam said. "But I get that you didn't start it."

"Naw," Jon said.

"So that was stupid too," Cam said. "What I did. No doubt."

Jon shrugged.

"So we cool?" Cam asked.

"Yeah."

"Check?"

From the video:

It's game point. Jon is up 14-13 — win by two — and Cam loses the ball off his foot. Jon gets it, and his fake makes Cam stumble slightly — the camera catches this — and the final action unfolds in slow motion: the two guys racing to the basket, both going up high, Jon lifting his finger-roll just beyond Cam's straining fingers. Turner catches this in a perfect closeup. A white hand, a black hand.

The ball slips through the net.

Next Bethany is on camera with the guys, asking if they're friends now and the boys giving each other gentle grief. Bethany asks how Chris made this happen and Jon says, "I heard about his dad."

Tension.

"Helmand Province," Cam says. "Hell ... man."

*Jon tries to say the right thing. "He did it for you and me — you know?"
When Cam boils up and almost spills over, the camera zooms in to catch the
glisten of tears in his eyes.*

*After Cam has turned and stalked away, there is silence. Turner lets it last
for several seconds. At last a new, deep music comes up in the silence, inside
the footsteps of a boy walking away and everyone else just breathing. The sad,
sweet music that Emily made swells up and fills everything — and now it stops.*

Bethany stands alone on the court.

*"This is Bethany DeMere," she says. "Coming to you from a place every
middle schooler knows. A place that kids here ... call Darkland."*

*Emily's music rises, pushing up louder and louder as the camera returns to
Cam disappearing up the road. Then, one last time, the music stops.*

The screen goes dark.

I sat for a long time, just staring at the screen. What they did — it
had really hit me. This film was something. I wasn't sure how I felt about
it — I felt a lot of ways — but it was *something*.

I felt the way you do when you've watched a really good movie — I
mean a really good movie, when you sit there staring as the credits roll,
and you're still *right there* and so are the feelings, and you'll carry them
through the lobby and out into the street, into your life for a while.

My phone buzzed three times. It was Elliot.

Did you SEE that???

27.

Bitchany

The next morning a lot more girls came in wearing boots. Most had them on over jeans, but the top girls, always a step ahead, were now pairing the boots with tights (or leggings, or whatever they're called) and short skirts. It was a pretty hot look. But as we came in, the buzz in the halls was not about fashion or footwear.

It was about the film.

"That video your friends made — that is *so* cool," Allison the theatrical girl said to me at my locker. She started talking fast: "It's so sophisticated, with the camera angles and the jump-cuts and ohmygod, the *music*. It's amazing — I mean really. Don't you think?"

That video your friends made. It was like I wasn't even on the team.

"That girl is a quiet little genius," Allison was saying. "How does she come *up* with that stuff?"

"Uh, I don't know." I didn't, either. I had no clue.

"I'm telling everybody about it," Allison said. "I wrote about it on Facebook, I put up a link, I texted people. Everyone should see this."

"You think so?"

"I do! You know, your friends are really talented, Russell. Even Bethany — I mean, on camera that girl *has* it. Some people just do, you know? Anyway, we should put our tables together sometime. At lunch, you know? Tell your friends to come sit with us."

"Well ..."

"No, really! Let's do it," Allison said, and the bell rang. "See you!"

She rushed off and so did everyone else, and I closed my locker thinking, *Sure, right — let me send my talented friends off to the talented table. And I'll sit there with, who ... Elliot? No, he'd go with Emily. And he's talented too, in his interplanetary way.*

Some people just are, you know?

At lunch, the Out Crowd was all there — me, Turner, Emily and Elliot, who had on a purple Froot Loops t-shirt. Everyone but Janelle, who didn't seem to be in school.

Things were different. For one, people kept *stopping by*.

"Hey guys, that video is intense."

"I saw that thing last night? On YouTube? Whoa."

"Yo, White, *nice*." That one had a hand out for high-fiving, which Turner did.

One thing I really liked was the attention Emily was getting. She deserved it. She looked at her lap as Elliot said, "People have been saying stuff to her all morning. Mr. Foley came out from the music room to stop her in the hall. He raved so much he made her late for second block."

"He wasn't *raving*," Em said, blushing fiercely.

"He totally was," Elliot said to me. "He said it was the most striking work he's ever heard by a middle schooler. He said, 'If anyone else in this school had claimed to have composed that music, I would have felt sure they'd lifted or sampled it. But I could hear your ear in that work. I knew it was all you.'"

I leaned over to Em. "You did a nice job," I said. "I was proud of you."

"Thank you. Did you really think it was good?"

"Oh god. It was amazing."

She nodded, then looked at Elliot. "Now *please* stop talking about it," she said.

He shrugged. But he was glowing, Froot Loops shirt and all.

The next one to stop by was, of all people, Bethany, carrying her tray. "Um, you guys mind if I sit?"

"Do," Turner said, and she plopped down next to him.

"Things are weird today," Bethany said to us, ignoring the fact that she'd never sat with us before. "Hi, Emily."

"Hello," Em said, looking at her thoughtfully.

Turner said, "What's up?"

"Something's going on," Bethany said.

"Yeah," I said. "You're famous."

"What? No — not that. I walk down the hall and girls *bump* me."

"In a friendly way?"

"No. Not a friendly way."

Turner said, "Which girls?"

"Those girls. And their wannabe friends. And they *say* stuff."

"Like ..."

"Well, they whisper, just loud enough to make sure I hear it. Stuff like, 'She is *so* conceited.' 'Who *does* she think she is?' I mean — just because we did a good thing, a real thing, does that mean I have to be the

143

new target? What is *wrong* with people?"

"Well," said Elliot, "they thought they'd stopped us dead, but now you're back with this amazing film. They have to do something."

Bethany was nodding intently now, like she had an idea. She turned to Turner: "We said we'd keep going, right? You said we'd film the reaction to this. Like do interviews."

"Yeah. You want to?"

She nodded. "I want to go up to Nicole Pearl."

"The one with the dating project? Why her?"

"We were friends since fourth grade — but ever since I got banned from the group, she hasn't talked to me even once," Bethany said. "Then today she was one of the ones going, 'She thinks she's *so* ...' whatever. I just want to ask her what's up. I mean, are we friends or not?"

"She's in the group, right?"

"Oh, she's inner-circle."

"Let's do it," Turner said.

I said to Bethany, "Isn't it a little risky for you to sit with us? I mean, we're not exactly social high ground."

"You guys are a little ... different," Bethany said. "But you're not going to go all weird just because there's some new whispering campaign. Anyway I had to sit somewhere. I was sitting with your friend — but that's over."

"What do you mean?"

She tilted her head toward the front of the room. I looked up and there, sitting at the Royalty table beside Serena, was Cat.

"Looks like they've got a new recruit," Bethany said. "Good luck with *that*."

After school, so much happened so fast.

In the hall, through the crowd, I saw Serena and Lauren coming out of the girls' room. I walked up fast and got in their way.

Lauren had on deluxe brown boots, purple leggings and a simple gray dress like a clingy t-shirt with a low-hanging belt. Serena was all in black, from her v-neck blouse and her long-tailed sweater — buttoned just once at the cleavage — to her short skirt and leggings and the high suede boots. They tried to step around me, but I shifted to block them.

"What are you doing?" Lauren asked patiently, as if I was mentally challenged and she was kind.

"I was gonna ask *you*," I said. Serena gazed past me, like there was something more interesting up the hall.

"Look, I get that you two have this need to play fashion police and rumorizer," I said — "but why don't you leave my friend alone?"

Lauren looked at me wide-eyed. "You have a *friend?*"

"You know who I mean," I said. "Anyway, she knows."

Lauren glanced at Serena, who shrugged. "We're kind of busy," Lauren said to me.

"You know," I said to Serena, "Cat's got some serious stuff going on right now — she doesn't need you playing your stupid power games. I mean you're a little ridiculous, all right?"

Lauren said, "Ex*cuse* you?" Then she snorted and stalked off. Now it was just me and Serena. She leaned in close.

"You think you're her friend," she hissed in my ear — "but *you* gave up her secret. I wonder. How would she feel if I told her you did that?"

For a second I was speechless. Serena stepped back and gave me that little smile. Then she stepped around me and strode to where Lauren was waiting. As they strutted away I heard them whisper, giggle and laugh.

I went to my locker in a worsening mood. When I opened it, on the floor of the locker — well, not exactly the floor: on top of the wadded mass down there of socks, paper bags, balled-up quizzes and worksheets, a sweatshirt and empty juice bottles — was a folded piece of paper.

It wasn't mine. I didn't fold anything nicely. It must have been slid in through the slats in the door. I unfolded it.

A lot of people want you to keep going.
I can help.
Meet me at 2:55 in the library.
Just you!

I ducked into a classroom to look at a clock. It was 2:45. I took one more look at the note, folded it and stuck it in my pocket. I heard, "Hey Russell."

It was Turner, hurrying up. He had his camera in his hand. "Look at this," he said. He tapped some buttons and showed me the screen:

In the hall, Bethany walks up to a thin-lipped pretty girl with long, light-brown hair.
"Hi Nicole."

The girl gives her the "Do I know you?" look.

"I just wondered," Bethany says. "Um ... I mean we were friends from fourth grade, right? Maybe even best friends. So I wonder why in the last week you haven't spoken to me at all. You act like you don't know me."

"No I don't."

"Yes you do. You just did! I just wonder why?"

Nicole looks around for backup, but doesn't have any. She turns back angrily.

"You were never my real friend," she says — "you were never anybody's real friend. I think you totally deserve what you got. I can't believe you're even talking to me!"

She sees someone up the hall, and steps around Bethany without another word. Turner's camera follows Nicole as she joins two other girls. Their faces wrinkle as they look back at Bethany.

"Were you talking to her?"

"Oh god, she tried, but please."

They snicker and walk off. "Good luck with your reputation, Bitchany," one says, and they all laugh. The camera shows Bethany from behind, standing and watching them go.

"Yikes," I said. "When'd that happen?"

"Between fifth and sixth block," Turner said.

"What'd Bethany say after?"

"She didn't. She just walked to class."

Jon Blanchette, Burke Brown and Chris walked by. Burke was an athlete, too — but he was shorter than Jon and Chris, sharp-faced and angry. He saw Turner and his eyes lit up.

"Hey, yo — way to catch the ghetto boy *crying*. He is so burned — he can *never* come back here!"

I thought, *What?*

Jon's glance flicked my way. Then he said to Burke, "I know!" And he laughed.

"You stuffed that loser," Burke said. "He's a frickin' *girl!*"

Jon laughed again, but Chris stopped as his buddies rumbled down the hall. Chris looked at me, then back at them. He sighed, shook his head and shrugged. Then he went to catch up with them.

Okay, now I was mad. I had promised not to tell anybody that Jon had cried in his kitchen, and he knew I hadn't told. Now he'd say that crap and laugh, just to be cool with his idiot friend?

"This stuff is out of control," I said to Turner.

"Tell me about it," he said. "That's why we're doing this."

"I don't feel like I'm doing anything. You guys did that movie and ... I don't know, maybe you and Bethany are together now."

Turner squinted. "What?"

"You know."

"No," he said. "I mean, in the project we do okay. But ... her and me?"

"I don't know. It just seems like you're pretty close."

He looked at me oddly. Then he started walking away.

I caught up. Turner was walking fast. He pulled out his minicam. "If you want to do something," he said, "get us material. Video. Borrow one of these from Mr. Dallas. Go up to people and ask how they felt about the film. About the rumor. You know."

"Anybody?"

"Why not?"

The main hall was full of the usual end-of-school nuttiness. A skinny seventh grader came up with a dollar crumpled in his hand.

"You guys got four quarters for a dollar?" he said.

"Uh ... no," I said.

"I don't have *any* money," Turner said to him. The kid shrugged and hurried off.

"He does that every day," Turner said.

A seventh-grade girl with kinky red hair tore across the lobby at a frantic run. Mrs. Capelli, our principal, popped out of the main office.

"Dawn, walk!"

"Okay!" Dawn yelled as she disappeared running down the hall. Mrs. Capelli stayed out here, watching the milling-around and minor mayhem. Our principal was a short person who always stood very straight, like she was trying to look taller. She sighed and shook her head. Then she spotted Turner.

"*Mister* White," she said.

"Hello, Mrs. Capelli."

She peered at him. "This new YouTube offering of yours is getting quite the buzz. I'm not sure if I should say congratulations."

"Did you see it?"

"Well, not yet. But I'm told it was shot partly on school grounds."

Turner nodded. "On Sunday. Outside. Mostly it's at the School Street park."

"And I'm told you related an incident that did occur at school."

He nodded again. She squinted. "Are you sure that's wise?"

He shrugged. "We tried to get it on the school news, but they turned us down."

"Well ... perhaps they had a point?"

"You haven't even seen it, Mrs. Capelli," Turner said. "Plus YouTube is free speech, right?"

"Uh huh." She shook her head and looked at me. "These Internet rumors and personal attacks are the bane of my life these days. You have no idea."

"But this is about how bad that stuff is," I said. "How much trouble a rumor caused."

"Uh huh," she said again, skeptically.

There was a buzzing on Turner's person. Mrs. Capelli scanned him like a sniffing bloodhound; he rushed across the hall and out the front doors. As I went to follow, the principal called after me: "You tell him, next time he loses that phone for a week!"

Outside on the steps Turner was reading a text. When I came up, he showed it. It was from Bethany:

This is getting ugly & strange. I was in the girls room before last block and I came out of a stall & Cayenne Sheffield was there with her cell out! She took a photo then she ran out and I heard laughing. I think she was waiting for me like they followed me 2 do that!

"Weird," I said.

"They're up to something. Cayenne's inner-circle too." Turner hurried down the steps.

"Where are you going?"

"I want to see how many hits the film got," he called back as he went.

I didn't have my cell. "Hey," I yelled, "what time is it?"

He checked. "Two fifty-nine!"

Holy crap — the library.

I ran back through the lobby. Mrs. Capelli called, "Mr. Trainor, walk!"

"Okay!"

28.

The Skater

I rushed into the library but it was empty. Just one kid was coming out, a fairly cute girl with short, bouncing dark hair. "In the computer lab in two minutes," she murmured as she passed.

I turned, surprised.

"Don't follow me," the girl said without looking back.

Well, okay.

Two minutes later I stepped into the computer lab. Mr. Dallas, in here alone, swiveled from a terminal. "Russ T," he said. "How's that project?"

"Uh, well ..." I was looking around. No dark-haired girl.

"I heard you guys sidestepped the authority figures," he said.

"Pardon?"

"That video the news committee wouldn't air. You put it on You-Tube."

"Oh. Yeah."

"Clever! I tell you what, *no one* controls the flow of information any more. Anyone who's got something to say can share it with the world — and no government, no media machine, no ruling class can block that. You guys are growing up with powers to communicate and connect that are totally new in history. I wonder what you'll *do* with those powers. What will you use them for?"

"Um ... huh?"

"I know, I know. You're not paying the least attention to me, and I happen to know why. A certain bright-eyed female came in and left you this."

Mr. D. held out another folded piece of paper. "Very old-school, by the way," he said as I took it. "A good old paper note."

Unfolded, it said: *Come to Crazy for Crepes, ok? I'll come in after you do. Don't leave.*

Mr. D was watching me in a sparkly way.

"I better go," I said.

"Sure. Hey, good luck with your project! Let me know if I can help."

149

I stopped. "Actually, I was thinking I might try using one of those minicams."

"Not a problem. Stop in tomorrow morning. I'll give you the briefing and you can sign one out."

"Okay. Are you here early?"

"Are you kidding? I'm in first thing. I love this job!"

Crazy for Crepes was a funky little place; they did thin, rolled-up pancakes that were really good but kind of expensive. The menu, written in chalk on a blackboard behind the counter, looked incredible and I was totally starving — but nothing was under five bucks and I only had three. I went to the cooler and got a bottle of lemonade and ice tea.

"How much is this?" I asked the girl behind the counter, who had purple-streaked hair.

"Um, $1.99."

"Okay." My stomach groaned. At least this was sweet.

People were eating at these polished-up picnic tables that had long benches. I sat at an empty table, sipped my drink and gazed up longingly at that chalkboard. They had chocolate crepes, cinnamon sugar crepes, Nutella and banana crepes, hot apple-pie crepes, and whoa the chocobananastravaganza, with bananas, chocolate sauce, whipped cream, walnuts, cherries ... oh *god* ...

"Which one?"

"Huh?" My head jerked up. Grinning down at me was a girl with dark-brown hair cut below her ears, a light splay of freckles across her nose, and — Mr. D. was right — bright blue eyes.

"I *love* this place and I have new craves on a regular basis," she said. "Which do you want? I have cash."

"Oh. Uh ... the choco ... chocoban ..."

"Chocobananastravaganza? Oh man, that's jumping in the *deep* end," she said. "Well, why not? Hang on a sec."

She marched up to the counter, where the purple girl lit up to see her. They chatted and laughed, then the bright-eyed girl paid and came back with plates, napkins and forks.

"It'll be just a minute. Try to hold on," she said as she sat down across from me. When she smiled she lit up, like from the inside.

"Sorry for the skullduggery," she said, and stuck out her hand. "I'm Kennedy."

"Um, hi. Russell."

"Oh, I know. You're a semi-notorious character."

"I am?"

"Sure. You and the Odd Pod."

"The what?"

"The Odd Pod. That's what some kids call the group you sit with. At lunch."

"Oh yeah? We call ourselves the Out Crowd."

"Huh." She nodded. "I like that, too."

The chocobananastravaganza came. "Is this not a glorious creation?" she said.

"I was thinking the same thing."

Her fork was up. "Never mind the plates — I'll take my side, you take yours, okay? Meet you in the middle."

I nodded eagerly — and for several minutes we leaned close over the table, communicating only through grunts (mine) and moans (hers). It was unbelievable. I mean the dessert, mostly.

Finally I emerged. "So what's with the scavenger hunt?" I asked. I went to wipe my mouth on my sleeve, then caught myself. Used a napkin.

"Duwhoom?" She was still chewing.

"You know. *Meet me here, now go there ...*"

She leaned over the table. "I needed to make sure they weren't watching."

"They?"

"You know, the wicked witchettes. The brides of evil."

"Oh. Right. Do they watch you?"

"They watch *you*. And your friends," she said. "They ignore me because I'm a skater."

"You're ... an ice skater?"

"No, I mean I skate from group to group. I have different friends. I'm not *cliquey*."

I remembered something. "You said a lot of people want us to keep going."

"They do, you know — a lot of people. They just can't say so because they're fearful of the brides. Which a person might think your group would be, too, after that first nasty retaliation."

"You mean the rumor thing? After the prank thing?"

"Yep — those things. Most people would have got the message. *Do not mess with us, we are* way *too evil and ruthless for you.* But not the Odd

Pod."

"We're basically from other planets," I said. "Also they pissed us off. And we have this project. It's kind of complex."

"*Everything* is complex," she said. "The thing is, right now you're pretty much stumbling around in the dark. But that's where the brides live, in the dark places where regular people get scared. They're like vampire bats. With radar."

"I think it's sonar."

"What?"

"Sonar. The way bats send out sounds in the dark, then listen for the echoes? It's sonar."

"Okay, but see, I'm saying those girls can hit you out of nowhere. They will, too. That gay rumor was nothing for them. With this new video, you're escalating, and I mean big-time. They are *going* to retaliate. You need to know what you're doing."

"What are we doing?"

"You're taking on the most powerful unit in this school," she said. "They are well-organized, and they have no qualms. No scruples. A lot of people would like to see them broken, or exposed, and you guys might be just clever *and* clueless enough — it's an interesting combination — to maybe pull it off. But you need help. That's where I come in."

"Okay. But why you?"

The sparky smile opened across her face. I liked that smile.

"Because I skate, Russell! I go here, sit there, I talk to everyone, and nobody thinks it's strange. I'm just like that." She leaned over the table. "So I can tell you some things you need to know. If you want me to."

I had seen her around, I realized it now — and she was right: she could be anywhere. She was friendly enough, and cute enough, that she could talk to anyone.

"Okay," I said. "What should we know?"

"You should know about *them*. Are you ready? You might want to take a few notes. This'll get a little complicated."

"Uh, yeah. I have my stuff." I zipped open my backpack, found a blank page in my ratty Language Arts notebook.

This would be good for the project. I was onto something, I could feel it.

"Okay," Kennedy said. "There are five in the inner group. They also have other girls that they let sit with them, and do stuff for them. Those can be candidates — people they're grooming, testing, finding stuff out

152

about, seeing if they can control. Because this is *all* about control. Are you with me so far?"

I grunted, and wrote down *Five. Inner group. Control.*

"Now in the five, there are roles. This is an *organization*, Russell. First there's Rachel Holzinger. She's the intelligence agent."

"Who?"

"Ah, see — you don't even notice her. She's the only one in the inner group who's allowed to not be hot. She's a skinny-faced girl, not tall, brown straight hair. Quick eyes. Can you picture her now?"

"I ... kind of." I could see a girl like that, sitting at the table. Kennedy was right, she wasn't eye-catching. But she was there.

"Rachel finds out what the top girls need to know. Like maybe someone did something they wish they hadn't."

"Like what?"

Kennedy shrugged. "I don't know ... maybe a girl is bulimic so she throws up her lunch in the girls' room, or she sneaks vodka into school in a juice bottle. Or maybe she shoplifts makeup and hair supplies from the Rite-Aid — not because she can't afford those things, but just because this is something she does. You see?"

I didn't see. "Girls do stuff like that?"

Kennedy grinned. "See, this is what's so sweet about you and your friends," she said. "It's like you've been living on an island."

I thought, *Did she just call me sweet?*

"The thing is," she said, "girls who really need to be attractive, who need to be popular, who really really need to be in *this* group — these are basically the most whacked-out insecure people in our school. They don't look that way, but they are. You know why?"

"Why?"

"Because they have secrets, and they will do *anything*. They may not know why they have to steal the makeup or mix the vodka with the juice or stick their finger down their throat, or do ... certain things for certain guys, but they do, and they have to keep their secrets *and* look good doing it. These girls are barely keeping the lid on their lives. The ones right below the absolute top, they are *desperate* — and they can never seem that way for a second.

"So Rachel finds out stuff," she said, "then she passes that info to the top. By the time a girl figures out she cannot trust Rachel, that Rachel is a ferret and a sneak, it's too late. Are you getting this?"

"Yeah." I'd written *Rachel. Intelligence. Sneak.*

153

"Okay. Next there's Nicole Pearl."

"Right." That was Bethany's former sort of friend. "What's she do?"

"She's the action girl. If the top witchettes want to carry out a plot, like say spread a rumor that someone is cheating on her boyfriend, because it's a couple the group decides to break up — which happens a lot, by the way — then Nicole will set that in motion. She'll tell people what the girls need them to do, like pass a text along or whisper something nasty in the halls. She's a networker. She's very good at it."

"Okay." *Nicole. Networker. Nasty.*

"Then there's Cayenne Sheffield. Now, Cayenne is interesting to me. She's the one with the strawberry blonde hair and the cute smile who studies what Lauren wore today so she can wear something very similar tomorrow. She's the most recent one in the top group, and she knows she's insecure in it.

"I figure Cayenne is either the weak link or the absolutely most ruthless one," Kennedy said. "Because she will do *anything*. These girls know they could be out at any random moment. That's key to the top girls' control."

"How do you know these girls so well?"

Kennedy looked almost proud. "I'm a skater. Sometimes I even sit with them."

I couldn't believe it. "Do you like these girls?"

Her eyes flashed. "*Nobody* likes them. Everyone is *scared* of these girls. They don't care what's true and what isn't — they don't care about you, your friendships, or your relationship if you have one. They'll spread some story just to prove they can mess with you. It's all about fear, control and lies — and it all comes from these five."

"Okay. Rachel, Nicole, Cayenne."

"Right. Next is the one everybody thinks is the queen — but that's another false front. This girl gets to dictate how to look and she gets to have the hottest boyfriend, but inside she's as petrified as the rest of them."

"I had a feeling about that," I said.

"You did?"

"Kind of. Also, Bethany said something about it."

"Ah yes, Bethany. The witchettes never really trusted her, and you know why? Because she was still kind of real. She didn't *want* to be real, but she wasn't totally ruled by insecurity and fear. See, if you don't have that darkness inside, it doesn't matter how good you look or how hard you try — when they're done with you, bang: you're out on your perky little butt wondering what's wrong with you. But it's because you're still partly real. They *hate* that.

"And that's why they hate you guys, okay? People might think they would ignore you, the Odd Pod — but you're a threat to them," Kennedy said. "Since all this started, I've been sort of watching you. And you guys may not be classically, um, popular, but you're clever and creative and you don't give off waves of fear and insecurity. I think you scare them a little. It's not obvious how they can destroy you — but they *will* try. They're looking for your weakness, and if they can find it they'll use it to shatter you."

"O ... kay," I said. "So what can we do?"

She looked at me carefully. "I'm going to mention something that may be, possibly, a little sensitive. Is that okay?"

"I don't know. I guess."

"Really? You sure?"

"Yes. Go."

"Okay. The top girls will pick out a new recruit, and it's not hard to see that when it happens. This new girl has to be really good-looking, and she has to be vulnerable in some way. They will detect this. I'm telling you, they are *good*.

"The new recruit will start to hang out with them," she said. "She'll sit with them. She'll be Lauren or Serena's new special friend."

"Okay," I said. "So maybe I know someone who's ..."

"Right," Kennedy said. "And if you ask me, this is when these girls are vulnerable, when they've got a new prospect. They don't yet totally control that person. So I mean, maybe that new person could be, kind of like, your eyes and ears. You see where I'm going with this?"

"You want me to recruit a spy?"

"Well ..."

"Isn't that a little sketchy?"

"Sketchy?" she said, wide-eyed. "Why?"

"I don't know ..."

"No, I get what you mean," Kennedy said — "but this is a chance to use their game against them. I mean it's possible, right? I don't know your relationship with ... you know ..."

"The recruit."

"Right. Something has told the witchettes this girl could be one of them. Are they right? Can Serena control this girl?"

This was deep. It was strange. "I don't know," I said. "I can maybe see how ..."

My cell buzzed three times. "Hang on," I said, taking it out.

From Turner:

22,763 hits

I stuck the phone back in my pocket.

"What is it?"

"Something weird. But not bad."

Then my cell buzzed four times. "Sorry again," I said, reaching for it as Kennedy grinned. Then her face fell as she watched me listen.

Cat was crying on the phone. I said, "What? What is it?"

"Can you come? Can you ... please help me?"

"Where are you?"

"At the park."

"On School Street?"

"Yes. Oh my god ..."

"What? What happened?"

"Russell, he *hit* me. He hit me really ... oh my god ..."

She was just sobbing, now.

"Stay there," I said. "I'll be right there."

I shut the phone and stood up from the table. "I have to go. Something's happened."

Kennedy looked worried. "Is it bad?"

I nodded. "It's ... our girl."

"The recruit?"

"Yeah."

"Did *they* do something?"

I shook my head. "Not them. I have to go."

"Can I do anything?"

"No. Thanks."

She grabbed my notebook, turned it her way, and scribbled.

"That's my cell," she said. "Go."

I ran out the door.

29.

Backhand

I got to the park on the run. At the edge of the basketball court I bent over, heaving for air. This was where Jon and Cam had played their game — but I was looking past the court now, out at the wet fields. I couldn't see her.

Beyond the fields was a small footbridge over a stream, with the Little League ballpark past that. As I walked I scanned carefully, from left to right and back. The little bridge creaked as I crossed it. The stream below was swollen brown.

The grass was thin and puddly on the baseball field; the signs of the Little League sponsors hung on the outfield fence, lonely in the offseason. World of Windshields, Tipson Tire, Bowl-o-Rama. I couldn't see her.

Then I heard her.

The sound came from somewhere in the infield. I walked that way, peering all around. Then, inside the dugout along the third-base line, I saw a shape.

The dugout was a long green shed, open at both ends with a thick screen across the front to protect the players. Stooping inside, I saw a concrete floor, a long wooden bench, and her.

She was slumped in the far corner on the bench, arms wrapped around her drawn-up legs and head on her knees. She was shaking, sobbing. She didn't look up. I padded over softly and sat down.

Middle school girls cry pretty often. You'll hear hiccupy sobs coming up the hall, and then a girl will rush past in a knot of her friends — or at a dance, a weepy one will hurtle by trailing others en route to the girls' room. Usually you see this and go, *Okay. It's drama, it's everyday.* But this was different.

This crying was deep and ragged, like something inside Cat was ripping. It was scary, how she sounded.

Finally she settled down a little. I said, "Can you tell me what happened?"

She nodded. But she didn't say anything. I said, "It's okay. I'm right here." She sat up a little but stayed slumped in that corner, like she was getting as far away as she could. From everything? From me?

She took a deep, shuddery breath.

"I said I wanted ... to come to his house. After school." Her breath came in little jerks. "I ... called him, but he said no. I said Richard I need to see you — but he said no. He said it wasn't safe. He said, *I'm telling you.* I said I didn't c-c-care, I wanted to *see* him. He said no!"

She stopped and looked past me. I turned. No one was there.

"I said I was coming — just for a minute," she said. "He swore at me really hard, like he never did before — and he hung up."

She pulled a tissue from her backpack. Wiped her face, blew her nose. "He called back and said I had to meet him at the Convenience Farms, *right now.* You know, the store where he used to hang around? He didn't even wait for an answer, he just hung up again. So I went there."

The place was a gas station and convenience store, a few blocks from here. I was familiar with it.

"When he got there," she said, "he was walking very fast, and his face ... it was strange. He didn't say hello or anything, he just kept walking right by me. Then he gave me this *look*, like I was supposed to come, too."

I nodded. I knew that look.

She said, "I asked him, 'Where are we going? Why won't you *talk* to me?' But he wouldn't say a word — he just kept walking along, so fast I almost had to run to keep up. And he had this look. It was so *strange.*"

She clutched herself and rocked. After a bit she said, "He brought me here. It's a place we came to sometimes, in the winter."

I looked out at the bleak, puddly field. They came here?

"As soon as he got me in here, he *turned* on me. He called me a stupid effing bitch — said I wasn't listening to him and didn't he have enough problems and what was wrong with me? He kept saying that — 'What is *wrong* with you? Don't you know I have to *be* there?' He got more and more worked up — he said, 'Who the eff do you think you are? Huh? *Who?* When I didn't know what to say and I started to cry, because I was scared, he swore really hard and he hit me."

"How? How?"

"Just like ..." She swiped her arm backhand; then she slumped in the corner again. She pulled up her knees and sobbed, hopelessly.

I felt like I'd stuck my finger in a light socket. Electric anger. I fought it back down.

"Are you all right? Did he hurt you?"

She nodded yes, shook her head no, then shrugged and pulled her arms over her head. Inside her own cocoon, she just wept.

My phone buzzed three times. It was Turner.

37,821

I sat there looking at the phone. "We need to get you home," I said. "I want to call CC."

Her arms opened, a crack. "What?"

"Can you give me CC's number? She can come in the car. Bring you home." I was shaking, I was so upset. But I had to hold it together, get her safe. "She won't be mad," I said — "she'll come get us."

I held up my phone. "Tell me her number. Okay?"

Staring past me, tears flowing, Cat took out her phone. She punched numbers, handed it to me and sat there, staring through the wire. I looked at the dismal, drippy field as I waited for CC to answer.

In the red Audi, we were silent. Cat huddled against the corner in back.

"Do you want to go home?" CC asked me.

"I ... you know ... I want to make sure she's okay," I said. "Is that all right? I don't need to go home right away."

"Yes. Thank you," she said as she drove.

I waited in the kitchen. Before CC took Cat upstairs, she had asked if I wanted a snack, but I shook my head. Now I sat at the table, looking out at the empty backyard.

The trees had faded into murky shadows. The first anger had vibrated through me. I felt mostly bleak, dismal, disappointed. Sad.

Why would he *do* that? Hadn't Cat stuck by him no matter what? Hadn't she wanted to go to his house just to make sure he was okay? Why would he get so mad? Why hurt *her*?

My cell buzzed three times. Turner again.

This thing is going crazy! We had over 18,000 hits in the last HOUR

I turned the phone off and shoved it in my pocket. Outside, it was getting dark. When I heard the two of them coming down the stairs, I sat up and tried to put on a positive expression. The hall door opened, and

159

CC led Cat into the kitchen.

My friend was pale. She'd had a shower, her hair was wet and stringy. She sat down across the table. Her right cheek had a spongy-looking bruise, a mass of tiny gray lines on her skin. The look in her soft, sad brown eyes ... it went right through me.

I'd expected CC to start whipping up a late merienda, but she sat down, too.

I asked Cat, carefully, "How are you?"

She shrugged. Touched her bruise. She said, "Do you ... do you think I can still be his friend? It's a really hard time for him right now. But ... if he can do this ..."

"When a man does this once, it is over." CC said this firmly to me, but really to Cat. "It has to be. If the man is forgiven, he will do it again. He will always do it again."

"It was so scary, Russell. *He* was so scary."

"It is hard," CC said, nodding. "But if you cannot be strong for yourself and also please someone else — then you must be strong for yourself."

I nodded. I totally agreed. But Cat just sat there, looking miserable and unsure, fingers on her bruise.

30.
An Alternate Universe

That night the phone and the Net went nuts.

By seven o'clock, the video had over 118,000 hits on YouTube. Facebook messages and texts were flying everywhere. After what I'd just been through, it felt like I'd stepped into an alternate universe.

Turner was forwarding us messages from all these people, who knows where they were. On his YouTube site, comments were getting posted one after another after another.

This is pure total amateur hour. If you think this proves anything, dream on!

I think the black kid should have punched the white kid in the face. That's what Id of done I wouldn't even THINK about it!

This is a beautiful salute to what our American families are going through for freedom. We all owe military families a big thank you — look at the pain in that boy's eyes! It just tears you up sometimes. THANK YOU for this wonderful film.

It can take children to show us what we really are. Vicious rumors, shattered families, ugly racism ... we're slipping into darkness and our kids are inheriting the whirlwind. Wake up people!!!

I dont get why anyones into this wierd little film. Its like ok theirs a black kid and a white kid and they play a game and the black kid looses and he crys, right? And were sposed to care about this WHY???

Last poster you'd be brain-dead if you HAD a brain, which I seriously doubt. Did you even watch this amazing story, which by the way is TRUE, ok? Your social conscience is on the level of your spelling ability, which appears to be way below zero. It's losers like you that are making the Internet a wasteland.

And on and on and on.

I wanted to be positive, to do something positive. I texted Turner:

Incredible! Does this mean you made it?

He wrote back:

I have no idea what's happening but thanks

I had an idea. I called Elliot. He said, "You believe this?"

"Yeah, no — listen, what's Emily's number? I need to call her about something."

"Okay, but she's a little freaked out right now. All these people are posting comments about her music. You know, Em's kind of shy."

"Um ... yes, Elliot. Is she okay?"

"Oh, she's *okay* — she just doesn't know what to make of all this. People are saying she's a genius, she's brilliant, they want to download the soundtrack. All of a sudden."

"Well, maybe she is a genius."

"Yeah, well what is that? What are you supposed to do if people call you that?"

"I sure wouldn't know."

"Well, anyway, go ahead and call her," Elliot said. "Just act normal, okay?"

"As opposed to ..."

"I don't know. Be regular."

I couldn't believe I was hearing "be regular" from Elliot Gekewicz.

"You want to ... what?"

On the phone, Emily's voice faded like she was shrinking away.

"I want us to go up to the girls in that group," I said — "get each of them on video, for the project. You know, like 'This is Nicole,' "This is Cayenne.' We can use a Flip cam tomorrow, I talked to Mr. D. We'll go up to them in the hall and ask a question, any question, with the camera on. Whatever they do or say, we'll have it on film. It'll be part of the project. Social pressures, right?"

"I can't go up to those girls," she said. "I think I would pass out."

"Well ..."

"I might pass out now."

"It's all right," I said. "Really."

"It's just ... we're hearing from all these people and, I mean, I get very anxious in social situations. My heart starts racing and I get really scared. I could do the music," she added eagerly.

"Sure," I said, though I couldn't see how music would fit, here.

"But you need someone," she said. "You don't want to go up to those girls all alone."

"Well, I mean it's not like ..."

"El would do it," she said.

"Huh? Elliot?"

"Yes. He would. He doesn't really understand about social pressures anyway. Russell, Amanda Burrell wants to interview me. For the music project."

"Well, of course."

"But I can't."

"Why not?"

"I just can't! She wants to put me on *camera*. I don't ... I wouldn't know what to say."

"Talk about your music," I said. "How'd you get into it?"

"I ... but ..." She was almost choking. "I *can't*."

"Okay, Em, it's okay. You don't have to if you don't want to."

But I thought it would be a shame if Emily wasn't in that music project somehow. I kind of hoped Amanda would keep trying.

"Sure," Elliot said on the phone when I asked him to help do the interviews. "That'll be *fun*."

I thought, *You know, it might just be.*

Kennedy texted me.

Everything OK?
Sort of.
U going to talk to her?

I had to stare at my phone a second, to remember she meant Cat. I thought, *Well, why not? It might take her mind off him.*

I guess so, I texted back.
Let me know what happens. Good luck!

163

"I can't go to school tomorrow," Cat said on the phone. She sounded better now. Stronger. "Everyone'll just look at me, at my face like this. It's nobody's business anyway."

"Right. You should stay home."

Then he can't meet you after school, I thought. *It'll be Wednesday. If he comes, you won't be there.*

"He's been calling," she said.

I sat up. "He has?"

"Yes."

"Have you answered?"

"No. I don't know what to say."

"What does he say?"

"He leaves messages. He says, 'Please call me. I need to talk with you.'"

"Huh."

"He does say please," she said. "And I'm *worried* about him. Where's his dad? What's going to happen?"

"I don't know," I said. "But if you let him get away with that, things will only get worse."

She sighed. "That's what Cecelia says."

"Well, it's true. Listen — I wanted to talk to you about something else."

"All right."

"I saw you sitting with Serena and her friends today. At lunch."

"Oh, yes. She and I are a lot alike."

"What? How?"

"Well ... she said to me, 'Never mind these blondies. We have *our* way.' That was nice, you know? And she wants to know about me — where I come from, what my family is like. She's interested, you know?"

I thought, *Of course she is.*

"Listen," I said. "That rumor — the gay thing that led to the fight. Serena did that. Her and her friends. They do stuff like that to people."

"Is there proof? That they started the rumor?"

"Well ... we know they did."

"Show me proof," she said.

"They kicked Bethany out. You *saw* that. You saw their text."

"Yes. But Bethany has not always been so nice herself."

I was thinking hard. This wasn't even my idea. What did I want Cat to do? What was best for her?

"I've just been so lonely this year," she said. "I've only had two good friends, and you're both males, you know? A girl needs girlfriends, Russell. It feels so much better to have a friend who understands you that way. Who gets you."

"What about Allison? She's a girl. She's your friend."

"Allison's been really nice to me, but I don't fit in with her theater friends — and she kind of talks a lot," Cat said. "Serena's not like that. She listens."

"Okay," I said, "but maybe ... I mean ... okay, we're doing our project on social pressures, right? Serena and her friends are the top group, no doubt. I guess it's an honor to be invited to sit with them, but I wonder if there'll be pressure. Will they start asking you to look a certain way, or maybe do certain things? I just kind of wonder. Will you let me know what it's like?"

"Let you know?"

"Well, yeah."

"You mean for your project, or just as friends?"

"Well, I mean ..."

"Wait," she said — "he's texting me."

I waited. When she came back on, her voice was different.

"They found his dad," she said. "He's been arrested."

"They found him? Where?"

"Outside the house. He was watching the house."

"Oh. Um ..."

"I have to call him, Russell," she said. "He needs me. I'll call you."

She hung up.

By the time I finally signed off and went to bed that night, *Darkland* had 147,038 hits on YouTube.

31.
In the Spotlight

When I came up to the front steps in the morning, kids were showing each other their phones. Turner saw me coming and rolled his eyes. He said, "Did you see it?"

"See what?"

He pulled out his smartphone, tapped keys and turned it to show me the screen. It had another forwarded text, but with no words this time, only a link: www.bitchanysworstquality.com.

The home page of bitchanysworstquality.com showed the girls' room photo of Bethany from yesterday. Snapped as she stepped out of a stall, she looked shocked, her mouth twisted and her forehead wrinkled in surprise. They definitely had snapped her not at her best.

Under the photo was a poll.

What is Bitchany's WORST QUALITY??
1. She's gross-looking
2. She's a slut
3. She thinks it's all about HER

They'd gotten somebody who was good at coding to set this up, so that each question had a little box beside it. Below the options, it said:

Click on your choice & you'll be counted. Vote today! Vote tonight! Look for the results here TOMORROW

I went, "Gack. Has she seen this?"

Turner nodded. "Hey, you know how many *hits* we have?"

He tapped his phone, and showed me a counter. I'd only glanced at it when the bell rang; it was over 200,000, for sure.

Before first block started I had signed out a Flip cam from Mr. D. He gave me a red one. Its color was fairly glaring, but I figured, fine. I wanted the girls to know we were filming. I wanted to see what they would do.

* * *

166

Between first and second blocks I got a text from Cat.

Please call me right away.

I went in the restroom, closed the door of a stall. Took a deep breath and called.

"I need to ask you something," she said.

"Like ..."

"A favor. I talked to him this morning."

I was sucking in air when she said, "I know! But listen, please. His dad's in custody, but Richard says they can't hold him if Ellen won't cooperate. He might be out tonight. He wants very, very much to talk to me."

"His *dad?*"

"No — Richard! He said he was really upset that I made him leave his house yesterday, because he had to be there in case his dad showed up. And he couldn't let me come over, because it wasn't safe. That does make sense, Russell."

"Yeah, but ..."

"He asked me to meet him after school today," she said.

"You know, just because he ..."

"I said no."

"What?"

"I did! I said I won't be alone with him."

"Well," I said. "All right."

"So I need you to come talk with him. With me and CC."

"*What?*"

"Russell, he sounded desperate. He says if he can't talk with me, he doesn't know what will happen. I ... said we could meet downtown."

"But I'm ..."

"*Please*, Russell. If you could have heard him — it's like his life is coming apart. His mom was in the hospital, his father's in jail, and he knows he hurt me. He's doesn't sound like the same person. Can it be so awful if we just listen to him? If you're there, and CC is too?"

The bell rang. I took another calming breath. I said, "I have to get to class. Where do you want to do this?"

"I don't know! Where should we go?"

"Crazy for Crepes is nice."

"Okay. After school!" She hung up.

167

After school. Yes. I know.

Then I wondered why I'd mentioned *that* place. What if Kennedy saw us?

That morning, word flashed all over school that Jon Blanchette had been dumped as Lauren Paine's boyfriend. One of her inner-circle girls had told him last night.

I was still irked at Jon for laughing about Cam. *Good,* I thought. *He deserves it.*

At lunch Bethany plopped down her tray. "Did you see that thing? That site?"

I said, "Yep. You okay?"

"Are you kidding? They are *desperate!*" She seemed almost happy.

"It doesn't bother you?"

Bethany turned to Turner. "How many hits now?"

He glanced around before pulling out his cell under the table.

"Two hundred twenty-two thousand, four hundred fifty two."

"And all they've got is a photo and some ridiculous poll," Bethany said.

"I wonder if people will actually vote," I said.

"I hope they do." She said to Turner, "It's in the project, right?"

He nodded. "I got screen shots. If they publish results, we'll get those too. It's excellent stuff, if you think about it."

"They're still dangerous," Emily said quietly.

Bethany snorted. "Yeah. Bring it *on.*"

Janelle was staring at Bethany with a puzzled look. Janelle had missed two days; she said she'd been sick. Lately, two days was like two universes. I realized how bizarre it must seem that Bethany was even sitting with us.

"I got a Flip cam from Mr. D," I said to Turner. "We're going to go up to the brides of evil — try to catch them separately. Put 'em on camera."

"The brides of evil — that's good! Where'd you get that?"

I shrugged. He said, "You're gonna do it with ..."

"With Elliot," I said. "What should we ask?"

"Ask if they feel threatened by the film," Bethany said. "Ask if they feel *overshadowed.*"

"What film?"

We all turned to look at Janelle. She said, "Well? What film?"

We just stared. "How sick were you?" Elliot asked.

She shrugged. "I didn't feel like doing much. Did I miss something?"

Turner said, "Well ..."

Elliot and I got our first chance right as lunch broke up.

Cayenne Sheffield was the last one left at the top table. She was gobbling chocolate pudding, spoon spoon spoon, eyes flicking around like she didn't want to get caught.

I said to Elliot, "Camera ready?"

"Ready," he said, fiddling with it and smiling. Give him a gadget, he was happy.

"Hi, Cayenne!"

She looked up, saw the camera and froze.

"You've got a little pudding there," I said, pointing to my face.

"What? Where? Is that thing on?"

Elliot said, "Yeah!"

She took out a little mirror, peered at her face. "I don't, like, see anything?"

"Oh," I said. "Yeah, I guess it's gone."

She glared at me. "What are you doing?"

"Interviews. For Language Arts. Interviewing key kids," I said.

"O ... kay?"

I had never spoken to Cayenne before. It appeared she said everything as a question.

"Can you tell me," I said, "who are your role models?"

"My ... role models?" Now she gave her head a little tilt and smiled, like she'd decided to be cute for the camera. She was wearing a gray t-shirt dress with a belt, like the one Lauren had worn the other day. "Okay, Angelina Jolie? 'Cause of that stuff she does in Africa?"

"How about here?"

She looked around. "Where?"

"Here. In this school. If you could be exactly like any one person in this school — if you could look and act and maybe dress like anyone ... who would that be?"

"Who ... are you serious?"

"Why not?"

"Are you trying to make me *look* bad?"

"Why would you say that?" I was starting to have fun.

"I don't know ... 'cause you think it might *help* you? With your *friends?*"

"How would this help me?"

"I don't *know? Okay?*" Behind her, the next lunch came thundering in through the doors.

"Don't you have, like, class?" she asked. "With the *special* kids?"

"Now was that nice, Cheyenne?"

"It's Cayenne? Okay?"

She stood up, turned her back and hurried away. Elliot zoomed in on her empty pudding cup.

"Hmm. Reality," he said, nodding as he shut off the camera. "I could get into this."

In Language Arts, Ms. Corbin's expectant look landed first on Amanda Burrell, up front with her guitar.

"Amanda, let's start our check-in with your team," Ms. Corbin said. "To remind you all, your web documentaries are due at the end of next week."

Mass groan.

"So how's the music project?"

Amanda started strumming hard. Ms. Corbin waited. Amanda stopped, looking around like she'd just realized we were there. "What?"

Richard Sunshine, the heavy kid on her team, piped up. "It's going okay," he said. "I'm doing a Garage Band tutorial."

"*You* are?" said Amanda.

"Well, we are," Richard said. "And we asked different kids who play instruments to be videotaped. We've got a girl playing oboe, a boy who does keyboards, and this guy who plays the didje."

"The what?"

"It's Australian — like a long bamboo thing," Richard said.

"It's not *like* a bamboo thing," Amanda said. "It *is* bamboo."

"Right," Richard said amiably. "You sort of blow into it. It moans." He swayed back and forth, playing an imaginary didgeridoo. "Plus we've got Amanda playing some of her ... own compositions."

"Frickin' *right*," Amanda said. "Puttin' 'em on YouTube after this. I'm gonna be the next one famous." She glared around, like she dared anyone to say different. "And I'm doin' some interviews," she said. "Tryin' to get key people to talk to me. It's not as easy as you'd think."

Emily stared fiercely at the floor.

"Are you asking ... nicely?" Ms. C asked.

"You bet your ... I mean, yes I am," she declared. Everyone grinned except Emily, who was as red as her shoes.

Ms. Corbin went around the room getting updates, some of them real, some of them obviously quickly dreamed up by kids who hadn't done much yet. Jon Blanchette said he and his sports-project team had been filming team practices and a pickup basketball game. He seemed a little dazed.

"Is that it, Jon?" Ms. Corbin asked.

"Well, I mean ... We're gonna do interviews."

"Okay. Will you do anything that takes you out of your comfort zone?"

"Out of what?"

"You know, stretching yourself. Are there any unusual athletes here that you might film or interview?"

"There was one," I volunteered. "A good basketball player. But he's not here any more." I stared at Jon. He didn't look back.

"Bethany?" Ms. Corbin said, "How's your team doing?"

"Oh, like everyone doesn't know *that*," said Baker Corrigan.

Everyone turned to look. "Yo, Baked's *awake*," some guy said. Baker grinned in a cocky way.

"People?" Ms. Corbin said. "I'd like to hear about their project."

"What's it like to be famous?" some kid in the back said to Bethany.

"Yeah — and to have dirty old men looking at you, and guess what *they're* doing," Baked said. This tipped the class into an uproar so loud that Otis, the big kid who always had his head on his arms, looked up and blinked.

"All right, *enough*," Ms. Corbin said. But she was losing us.

"Hey!" Otis glowered around at the suddenly silent class. "That's right," he said, and nodded to Ms. Corbin.

"Why ... thank you, Otis," Ms. Corbin said.

"No problem." We waited for Otis to put his head back down. But he looked at Bethany. "What are you gonna do next?" he asked. "To go with that video."

"Good question, Otis," Ms. Corbin said.

"Well," Bethany said. "We're also doing interviews. And there was a request for nasty texts ..."

"Oh yeah," said Baked. "That got *stomped*."

"Baker, you're quite lively today," Ms. Corbin said. "What do you mean?"

"Everybody knows what I mean. Those that are cool are those that rule."

This set everyone off — Baked Corrigan not only making sense, but rhyming! And he seemed so smug.

"Oh, give me a break." That was Jon. "Some guys think they're hot when everyone knows they're not."

"Oh yeah? And some guys are losers," Baked said. "Right pretty boy?"

"You know what, Corrigan? You're a jackass."

The class erupted. Baked said, "Yeah? You want to go?"

"How about right now?"

They both stood up. Ms. Corbin said in her loudest voice, "You two *sit*. Now!"

Baked and Jon slowly sat, glaring at each other. The class settled, electric with the tension. What was up between those two? Ms. Corbin was shaking her head.

"Jon Blanchette. Of all people. To the office, please. And I have to say I'm *very* disappointed."

Jon sighed, gathered up his stuff and shuffled out. Baker smirked at him. Amanda twanged a harsh chord. Ms. Corbin let out a long, slow sigh, then looked around at the Whatever Class. "Remember, people," she said — "your projects are due! End of next week. They're 60 percent of your semester grade!"

I had to do math problems, and a dichotomous-key chart for science. That's where you show how a bunch of either-or choices, like vertebrate/invertebrate, meateater/planteater, can lead you to any species of creature. Your choices lead you anywhere. I figured I'd better grab what time I could — especially because it might take my mind off this looming meeting at Crazy for Crepes.

Richie would show up and there I'd be. Would he flip out? Go into a rage? I had no idea, and I was trying not to think about this when I stepped into the library and saw Cat, sitting in there with Serena.

They were huddled over a table, talking so intently they didn't notice me. I ducked back among the shelves. I could hear Serena's low, caressing voice, turning up with questions as she drew gentle, excited-sounding answers from Cat.

I had two tall sets of bookshelves between me and their table. I could sidle over and stand there listening, but sooner or later they'd spot me through the shelves. Then I had an idea.

I reached into my backpack and pulled out the Flip. I pushed Record, and with the thing cupped in my hand I strolled along the aisle between the shelves. When I got to the spot closest to them, with only a bookshelf between us, I reached up quietly, quickly, and laid the minicam on top of the shelf. Its camera eye was pointed up at the ceiling, but the audio should pick up what the girls were saying.

You're spying on your friend, I thought as I walked out of the library. Cat, intent on Serena, never looked up.

Yep. It's come to this.

32.
One Friend

I figured I'd hang around out here in the hall until Cat and Serena left the library. Then I could duck back in and snag the camera before I headed to the meeting with Richie, which I really did not want to think about. I was going toward my locker, thinking I'd grab my math stuff and get some work done, when I turned the corner and saw Rachel Holzinger the intelligence agent.

She was by herself, loitering. She hadn't seen me. I ducked back. *Hmm.*

She had to be waiting for Serena. These girls rarely went anyplace alone. But she'd also been looking around like she was interested in something. In what — locker doors along an empty hall? I had no clue, but I figured it'd be more fun to accost Rachel, on camera, than to do math.

I strolled back into the library. I heard Serena say, "She has Internet and everything?" as I hurried between the shelves, reached up, and snatched the Flip. When I strode up to Rachel in the hall she got pop-eyed, like I'd caught her at something. I remembered: *She's a sneak.*

"Hey Rachel," I said — "I'm interviewing popular kids. For a Language Arts project."

"Uh ... yeah," she said. "I know." She glanced over my shoulder.

"Are you looking for Serena? She's in the library," I said.

"Uh huh," said Rachel, obviously knowing that, too. She had on jeans and a plain blue warmup jacket over a black t-shirt. She wasn't wearing the boots. It was like she was a plainclothes cop.

"Don't turn that on," she said as I turned the camera on.

"As a member of a really popular group," I said, lifting the camera, "what kind of pressures would you say you face?"

"Uh ..."

Rachel didn't want to be filmed. Her eyes kept flicking elsewhere, and she did not smile.

"I don't know," she said. "Isn't there someone else you could talk to?"

"But you're in the top group."

"Where do you get that idea?"

"Well ..."

"There aren't really groups here, not in that cliquey way," Rachel said. "People just have friends. Are you saying there's something wrong with that?"

"I was just wondering what kind of pressures you have."

"I would say mainly being judged and misunderstood — like right now," she said. "But I'm wondering what *you're* doing here."

"I go to school here," I said.

"Yeah, but you're waiting for somebody, right?" Her eyes glittered. "Are you still doing that?"

"I'm ... working on a project. Why? Are you gathering information?"

"I have no idea what you're talking about," Rachel said, and she spun and stalked away.

I was at my locker, putting the camera away, when I heard Cat's voice and then Serena's. When they turned the corner and saw me, they went silent. Serena smiled.

"Um — hi," Cat said. "Are you ready to go?"

I nodded as Serena slowed down to glide by. Her dancing eyes held mine for a second, then she glanced into my locker as I shut the door. She raised one eyebrow, like maybe she knew something. But that was how she always looked at you. Right?

No. Something was going on. Rachel hadn't been here by accident, and I was pretty sure Serena didn't do anything by accident. What did she want? And why that look?

"*Are* you ready?" Cat was peering oddly at me.

"Oh — yeah. Sure."

As we walked up to Crazy for Crepes, oh god there was Kennedy, just coming out. She spotted me, then Cat. She gave me a look, then held the door for Cat. Inside the cafe I could see CC, already waiting. No Richie, so far.

"Sooo," Kennedy said as she let the door drift closed. She and I were outside. "Progress?"

"I don't know," I said. "I can't really talk right now. Kind of a tense situation."

"Okay, okay. You got my number, right?"

I nodded. She pulled open the door.

"A friend?" Cat said when I came to the table. She sat beside CC.

"Yeah. I mean, I don't know."

CC leaned into the aisle, trying to see who we meant, but Kennedy had already walked away. "It's nothing," I said, then Cat's face tightened. I turned to see Richie push open the door.

He saw us three and stopped. He gave Cat an intense, questioning look. CC's expression hardened.

Richie walked toward us, his eyes fixed on Cat. I stood up to let him in. Then he was in my face.

"Hey," he said as he looked me up and down. "What's up?"

I shrugged. "I'm here."

"I see that."

I took a breath.

"She's my friend, Richie. She's a little scared right now."

Suddenly there was pain in his eyes. He glanced down at Cat — she started to reach for his hand, then pulled hers back. The bruise on her cheek was a gray shadow. As he sat down very slowly, Richie looked intensely into Cat's face, like the two of them were the only ones here.

"Richard," she said. "This is my yaya, CC. I told you about her."

"Uh ... yeah. Hey." He held out his hand. CC looked at it for a second, then shook it once. I sat down quick. There was silence.

After a second, CC said, "You are looking at this girl. But so are we. We also see her."

Richie put one hand on the table. Cat's fingers darted forward again, then stopped. In a steady voice, CC said, "We see what you did to her, young man."

175

Richie's mouth clenched. Cat pulled her hand back. "Richard," she said, very softly, "I know what you're going through is really hard, but ... what happened yesterday ... it was so scary."

"I know," he said, trying to hold her eyes. "I ..."

"You said you'd never do that," Cat said, urgently now. "You said you'd never! What am I supposed to *do?*"

Richie shook his head. "Cat," he said. "God. I am so ... I mean I don't know what ..." He glanced at me and CC, and blew out air. "Could you guys, like, go order food or something? Just for a second?"

CC said fiercely, "Do you not understand? This girl is not safe with you. She cannot *be* with you. I am here to tell you this. For her family."

"What?" Richie's head jerked back. "What's her *family* got to do with it?"

"Her family has everything to do with it!" CC said, "I don't understand Americans. Do you think the things you do affect only yourselves? Everything about this girl reflects on her family. She *is* her family — and young man, you are *your* family."

Richie leapt up. And there ... was the rage.

"The hell I am! I'm *me*, all right? Just me. I don't even ... I don't know who you think you are, but you can't tell me *shit!*"

Then he froze. He gasped. "I ... "

CC turned to Cat. "Do you see this? Do you see? He cannot control it."

Cat was reaching for Richie with both hands. "Richard, I know it's hard, it's so hard. But ..."

"So I've got nothing, right? Nothing. Is that what you want?"

"What? No! I just ..."

"The only reason I can be here is 'cause my dad's in custody — but they're gonna let him out," he said, looming over us. "The cops wanted my mom to at least take out a relief-from-abuse order but she won't, okay? She says it's his house, we're his family, he belongs with us. She says, 'He's having a really hard time right now.' And that's all *you* want to say?"

Glaring ferociously at Cat, he said, "You have no idea, all right? None of you do! If you think I'm my family you're *crazy*," he said to CC.

The whole restaurant had fallen silent. Everyone watched. Richie started backing up the aisle.

"I have to go home and stay there," he said to us. "If I do anything, this'll happen again, but if I'm not there ..." He shook his head. "And I thought I had *one friend*, who understood and would be there even if I made a ... a mistake, all right? I made a mistake, okay? And I came here to say I was sorry, but never mind, all right? Just *forget* it."

He spun away. Cat said, "Richard ..." but he was already walking up the aisle.

He shoved open the glass door and stalked away.

CC had given me some cash and sent me up to get us something while she talked, quietly but urgently, at the table with Cat. I was looking up at the chalkboard menu when my cell went off. It was Janelle.

"Hey," I said.

"You remember where Ms. Avery's place is. Right?"

"Huh?"

"Don't 'huh' me," Janelle said. "You remember?"

"Sure. I'm a little ways away from there, actually. I'm kind of ..."

"You need to get over here."

"What?"

"You need to get *over* here. I mean now."

"Um ... look, Janelle ... "

"And you need to call the White boy and that curly-blonde girl. Tell them how to get there, and say they need to *be* here — both of them. In half an hour. Or less."

"But why?"

"You will find *out* why," she said. "Me and Ms. Avery need to have a conversation with you. This is serious."

"Well, okay."

"Half an hour," she said. "Tops."

"I don't even know where Bethany lives."

"I don't care where she lives. You get her over here. This is *serious*."

"You did mention that."

"Russell, I am not playin' with you. You want me to put Ms. Avery on the phone?"

"No! I'll call them."

"You do that."

She hung up.

I had never seen Bethany seem so insecure. Turner was looking around at Ms. Avery's living room like he was making mental notes for a movie set. Bethany sat quietly, hands clasped in her lap.

177

Ms. Avery was polite. She brought us lemonade. We perched on chairs and gripped our glasses. Ms. Avery sat down and fixed us with her eyes.

"Did you ask my nephew's permission to put that film on the Internet?"

Bethany and Turner looked at each other. "Well," Bethany said ...

Ms. Avery waited, but Bethany swallowed and didn't say more. Ms. Avery turned to Turner.

"You're supposed to be his friend. Why didn't you check this out with him?"

"Um ..." Turner's eyes flickered. "I just ... I haven't called him. I know that's bad."

"Let me put this to you straight," Ms. Avery said. She was controlled, but whoa. She was mad.

"You put together a video," she said, "nicely crafted by the way" — Turner kind of winced, then nodded — "which reports to the world, first of all, that my nephew is rumored to be homosexual."

"He denied that," Bethany said. "It was in there."

"Yes. But once a big spicy rumor is out there, even if it's denied, what do you think people remember? The denial or the rumor?"

"We never believed it," Bethany said.

"Are you going to answer my question?"

They didn't.

"How many people have seen this so far?"

Turner blushed. "On YouTube ... 272,354 hits. That was almost an hour ago."

Ms. Avery's eyes bulged. She took a breath. "So. All right. Your film goes on to portray my nephew as a perpetrator of violent assault. There's no denying he let his emotions take over and he made a very serious mistake — but does that boy, with all he's been through, really deserve to have, what did you say, over a quarter million *people* know that about him?"

Ms. Avery looked at Turner, then at Bethany. "And what happens when he applies for a job someday? Don't you think his image has been, how do you put it ...?"

"Tagged," Janelle said. "On Facebook. The video's posted there, and people can tag him."

"So if anyone, I mean *anyone*, should google my nephew's name, any time for the rest of his life, what's going to come up?"

Bethany and Turner shifted and fidgeted. So did I. None of us had thought about any of this.

"And," Janelle added, "he pretty much cried. How do you think a young man who just lost his daddy is going to feel to know the whole world can watch him *cry* about it?"

That question hung in the air between us, and just fell to the ground. Bethany looked shell-shocked. Turner was in pain; you could see it in his eyes. Cam was his friend. I think Turner had been swept up in what they were doing with the project, and in what happened. To have a film, *his* film, catch fire like that — it had been his dream.

Now the dream had caved in. You could see it in his eyes.

"We didn't think about that, Ms. Avery," he said. "I feel real bad. We're just eighth graders."

"*I* know that," she said — "but the Internet doesn't care how old or young you are. You post something and it's on there forever. Unless you do the right thing."

She crossed her arms, and looked from one kid to the other. She waited. Bethany looked confused; then, as it dawned on her what Ms. Avery meant, she flushed red.

"You want us to take it *down?*"

"My understanding is that on YouTube, the originator of a posting can withdraw the video and block further access to it. This happens fairly often, in cases such as copyright infringement. It is, if I understand right, possible for you to do this."

She swung her gaze to Turner. He swallowed. "Well," he said — "even taking it down won't get it off completely. You can't know who's archived it, who's been able to pull in the video. Once something is posted, you can't guarantee ..."

"But you can do what *you* can do," Ms. Avery said. "That's all you can ever do, isn't that true? You can do the right thing that *you* can do."

Turner stared at the floor for a silent while. Then he looked up at her. "Do you have wireless?"

Ms. Avery nodded. "I have a computer. It's not that new ..."

"That's okay — I've got my laptop." Turner said. "Is there a password?"

"Oh yes. This house ... it has to be secure," Ms. Avery said.

Turner opened his backpack and pulled out his laptop. Bethany was gaping at him. Turner clicked a few keys, then turned the computer toward Ms. Avery.

"Ma'am, if you could just enter the password, I won't know what it is."

She nodded, then took the machine into the other room.

"Are you *doing* this?" Bethany whispered when Ms. Avery was gone.

"Well, yeah. She's right, don't you see it?"

"But this ruins everything."

"No it doesn't," Turner said. "It's just a video, Bethany."

She sat back — but not like she was mad, not really. She was just blown away. She looked at Turner, who was sitting there waiting for his laptop. He was very calm.

Bethany turned to me. "What do we do now?"

Before I could say, "I have no idea," Ms. Avery strode back into the room with the computer. "You're online," she said, handing it to Turner. He nodded, and went to work.

After Turner and Bethany had gone, I still sat there. A lot of things didn't feel so good right then — and something especially was bothering me. I didn't even know what it was. My stomach just felt tight. And sore.

Ms. Avery came back. She looked at Janelle looking at me. Then she sat down.

"Thank you for bringing them over," she said. "I thought they faced up to this rather bravely."

I nodded. Even Bethany, once she'd accepted it, had been surprisingly graceful.

"Yo Russell," Janelle said. "Maybe I shouldn't have been so hard on you, on the phone."

"No. That was okay."

"All right," she said. "So what isn't?"

"Huh?" I looked up. They were both watching me.

"*Something's* not okay," Janelle said. "If you want to, you could tell us what it is."

"I just ..." I shook my head. "I don't know. I really don't."

"So just talk," Ms. Avery said gently. "It'll feel better."

I opened my mouth, and this is what came out:

"What happens when a guy's dad got arrested, for hurting his mom, I mean the kid's mom — but his mom won't testify, so now the dad is getting out and coming home? What happens then?"

They gave each other a quick look. Ms. Avery said, "Do you know someone who's in a situation like that?"

180

"Yeah," I said. "And this kid, I mean this guy, he's sort of stuck in the middle. The dad said if the mom tries to leave he'll kill her."

Ms. Avery nodded. "You say the dad's in custody?"

"Well, yeah. But they have to let him go."

"Is there a relief-from-abuse order?"

"No — the mom won't ask for one. She's home cleaning."

This all sounded so bizarre. But Ms. Avery just said, "Russell, are you in touch with this boy?"

"I just saw him. He stays at my house sometimes. Why?"

"Well, I'm going to tell you what I do," Ms. Avery said. "You don't know that, I think."

"What you do?"

"Yes. I run a shelter. It's a place for women who are being hurt by their partners. It's a secret place — we have to keep its location secure, so that people who might want to find and hurt these women, can't. That's why I'm security-minded, you see. Do you see?"

"I ... yeah. Yes."

"Have you heard of places like this before?"

"Kind of. I saw a movie once. This guy wanted to find Julia Roberts and kill her or something. He was her husband but he terrorized her."

"Yes, I know that movie. Well, this happens in real life, a lot more often than you might think — and my job is to help these women. If a woman's in danger, I can talk with her. I can also talk to a family member who might be wanting to protect this woman. Who might feel caught in the middle."

"Okay."

"I'm going to give you my card," Ms. Avery said. "I want you to give it to your friend — or get him my phone number. I want you to do this as soon as you can. Are you able to do that? You say this boy's upset."

"Oh yes."

"Is he upset with you?"

"I'm not sure. Maybe."

"I don't want you to do anything that's dangerous for you," she said.

I didn't know Richie's cell number. But I knew where he lived.

I thought, *Don't think about it. Some things are important.*

"I can do it," I said.

PART FOUR

The Rebellion

33.
Chains

The curtains were all closed inside the front windows of Richie's house. I was standing across the street, hearing the sounds of birds. I remembered the sound of sirens.

Don't think about it, I thought.

I walked up to the porch. I'd come here right from Mrs. Avery's; my mom would be expecting me home for dinner in half an hour. I didn't have a lot of time, and I didn't know what would happen. If Richie opened this door, would he be out-of-his-mind angry? Would he take it out on me?

Don't think. Ring the bell.

When I did, I heard an old-fashioned church-bell sound inside. Nothing else happened. On both sides of the door, narrow curtains were closed. I rang again. The curtain to the right rippled. I saw someone's eye. Then the fabric closed.

After a minute I heard footsteps. The door clicked, and opened just a bit. Richie sidled out and shut it carefully, quietly. He stood out here and stared at me. My heart was pounding.

"Um," I said, "I just need to talk to you."

He looked me up and down with narrowed eyes. I couldn't tell how he was. He jammed his hands in his jacket pockets, then walked off the porch. He looked back and jerked his head — the *follow me* command.

I followed him around the side of his house.

Richie's backyard was kind of a mess. It had a rusty grill, ragged grass, a red pail full of cigarette butts, and, of all things, an old wooden swing set. He sat down on one of the two swings. I sat on the other. My swing creaked, and I held onto the chains like a kid. Richie leaned forward, feet flat on the ground. He stared off.

Okay. I had one chance to get this out. But what? I'd been so intent on not thinking that I had no idea what to say.

"Um ... that was rough today," I said. He blew out air, like I'd never know. Then he grabbed one thumb with the other hand and started twisting it. He sat there hunched over on the swing, just wrenching his thumb back and forth.

"Look," I said — "I have this thing I wanted to bring you. I was talking to ..."

"I screwed up everything," he said. "Didn't I? *Everything*." He shook his head hard, like he couldn't believe it.

I shrugged. "I don't know if ..."

"No — I did. I *did*. How could I *do* that to her? And then ... oh man ... at that restaurant I might've had a chance. I was gonna say how bad I felt, I was going to say *sorry*, I don't know how it *happened*, and then ..."

Bam, he punched his palm hard. Then he just let his arms fall. He groaned, shook his head and stared at the scooped-out, bare ground below the swing.

I told him a little about Ms. Avery. "She knows what people go through," I said. "I mean, in families. Like this."

"You think she'll ever speak to me again?"

"Um ..."

"I can't *do* this to her." He jerked my way; his chains creaked. "She's a sweet girl, you know?"

"Yes."

"She doesn't deserve it," he said. "She can't be *in* it. I have to keep it away from her. I have to." He gripped his chains and stared off.

"Um," I said — "so, like, I brought that lady's card." I held it out. "You want it?"

"Huh? Oh. Yeah, right." He took it without looking at it.

"Will you call her?"

"I don't know if I should, man. I mean ... how can this be any good for her? You saw what happened."

"I meant her," I said, nodding toward the card in his hand.

"Oh. Well, I don't know."

"It might be good."

"Huh. Well — listen, you got to go." Suddenly he was agitated, looking around. "He could be home any ... you need to *go*, all right?"

"Okay."

As I stood up, my seat swung away, then it came back and bumped my legs. Richie's eyes flicked around, the way they had in my living room. I said, "What are you gonna do?"

His mouth got tight; he made a *pfah* sound, like there was nothing. I didn't know what else to say. I started backing away. "Good luck," I said, lamely.

Richie didn't look up. I left him sitting on that old swing, in his bedraggled back yard.

After dinner I remembered what I had. The *audio*. I dug the mincam out of the backpack, and loaded its one recorded file onto my MacBook.

Serena: He told you he wouldn't, right? He said he never would. But then he did.
Cat: It was awful! It was ... it was ...
S: A nightmare.
C: Yes!
S: And you did not deserve it. All you did was care for him.
C: Yes.
S: You were there for him.
C: I was.
S: (quieter): You loved him.
(No answer.)
S: You still do.
C (faintly, after a silence): I don't know. I think ...
S: You did anything he wanted. Anything.
C: Well ...
S: Hitting you was *not* okay.
C: It was horrible. My yaya says if I don't end it, he'll do it again.
S. But you care about him.
C: It's so great how you understand!
S: You need your friends right now. Your real friends.
C: *He* does! He needs me.
S: There are things only you and he know. Things nobody else can find out about.
C: I've kept his privacy.
S: You've been loyal.
C: I was!
S: Tell me about your mom.
C: My mom?
S: I know she's so important. I mean, to you.
C: Oh yes. But lately ...
S: I don't even know her name.
C: It's Rose.
S: Oh, that's a pretty name. Did she take your dad's last name?
C: Yes, but she changed back. She's Rosario Mercado.

S: I remember last year, you told everyone she sings.

C: Yes! She has a beautiful voice.

S: Do you still get to hear it? Do you talk on the phone?

C: Oh sure. We Skype.

S: Really! She has Internet and everything?

C: (laughing): Of course! Filipinos are very sophisticated. We had a big protest movement that was organized almost all by texting, back when Americans were hardly using that at all.

S: (laughing too): Wow! So what's her Skype name?

The recording ended there.

Oh, no, I thought. *Cat.*

I called her. I said, "Have you heard from Richie?"

"No! Not since the restaurant."

"Have you tried to reach him?"

"I ..." She sighed. "Yes. I texted him. He hasn't answered at all. That's so not like him, Russell. Should I call?"

"I don't know. What about Serena? You're talking to her, right?"

"Oh, she is *so* great. She asks, she listens, she understands. I feel like she really knows me. Already!"

"But what about her? Do you know her?"

"Um ... I don't know. She's really nice. She's very unselfish."

"Un*selfish?*"

"Yes, Russell. She listens. She asks really good questions."

"Uh huh."

"Russell."

"Uh?"

"You were there today. At the restaurant. It helped."

"Oh. Well, whatever."

"But CC was so hard on him! Why did she have to be so hard on him?"

"Cat. He hit you."

"I know. I know."

My call-waiting beeped. It was, surprisingly, Janelle. "I got another call, Cat."

"Okay. Should I call him?"

"I don't know!"

"So," Janelle said — "did you get it to him? Her card?"

"Yes."

"How?"

"How'd I get it to him? I went over there."

She didn't say anything.

"I don't know if he'll call Cam's aunt," I said. "If he does, will you hear about it?"

"It's supposed to be all confidential," she said.

"Oh. Right. So ... have you heard from Cam?"

"Ms. A has."

"Is he okay?"

"It's hard to tell. He's not sayin' much."

"Does he know about the video?"

"Oh yeah. He knows."

"Is he okay about it?"

"Well," she said. "Let's just say it's a good thing you took it down."

"It wasn't me," I said. "I didn't make it, I didn't take it down."

"Yeah, well. When you went to that bully boy's house," she said. "Were you scared?"

"I don't know. A little."

Silence again.

"It's like watchin' a boy become a man," Janelle said.

"What?"

"Oh, nothing."

34.
Inquiring Minds

The next day the Out Crowd was a little down. I think we were tired. And losing the video, all that excitement and attention just going down the tubes ... it was a lot to lose.

At lunch we all toyed with our food. All except Janelle.

"You gonna eat that?"

"No. Here," I said, pushing my tray her way.

"Hey," Elliot said — "you guys made a splash. A big splash. People are gonna remember. I mean, what the hey?"

I winced. "What the *hey?* Who says 'What the hey?'"

Elliot grinned.

"What they'll remember is that we look like losers," Bethany said, staring at her fish patty. "People are saying to me, 'Oh, you got scared off, huh?' Like I'm scared of *them*."

"Well, the music was beautiful," I said. Emily blushed.

"Is," Elliot said. "The music still is."

"Hey, it's just one film," said Turner. "I can make more. We can make more."

"But that one was really something," I said. "It hit people. It was making people see."

He said, "You really think?"

"I do."

Turner nodded. "Nice."

Janelle said, "Yeah, well you should have thought before you made that thing."

We looked up sharply at her. Janelle was kind of stylish today, with a dark-red vest over a black, long-sleeve shirt. The purple hoodie was long gone. She shrugged. "What? You should have thought."

"They did think," Elliot said. "They worked really hard on that film. And I don't care what you say. It was great."

Big Chris stopped by, breaking the tension. "Russ Ell," he said, nodding to the others as he bumped fists with me. "Sorry about that thing," he said to us. "A lot of people really appreciated what you did. It burns

189

me that those kids did that."

"Did what?" Bethany said.

"Well ... I don't know. Whatever they did to get you to take it down."

"See?" Bethany said to the rest of us. "It's what people think. See?"

Chris, confused, backed away. Then I heard a familiar voice: "Is this the bunker? The bomb shelter?"

Kennedy was sliding into a chair with us, setting her tray down as if she did this every day. I felt a prickly mix of electricity and embarrassment.

"We're hunkered in the bunker," Elliot said, and grinned. "Final stronghold of the Coalition."

"The what?"

"Don't you get him started," Janelle said.

I wanted Kennedy to say hi to me, and I absolutely did not want her to say hi to me. She caught my eye and said, "Hey." My face got hot and I said something like "*Hayump.*" Janelle raised one eyebrow.

"So what happened?" Kennedy said to all of us. "Everybody's talking. Inquiring minds want to know."

"It's not what anyone thinks," Bethany said. "Hi Ken."

"Hey Bet. People think you got intimidated, or some such nonsense."

"It was ... more of a personal issue," Turner said.

"It wasn't them *at all*," Bethany added firmly.

"Okay. What do you mean, a personal issue?"

At first, nobody answered. Then Janelle said, "People have a right to privacy. Especially someone who just lost his daddy."

Kennedy looked at each of us. "That's what this was about — that boy's dad? That's why you took the video down?"

"It was about respect," Janelle said. "Doin' what's right. You okay with that?"

"Sure. Oh, yeah." Kennedy was not at all intimidated. Actually she seemed impressed. She leaned over the table. "But what about everyone else? They think the boot people won."

"We know they didn't," Emily said softly.

"Ohmygod, and your *music*," Kennedy said. "Everyone *loved* that. I mean really. People are still talking about it."

Emily stared fiercely at her shoes, which were purple today. Kennedy, sitting next to her, looked down too.

"Hey," she said. "I *like* those.

"Every day she wears a different color," said Elliot.

"That is *cool*," Kennedy said. "Do you wear the patterned ones? Or the plaid?"

It was something how Kennedy could just start talking to people. I thought, *She's a skater — she talks to everyone. She came to our table because stuff is happening, not because she likes me. Why would she like* **me**?

"I just like the solid colors," Emily said.

"She's got blue, red, yellow, orange," Elliot said, "green ..."

"These are aster purple," Emily told Kennedy. "They've got vivid blue, neon green, neon pink ..."

The bell rang. When Kennedy looked up, her blue eyes were sparkling.

"I'll see you guys around," she said to us.

We were crowding out of the cafetorium when Elliot said to me, "Let's not quit, okay?"

"Not quit what?"

"Doing those interviews. For your project. You still need to do that, right?"

"I guess."

"So let's do another one. It'd mean a lot to Em," he said. "She'll see we're not giving up. She put so much into that music, Russell — it's the best work she's done so far. She feels a little down that no one can hear it any more."

"Everybody's a little down," I said.

"Nevah surrendah. *Nevah!*" Elliot said, jabbing a forefinger in the air as the crowd swallowed him up.

That's how we wound up in the computer lab after school, studying a video.

At the end of the day we'd gone up to Nicole Pearl, third and last of the brown-boot lieutenants. We caught her alone at her locker.

Nicole was slim and good-looking, with clothes like Lauren's and long, straight brown hair. "She's the action girl," Kennedy had told me. The one who'd set a scheme in motion.

Nicole seemed almost glad to see us. She saw Elliot's camera and wasn't shy.

"Hey, guys," she said — "what's up?"

Elliot lifted the Flip. Its light came on.

191

"Hi," Nicole says to the camera.

"I guess you heard the Darkland video got taken down," I say.

"Oh, sure." She looks sympathetic. "Hey, you guys gave it a good try. I mean really. Honestly." She smiles at the camera.

"Honestly what?"

"Well, I mean, it could have been so much worse. For you guys, you know? But it's over now. We can all relax. Nothing more's gonna happen. Maybe we can be friends!"

"There," Elliot said as we watched. "Stop it right there."

"What?" I said as I paused the playback.

He reached for the trackpad, slid the Play cursor back. Again we saw Nicole say, "We can all relax. Nothing more's gonna happen. Maybe we can be friends!"

"Okay, that's just creepy," I said. "*Friends?*"

"Yeah, but look closer," he said. "When she says, 'Nothing more's gonna happen.' Do you see it?"

"See what?"

"Her eyes shift around. I think she's lying."

"I wouldn't be surprised," I said.

"Did you notice how pleased she was to be interviewed?"

"Yeah. Like she wanted us to do it."

"She *did* want us to do it," Elliot said. "See, right now, just when you think the battle's over — this is when the Scourge hits you hardest. When you've let down, they go for the kill."

"Dude," I said. "I thought you were getting into reality."

"This is reality. Let's watch it again!"

"Did you hear the latest?" Kennedy said on the phone, right before dinner. I'd been looking at silly videos when my cell sounded its call alert. (I'd put in new alert sounds, different ones for calls and texts. It was quicker than waiting to count buzzes, especially with so much going on.)

"The latest what?"

"Lauren Paine's going with Baker Corrigan," she said.

"Are you serious? *Baked?*"

"Do you know him?"

"He's in my LA class. That's interesting."

"Why?"

"Well, him and Jon Blanchette almost had a fight in class today.

Corrigan was all cocky, I didn't know why, and Blanchette suddenly got mad."

"Well, this would be why," she said. "Baker's his replacement. The new top boyfriend."

"But *why?*" Jon and Lauren, our two best-looking blondes, had fit together. But Lauren and Baked?

She said, "What do you know about him?"

"Until today I didn't know if he could make sense," I said. "In class he would just blurt random words. If he isn't stoned he sure is strange."

"What I heard is, that rumor is true," she said. "He deals."

"Really? Weed?"

"Word is."

"Huh. But Lauren's not into that. Is she?"

"I can't imagine," Kennedy said — "but girls do like the bad boys. Hey, how's your friend? The recruit?"

"Very stressed."

"She was sitting with them again today."

"Yeah. She does now."

"She hasn't bought the boots, though," Kennedy said. "Did you notice?"

"Huh. I didn't, actually."

"Well, I did. It might mean she hasn't totally bought in yet."

"I don't know," I said. "I don't think she has the option to just go buy stuff."

"Yeah, but I *might* be right," Kennedy said. "Did you try asking what they're talking to her about?"

"I did find out some," I said, without admitting how. "Serena's asking Cat a lot of questions. Cat's so happy to have a *girl*friend, someone she thinks she can really talk to. I think Serena's getting her to tell some pretty personal stuff."

"Yup. That's what she does. Hey, I love those sneakers!"

Kennedy sort of jumped around, focus-wise. I wondered if she had ADD.

"You did seem to like them," I said.

"I already got a pair. In *vivid* blue."

"Uh huh."

"I ... sort of have an idea," she said.

"About what?"

"You'll see. It might be nothing."

"If it's nothing, how will I see?"

"If it's not nothing, we'll both see," she said.

Okay, girls were confusing. But sometimes very interesting. We kept talking till my mom came in puffed up with the shut-it-down-and-come-to-dinner command.

Then later, we talked again.

"How come Bethany called you Ken?"

"Oh, she always calls me that. We've known each other a while."

"Does it bother you to be called a guy's name?"

"No, no — I don't care what people call me. That's the ticket to freedom, Russell."

"Freedom? From what?"

"From the little fear boxes people get stuck in," Kennedy said. "See, everyone our age — especially the girls, but not *just* the girls — they're so worried about what anyone else thinks about them. That's why the boot people have so much power with their rumors. But if you don't care what people say, hey!" She laughed. "You're free."

"Yeah," I said, laughing too. "You can come sit with us."

"That's right! See, that's why people are looking to you guys," she said. "You don't realize it because you're all so lovably clueless, but you are in the spotlight right now. People don't want to see you quit. I know this, see, because I talk to people."

"We were kinda down today," I said. "I think you brightened us up."

"Yeah, well," she said, "check me tomorrow."

"What do you mean?"

"You'll see."

I got off the phone and sat there thinking, *Did she say* lovably *clueless?*

35.
My True Friend

Kennedy showed up Friday morning wearing new blue canvas lows. That was fine, they were sort of stylish in a funky way, but so? Yet I couldn't help watching her — and she seemed to be everywhere. I saw her in the halls, I observed her in the lunchroom, and she was constantly talking to people. Mostly girls, but also guys. What seemed odd was, as she talked to people she would show off her shoes. She'd fan her hands down at the sneakers as if she was a game-show model and they were the prize. Then she'd grin her sparkly smile.

I didn't get it. If you wore something new that you thought was fairly cool, wouldn't it wreck the whole impression if you went around all day *pointing* at it? It didn't seem like her, either. She'd just told me she didn't care what people thought. Wouldn't this have applied also to apparel? Or were all girls just weird about shoes?

Whatever the reason, every time I saw Kennedy, this was what she was doing. I don't even think she ate lunch. She just skated, talked to people, and showed off her sneakers.

In the mid-morning break, Turner pulled me into the under-the-stairs hiding place.

We stooped in, then stood up. I said, "What are we doing *here?*"

"I want to hide a camera in here," he said, looking around. "Pick up whatever happens, you know? Hey, look at this."

He pulled out his smartphone; on its screen was bitchanysworstquality.com. The site still featured the bathroom photo of Bethany, but they'd put a big red X over it. And below the picture, in large purple letters, they'd put:

CANCELLED
Your Voice Was Heard!

"Well, that's stupid," I said.
"I think it means something."
"Like what?"

"Well, they did that poll, right? The whole worst-quality thing," Turner said. "They said they'd publish the results the next day, right? And the next day was yesterday. They didn't do anything. Now today they do this. *Just* this."

"So ..."

"So they *didn't post the results*. The vote, or whatever. What does that mean?"

"I have no idea. I am lovably clueless."

Turner gave me a puzzled look. Then he said, "I think it means they didn't get any votes. Or hardly any."

"Couldn't they just make something up?"

"Yes, but they *didn't*. It means something, Russell. I have this feeling it means something."

We poked our heads out in the hall. Coast was clear. We stepped out and started walking.

"So," I said. "Project's due a week from today."

"Yeah. I want to do more shooting — I feel like we don't have enough. What about you?"

"Well, we interviewed all three lieutenant girls in the boot group. On camera."

"Hey" — Turner grinned — "the boot group. I could film the boots. The actual boots, you know?"

"What would that say?"

"I don't know. Spread of conformity? Social fashion pressures? We could interview girls who have them. 'Did you feel pressured to wear these?'"

I thought. We walked.

"I guess I don't really care about girls' shoes that much," I said. "I feel like I'm the only one."

"Well, I think it's interesting. I might do something."

As we were walking fast but trying to act natural, the PA came on.

"Please pardon the interruption. If anyone is good at untying difficult knots, please come to the guidance office. Thank you."

At the end of school, I was at my locker when Big Chris came up.

"Russ Ell. I need to confer with you, man."

"Okay." I shut the locker. "Sup?"

"Funny thing. Blanchette wants to talk to you."

"Jon?" This was weird. "About what?"

"Well, that's it — he won't say. Listen, him and I have baseball practice right now, but he wanted me to ask you — how about meeting us at the b-ball court tomorrow morning? At the park. We could shoot some, or whatever."

"Um ... I'm actually a little annoyed with Jon," I said.

"I know. And I know why," he said. "That was not cool, when he laughed like that. I think he feels bad. That might be what this is about, I don't know."

I said all right. I'd be there.

"I was watching you today," I said on the phone, that night. Then I got nervous, that I'd said that.

But she giggled. "Oh yes?"

"Yeah. I mean, you were talking to people all over. What were you up to, anyway?"

"I told you. I skate."

"Yeah, but no. You were up to something."

She got coy. "Like I said before, maybe you'll see. Maybe we'll both see."

"Both see what?"

"If I told you, it wouldn't be any fun, would it?"

I was trying to think of something clever when she said, "I like that you were watching me."

"Well, I noticed something."

"Oh yes?"

"I did."

"What did you notice?"

"Well," I said, "it's like ... it sounds weird to say it, but ... you're popular."

"I don't know," she said. "I know a lot of people."

"No, you're *popular*. People smile when you come over. They like to talk to you."

"And this is what? Shocking?"

"No, but I mean, you're not *feared* popular. You're liked popular."

"Well ..." She laughed. "Did you not realize this is possible, Russell?"

"In our school? In Darkland? No, I mean there are a couple of people. But basically it's pretty rare."

"Oh, I don't know. Certain kids draw attention because they're all statusy and they'll hurt you, sure — but that's not the only way to be somebody. I mean, basically it's up to you, right? If people talk to you, what do you talk about? If you talk about somebody, what do you say? The thing is, whatever you do you're stuck with it."

"You're stuck with ..."

"With you! Know what I mean?"

"Um ... not exactly."

"Okay," she said. "It's like ... I could move away. Go somewhere else, you know? Get new friends."

"What? No."

"I'm not, don't worry!" She laughed. "But what I'm saying — you're cute, by the way — I'm saying that even if I did, I'd still be me. I can't move away from me. And I don't want to have to remember that I crushed people for fun just because I could. *If* I could."

"I don't think you could," I said.

She chuckled. "Hey, I'm just me."

"That's for real," I said.

I liked talking to Kennedy, hearing her voice. Some people it was okay to just text; but not her. "I like that you're you," I said. Then I thought, *Did I say that out **loud**?*

"Thank you, Russell," she said softly. "I like that you're you, too."

Saturday morning the court was dry. Chris and Blanchette were there already, shooting baskets in a goofing-around, backboard-clanging way. When Jon saw me he straightened up and took an awkward shot. It didn't go in.

I said, "Hey guys."

"Russ Ell." Chris bounced-passed the ball. I caught it and put up a shot that bonked up high off the back of the rim, then actually fell through.

"Hey, you should play AAU ball with us this summer," Chris said. "You're gettin' tall."

"Except I suck."

"But we have an excellent coach," Chris said. "He's a good dude, he's got like three foster kids. You could learn."

"Well, I don't know."

We shot a while. Jon was silent. Chris and I chatted. "So," I said. "High school."

He grinned. "Football!"

"Yeah?"

"Oh yeah. Linebacker or defensive end, baby. I'm gonna *flatten* people. You?"

"I don't know — it's like I can't see that far ahead. You know Darkland doesn't even do an eighth grade graduation? I think we should get a medal for surviving that place."

Chris laughed, then we both looked at Blanchette. Jon said, "What?"

"I don't know," I said. "What's up?"

Jon gripped the ball hard. "I need to ... It's like I need to tell you something, but I'm not really sure what it is."

Chris cleared his throat.

"Oh," Jon said. "Uh, listen, man. The other day. When Burke said that stupid thing about your friend and I laughed. That was really lame. I mean, Burke can be edgy sometimes — but when he said I smoked that kid, and I laughed about it ... I mean, that was not cool."

He hadn't looked up at me. Now he did.

"I feel bad about it," he said.

"But it wasn't just about who won that game," I said. "Burke mocked Cam for getting emotional."

"I know. And I got emotional that time, and you never said anything," Jon said with a look to Chris, who nodded. "What I'm saying is ... it wasn't right. What I did."

Jon had lost his golden-boy glow, lately. I almost felt bad for him. "No problem," I said. "It's good you said something."

"How is he? I mean Cam," Jon said. "He just like left."

"Yeah. He was living here with his aunt, now he's back with his mom. I'm not totally sure how he is."

"Did he leave because of ... what happened?"

"I think it was because of a lot of things."

"Man, it's bad if we made things worse for a kid who lost his dad," Jon said. "I thought we had a great game. It was like we worked things out — and that video was cool." He grinned. "I was a star, man! Then you took it *down!*"

"Not me, but yeah. Because of Cam. His aunt and my friend Janelle were afraid it would be hurtful to him."

"Huh. Yeah, I get that. So ... you think he'll be okay?"

"I hope so."

"He's a tough kid," Jon said. "Seemed like."

"Yeah."

"Say hi for me, okay? I mean if you can."

"All right," I said. "If I can."

I figured that was it, what he wanted to talk about. But Jon bounced the ball hard off the asphalt, caught it and said, "There's something else."

"There is?"

"Yeah. It's like ... I think something's going on with those girls. Lauren and Serena and them. I think they might be up to something."

"They're always up to something."

"Yeah, but — this thing about dumping me," he said. "I mean, for Corrigan? That kid's only good for one thing, and everyone knows it. And Lauren's not into getting high, okay? She's into two things. Appearance and using people. That's it."

Chris and I waited. Jon, gripping his ball, said, "I know this sounds bad, like I'm annoyed that I got ... you know. Rejected or whatever. But I *know* that girl. And when she sent Cayenne to tell me we were broken up ..."

"You and Cayenne were broken up?"

"No, me and Lauren. But Cayenne, when she came to tell me, she said, 'It's okay, Jon, it's just for a while.' That's what she said, 'for a while.' Then she said, 'She's going with Baker now, but it's not like it seems.' I said, 'What do you mean?' She said, 'I can't *tell* you,' like it was some big secret. She said, 'I can't tell you, but those weird kids are going to be totally destroyed.'"

Jon looked at me. I said, "Those weird kids."

"Yeah."

"Meaning ... us?"

"Well, no offense, but yeah. They *hate* you guys."

"So if they're up to something, what is it?"

"I have no idea," Jon said. "I just thought you should know."

"Serena says you're my true friend," Cat said on the phone.

"What?"

"See? She's a good person, Russell. She really cares."

"Oh right. I bet people said that about Hitler. 'He's so *sincere*.'"

"Well, you can be prejudiced if you want, but she *said* you're my true friend," Cat said. "She said I should be spending time with you again."

"She said that?"

"She did! She says when you're under a lot of stress, you have to hold onto things. You know, things that are there for you."

"So I'm a thing?"

"No! Russell, she's on your side, all right? She says how great it was, the way we used to get together. After band."

"You told her about that?"

"Well ... I might have. I mean, in a positive way."

"Oh god. Cat."

"What? She cares, Russell."

"Oh yes. She's *such* a good listener. You didn't give her any passwords or anything, did you? Like for your Facebook?"

"No! Russell, you're being totally close-minded about this. She says you and I should, you know, get back to that."

"To what?"

"To meeting. After band. You know, that really was great — it was something I could rely on. I could always count on you, Russell. I ... appreciated it. I liked how we would talk."

"We're talking now."

"But that was like a ritual, you know? It was really reassuring. Serena's right — I need the things I can count on, right now. Would you ... I mean, would you ever ... would you even consider just doing that again? I know it's silly, but ..."

I could hear her getting shaky, and I did not want her to cry. I knew I'd let her down once before, turned my back when she needed me. That, I decided, was not going to happen again.

"Okay," I said. "Monday after band. I'll be there."

Sunday afternoon I got a call. I didn't know the number. But I knew the voice.

"Hey."

"Um, Richie. What's up?"

"Nothin' good. Listen, I need a favor."

"A favor? From me?"

"Yeah. It would involve you stopping by."

"Okay."

"You could do that."

"I could. When?"

"I was thinking now."

This led to me sitting on that swing again, in his backyard. That's what he had told me to do: come sit on the swing. He'd be watching.

The back door opened and Richie came out. He was holding a black backpack, the kind you'd bring to school full of stuff. His looked almost empty.

"Come on," he said, walking past the swing set.

We walked up the street, around the corner. When we were out of sight of his house, he stopped. Held out the backpack.

"I need you to take this."

"Why? What's in it?"

"Nothing illegal, don't worry. Just ... if you could stash the bag in your garage, that'd be cool. I might want to come and ... you know. Use it maybe."

I took the backpack. I could feel something large, flattish and round-ish in there.

"It's your face," I said. "Your mask."

He tilted his head, like, *Maybe.*

I could feel something else, in the bottom. Something small and narrow.

"Richie. Your knife."

He nodded.

"But why?"

"It doesn't matter, all right? Just put it someplace nobody sees. You can do that."

"Yeah. But these things are important to you. I know they are."

He shrugged. I said, "Is everything ... okay?" He blew a scornful snort. I said, "Did you — that lady. The one whose card I gave you. Did you call her?"

He shook his head. "I gotta go," he said. "I don't want you following. You understand."

"All right. But ... you could call her."

Walking away, he waved without turning around.

I didn't open the backpack until I got inside the garage.

The mask was still rough, like he hadn't worked on it much. His grandpa's old folding knife had a brown nubbly handle. Richie had put it inside a ziploc bag, for extra protection.

Holding the bagged, folded knife in my hand, I wondered why I had this. Why didn't he want it at home? I sat there wondering, trying to understand.

Richie was caught in the middle, and he knew he couldn't do anything. Cat had told me that things over there went in cycles. Richie's dad would be all sorry and his mom would make everything nice, but then the tension would start building again. It always would — and now that his dad was back, it had to be building. Had to be. His mom was scared to run, so Richie couldn't leave either. He could only stay there, so maybe people would stay alive.

No way could I imagine what that would be like. But it made sense that he wouldn't want to have a weapon, if he was afraid he might use it.

Then I thought about Richie sitting on the floor in our guest room, privately carving his mask. I thought how he lit up when he told me about it, when he showed me his grandfather's knife. It was the only time I ever saw him excited in a good way. So maybe he wanted to keep some important part of himself safe. Put it in hiding, right?

Or *maybe* ... maybe he hoped I would tell Cat about this. Maybe he wanted her to know what he'd given up so she'd feel bad. Maybe this was some strange way of sending her a message.

Basically I had no idea. I just had the knife. I slipped it into the back-pack, and put that on a high shelf behind a camping stove. It would be safe there. We didn't go camping any more.

Sunday night I'd said I would call Kennedy, but instead I did home-work. I didn't want to let anything spill out about meeting Cat, or about Richie and the knife.

But she called. We talked for a while, again. I didn't say anything about Cat or Richie, but at one point I did say, "I tend to feel clueless." Even that felt like too much — I was scared that if she really knew me, she wouldn't like me.

"No," Kennedy said — "I know you think that, but you know what I see? I see how you're always trying to figure out what's really going on. A lot of people are constantly wondering what other people think about them, you know? They're trying to see themselves in everyone else's eyes, so they can figure out how to act. It's chronic. It's everywhere."

"Well, sure."

"But you're not like that," she said. "You may think you're clueless, but what you're *looking* for are clues to what's true. What's real. I liked that about you right away."

"Huh."

"It's okay to be you, Russell," she said gently. "Maybe you don't see that yet, but I do. It's okay to be you."

I mumbled something. We talked a while longer, then I hung up feeling confused. It was nice, what she'd said — I had never thought about it that way. But even when she said I was looking for the truth, there were things that were true that I wasn't telling her. Like about hiding Richie's knife. And about meeting Cat tomorrow after school.

See? It was confusing.

36.
Orchestra

Monday morning when I came in the front hall, she was there. She saw me and came up grinning.

"Notice anything?"

"Such as ..."

"Ah! Not me. Look around."

Kennedy turned, to scan with me the crowd that trooped in the doors. Kids were all around us now. She said, "See anything ... colorful?"

Then I did. Some kids were coming in wearing colored low sneakers. They walked by us in reds, yellows, purples, oranges. Not a huge number of people, but ... more than a few.

This was odd. Until now, Emily had been pretty unique in her style. I thought some alternative kids had worn those weird-patterned ones — but plain-colored canvas lows? Only Emily.

Not now. A larger number of girls were wearing the brown boots, just like last week. But this morning you couldn't help noticing the new, interesting sneaker-color minority.

Kennedy was grinning. I said, "This is what you were up to?"

She cocked her head, spread her hands.

"So," I said. "People, like, went out and bought these? Over the weekend?"

"I think they actually did."

"Just because you said, 'Hey these are cool'?"

"I did say they're cool. I also said why."

"Why?"

"Think about it," Kennedy said as she turned to walk down the hall. I watched her go. I liked how she walked. She was wearing her vivid blues.

"All right people, I want updates," Ms. Corbin said. "Your deadline is *Friday*. Group leaders? What's going on?"

There was energy in the room. Our desks were clustered in teams again. And stuff was happening.

"We want to do interviews," said Nicole Pearl, director of the dating project. "Like ask people candid questions."

"Such as?"

"Like, 'What do you think about dating? At this age?' Ask for people's opinions and stuff."

"It's okay to ask personal questions," Ms. Corbin said, "as long as you tell people they're being interviewed, and being recorded. That way they know to be careful."

"Okay."

"Fine, good. Jon? Sports?"

Jon shrugged. "We're shootin' a couple games."

"Is that it?"

He sat up. "No. We've been filming things."

"Okay. Friday's the day."

"I know. We're good."

"All right. Music? Amanda?"

"We got excellent vids of kids playin' stuff, along with the demos and instructional things," Amanda said. "But, like, it's okay to interview someone who's on another team, right?"

"I don't see why not. Who'd you have in mind?"

"Well, there's this person I've been *trying* to talk with ..." She glanced at Emily, who blushed.

"I think that would be highly appropo," Ms. Corbin said. "Social pressures group?"

"I'm gonna do footwear," Turner said.

"Um ... footwear?"

"Yeah. It's appropo."

"Well, if you say so. So everyone's on track? I'll let you get to work, but remember: Friday!"

"Can we do interviews now?"

"If your subjects agree, sure. All right, people — don't waste this time!"

* * *

A girl named Camilla, who was on the dating team, came up to us with a silver minicam.

"Um, Bethany?"

"Oh. Hi."

"Could I like ... interview you?"

"Me? Why me?" Bethany acted puzzled, but you could tell she was pleased.

"Well, you're, you know. Pretty well-known."

Camilla was a sweet girl, shy. She looked back at her group. Nicole glanced up, then looked away. "It was an idea we had," Camilla said. "Because you're popular."

"Well, okay." Bethany couldn't not smile. "This'll just take a minute," she said to Turner and me.

As she and Bethany went out in the hall, Amanda came over. She said, "Hey, ah ... Emily?"

Emily looked urgently at me, and didn't answer.

I said, "Hi, Amanda."

"Russell, what's up." Amanda glanced at Emily, then she turned back to me. "Could I maybe talk to you? In the hall?"

A minute later, we came back. I sat down by Em. Amanda hung back, watching. "You know," I said softly, "it would be way wrong if you're not in the music project."

"I just ..." Emily sighed. "I don't know what it is, Russell. I can play music in front of people, but talking ... and to a camera ..." She shook her head. "I just get so bound up inside."

"Okay, so — hey, I know," I said. "What if she uses one of those audio recorders? The ones that look like space blasters? I mean, talking into something like that — it's just funny."

She thought. She smiled. "Maybe I could," she said.

When Em and Amanda had gone into the hall, I said to Turner, "Are you really going to do interviews about shoes?"

"Yeah. I'm gonna go up to people and say, 'Why are you wearing those?'"

"Any people?"

"No, girls wearing boots. And kids wearing sneakers."

"So ... you noticed about the sneakers."

"Yeah. It's a thing, suddenly. How'd that happen? Isn't fashion a kind of social pressure? It could be interesting, don't you think?"

"Yeah, I guess. You need help?"

"Well, if you want you could ask the questions."

"Yeah, okay. Now?"

"Give me a minute." He was fiddling with the camera. So I went out in the hall to watch the interviews.

The blue blaster that Amanda was holding out toward her was just silly enough to help Emily relax. Amanda said, "Can we do like a bio phase? How old were you when you started playing?"

Emily blushed. "I ... I think four."

"*Four?* Like, what, playing piano?"

"No. Um ... I plonked things."

"You ... plonked things."

"See, it's just too strange." Emily looked around, for escape.

"Hey, *I'm* strange. You're talented," Amanda said. "I mean, Emily, you're the most gifted musician in this school. The music you did on that video was *incredible*. People want to know how you do it — where it comes from, you know? You could inspire people to play, just by telling your story or whatever."

"But ..."

"You can do it, Em," I said gently, moving in for support. "She's right, it'll mean something. What did you plonk?"

"I ... would go around the house. I had this wooden spoon, and I would plonk on things. Pots, pans, glasses. See, it's weird."

"No," Amanda said, "it's *cool*. Then what?"

"Well ... the ones I liked, I would take them into my room. I had things from all around the house. Anything I liked the sound of, I'd bring it in. I'd sit there on the floor, playing on everything."

"And your parents let you do this?" Amanda said.

"Well, they weren't my ..."

"*My* parents never would have," Amanda interrupted. "They're total losers. That's why I live with my grandma."

"You live with your grandma?"

"Yeah. She's all right."

"I ... don't live with my parents either," Emily said. "Not my real parents."

"Oh yeah?" Amanda glanced around. She shut off the blaster, spoke more quietly. "Your parents ... did they do stuff to you? Bad stuff?"

"No. I don't think so."

"Mine were selling drugs," Amanda said. "That's why I got put with my grandma. I don't even *see* my mom, and my dad's like in jail now."

"That's awful!"

"Nah, I'm cool. So what about yours? They didn't die or anything."

"I don't think so," Emily said. "Can we talk about music again?"

"Yeah. Let me turn this back on. Okay, go ahead."

"When I was about four," Emily said, "I got put with the people I live with now. I call them my mom and dad, but they're really my foster parents. So they'd come into my room and I'd be sitting there, this little girl who hadn't said a word — I'd be sitting on the floor in the middle of a sort of orchestra. I'd have pots and pans, cups, tools, a bottle of Flintstones vitamins that I'd shake. I even had a metal lid from an old garbage can. That was my gong!"

For the first time, she smiled. "I'd play and play. That's how I got started."

But Amanda was squinting, looking puzzled. "Back there. You said ... did you say you hadn't said a word?"

"You did say that," I said to Em. "What did you mean?"

She blushed. "I didn't talk."

Amanda said, "Not at all?"

Emily shook her head.

"Like ... for how long?"

Emily shrugged. "Two years."

"Two *years?*"

Emily blushed deeper, and clammed up completely.

I said, "Em. I never knew that."

She didn't answer. "Em," I said, "what about your real mom and dad? What happened to them?"

She shrugged.

I said, "You don't know?"

She shook her head.

I said, "What happened? Did they do something?"

"They ... would leave me."

"Leave you?"

"Uh huh."

"Where?"

"In the house."

"For ... how long?"

Emily shrugged. "For weekends."

Amanda stared. Then she asked, softly, "How old were you?"

"Like two. And ... three."

"Two years old? What were they *doing?*"

"I don't know. Partying."

Amanda said, "Didn't they come back?"

"Oh yes. But they had, you know, these friends, people were drinking ... I don't really know. I was little. I remember a lot of noise. Then it would just be me."

"Would they leave you *food?*"

"Yes." She shrugged. "Like cereal. I guess one time, a neighbor came by. When I was by myself. She reported it. That's when I got taken away."

"Didn't your parents come looking for you?"

Emily looked down. "I think they came home. When I wasn't there, they realized they were going to get in trouble. And that was that."

"What do you mean?"

She shrugged. "They just ... I don't know. They disappeared."

"They *left?*"

Emily nodded. "So when I came to my foster parents, I didn't really talk. Eventually I started making words, but I started with my sounds. I was always changing and improving my orchestra, you know? And my foster parents just let me. Even though it meant they'd go to cook dinner and there'd be no pots. Can you imagine?"

Emily was smiling now; but Amanda, this hard-attitude girl, just looked at her. She shook her head, and switched off the recorder.

"Thanks, Emily," she said softly. "Really. Thanks."

Around the corner, Bethany was a natural. She smiled and talked so easily on camera.

"So," Camilla said, awkwardly, "this is, I think the last question. Do you ... I mean, like ... what about sex? Do you think kids our age should be having it?"

"Oh god, I don't *think* so!" Bethany pushed her fingers through her hair. "I mean, I think sex is probably a beautiful thing, but not without love."

"Would you ... do it?"

"Would I *do* it? Of course not. We're in eighth grade!"

Camilla nodded at her camera, shutting it off.

"Okay," she said. "Thanks a lot. Really. That was great."

"Oh, you're welcome." Bethany turned to me, all twinkly like, *Wasn't I great?*

* * *

Video clips from my and Turner's shoe interviews, done in the hallways after school:

Girl named Mikaela, crinkly red hair, fairly hyper, orange sneakers.
"Oh, I love these shoes! You can be so individual. One of my friends gave me the idea. We went to the mall together on Saturday. I really really like orange. Don't you think they're great?"

Guy named James, athlete, dark-blue sneakers, kind of embarrassed.
"Oh well, I wouldn't wear them to play or anything. They're just street shoes."
"They look new."
"Oh yeah."
"Where'd you get the idea to get them?
"Oh, from my girlfriend. She said it was the thing, and she was excited and ... I kind of like it when she's excited. Plus they're personal. You choose your color, right? I mean, obviously guys aren't gonna wear pastels or whatever. But these are all right."

Girl, Erika, long brown hair, seems wary, brown boots.
"I just ... like them. Why?"
"Well, it seems like a lot of girls started wearing them."
"Maybe. So?"
"Well, did you feel pressured to wear them?"
"No! I like these. Why are you asking, anyway?"
"We're doing a web documentary about social pressures. Did you think if you wore the boots, you could be accepted into certain groups?"
"I don't know what you're talking about. I really can't be seen ... I really don't have time. Sorry."
As she hustles off, she glances around to see if anyone's noticed.

Isaac, the alternative kid Bethany tried to interview before, has on sneakers patterned in crisscrossed red-white-and-black plaid. He looks down at them.
"It's fairly ironic," he says.
"What is?"
"Well, these shoes are suddenly this alternative to conformity, right? You wear your own color, or pattern or whatever. But everyone ran out and got basically the same shoes. Same brand, same model."

"But so did you."

*"Yeah." He grins. "But mine are **cool**."*

Afterward, I was back in the library. Cat was at band and I was waiting. It was strange. I'd done this all year, but now it just wasn't the same.

For one thing, Kennedy had asked if we could meet for crepes after school. I'd said sure, okay, but I couldn't do it till four o'clock.

"Why not?"

"I ... just have to do something."

A silence. "All right," she said. "Fine. I'll see you then."

So I knew, when I got there, I would be queried. What would I say? What would she say?

Cat and me — we're friends, I said to myself. It was like I was rehearsing. But it wasn't an excuse.

It was true.

After band ended, everyone else flowed out like always; then that sad, sweet sound of her saxophone came rolling up the hall. After Cat stopped playing, I went out, opened my locker, and stood there acting interested in the mess inside.

"Did you like it?" she asked, hurrying up. Her face was flushed.

"Did I like ..."

"That song. It's the one I'm playing in the concert, with Emily. Remember we talked about it? 'Someone to Watch Over Me.'"

"Oh, yeah. Is that the one? It's beautiful."

It really was — and so, I had to admit, was she. Cat's bruise had healed and her eyes were bright, her cheeks were flushed, and her long black hair shone so deeply that I almost ached all over again. Almost.

"Thanks for doing this," she said. "It means a lot."

I shut my locker and reached for her sax case. "Like old times," I said.

She laughed. "CC is right. You are the gentleman."

Our voices sounded echoey as we walked. I said, "Is he waiting for you? Out there?"

"No! He won't even *answer* me."

"Not still?"

"Not at all. I don't know if he's mad at me, I don't know if he's okay, I don't know if his dad came home ..."

"He did."

"What? How do you know?"

211

"I went to his house."

She stopped dead. "You *did?* How is he? What did you see? Why did you go there?"

"Whoa! I went because he asked me."

"He did? Why? Did he ask about me?"

"Well ... um ..."

She sagged. "Okay. But ... how did he seem?"

"All right. Kind of heavy. Serious."

She nodded. "That's how he gets. It's building up. I wish he would *talk* to me."

"Can I ... could I ask you something?"

"Okay."

I took a breath. "All those afternoons, when you left here with him." I took another breath. "Where did you go?"

"Mostly we went to a pizza place. He knows the guy who runs it. We played pool."

"You played *pool?*"

"Yes. Is that so strange? The pizza place had a pool table. And we just, I don't know, we spent time together."

"So you didn't ..."

She peered at me. "We didn't what?"

"Well ... I just figured you went back to his house. And ... you know."

"Russell! Is *that* what you thought?"

"Well, yeah. You mean you didn't?"

"Of course we didn't! I'm a good Filipina, Russell. I would never!"

"But isn't that what you were scared they'd find out?"

"I was scared of what they'd *think*. I was never worried about what I'd do."

"Wow."

"This is a *surprise* to you?"

"Well ... I just didn't know."

"Yeah. Well." She crossed her arms. "Now you do."

We pushed the front doors open. The red Audi was waiting by the sidewalk. For a sudden second I didn't want her to go.

"He did talk about you — before," I said. "I went to his house after we were in the restaurant. He said you didn't deserve what happened. He said you can't be *in* it. What do you think that meant?"

She shook her head, slowly and sadly. "Oh, Richard. He thinks he can do this all by himself. How can he think that?"

"Do what by himself?"

"I don't know — be in his room when it happens? Never talk to anyone about it? Russell, he'll try to get through this holding everything in, but it'll eat him up inside. He'll never be okay. How can he *do* that?"

I had no idea. So I blurted something. "He gave me his knife."

Her mouth fell open. "He *gave* it to you?"

"Well, he asked me to store it. In a safe place. The thing he was carving, too."

"Oh, Richard," she said. "Oh ... Richard ..."

"You have to be strong," I said. But she just sighed.

I figured if Kennedy was mad, she was mad. I would deal with it. When I got there, she'd already ordered a Chocobananastravaganza. She brought it from the counter and set it down without a word. We dove in and just ate.

"So," she finally said. "How is she?"

I stopped chewing. "Whuut?"

"Your friend. How is she?"

I swallowed. Kennedy's spark was there, but at the back of her eyes.

I said, "How did you ... um ... why did you think I was with her?"

"What else would you be all dorky and secret about?" Then she smiled. "It's okay, Russell. I know you had feelings. Maybe you still do. It's okay. You can be honest with me, all right?"

She reached across and put her hand on my hand. Her fingers curved over mine, then they tipped into my palm. Suddenly that part of my left hand, my warming palm and her fingers curling into it, was the whole heart of the world.

She was holding my eyes. "Tell me about it," she said.

So I did. I really did. I told her about waiting for Cat, all those months; I told her about Richie, about him punching me last year, about Cat's fixation on him, about Richie's mom and his dad and the emergency room and the knife. I told her about Richie hitting Cat. I told her everything. She kept her fingers curled in there and just listened.

When I was finally done, she sat and thought. Then she looked up at me.

"I want to go there."

"Where?"

"To the field. The place where he hit her. Where you went and rescued her."

"I didn't *rescue* her, I just went there."

"You did so, but whatever. I want to go there. Walk with me?"

When we were out the door, I held my hand out; then I felt a panicky twinge, like I'd stepped off a cliff. But she took my hand. My feet hit solid ground. We walked there together.

"It's just a dugout," I said when we got there.

"Oh, I know. I played here," she said.

"You did?"

"Sure. Youth league baseball, straight through. I only stopped when they said we had to start playing softball with all girls."

"What's wrong with that?"

"Nothing. I just wasn't interested."

She stooped to look into the dugout. Then she straightened up. Looked around.

"It's so weird to think of something like that happening here," she said. "I mean, here. Where kids play ball."

I looked around. "Yeah."

She was standing close. "I don't like you having that memory," she said.

"It's okay."

"No, really. I think we should make a different one."

"Uh ... huh?"

"Russell. There's no one here. You could possibly kiss me."

"I could?" Oh, I was dorky to the end.

"Possibly," she said, closing her eyes.

That night I was on a cloud. Then the lightning hit.

I was in my room when a text from Kennedy came in. She'd linked a video to this message:

OK this is bad. They've got this going ALL around.

I clicked on the video.

It's Bethany, in the hall.

"I think sex is beautiful," she says to the camera. "Without love, for sure."
She ripples her hair with her fingers. "Would I do it? Of course I would. We're in eighth grade!"

I sat there for a while, staring at the screen. This one was so low it was almost funny. Except it wasn't.

"I saw that interview," I said when I got Kennedy on the phone. "That's not what she said — only parts of it. They edited."

"Pretty skillfully, too," she said. "It's a little jerky if you look close, but most people don't look close. This thing is raging all over, Russell."

"Jeez."

"Bet's a bit of a preener, but she doesn't deserve this," Kennedy said. "I wrote a text. Let me know what you think. I'm asking everyone to forward this one, too."

Here's what hers said:

Are you tired of being ruled by rumors & fear? A lot of people are. So join the rebellion! Tomorrow wear color sneakers. Choose your OWN color. You have the POWER.

"What do you think?"

"Well ... we interviewed some kids about that today," I said. "I don't think they saw the sneakers as some rebel thing. They seemed to just like them."

"But why do they like them?"

"I don't know ... because they can be individual without being the only one?"

"Hey, works for me," she said. "And I guarantee you those girls don't like it, because they're not controlling it. We're saying to people, be *you!* Wear your color! Spit in their eye!"

"Wow. You're fierce," I said.

"And you *like* it."

"Oh yes."

"All right then. Let's see what happens tomorrow."

37.
A Bag of Poop

The next morning the eighth grade was in an uproar. Rumors and theories were flying.

"Bethany wouldn't say that! I heard it was chopped up. Rearranged."

"Of course she said it. You can *see* her say it!"

Some kids said the boot girls were writing down the names of everyone who wore colored sneakers to school today. My theory was that Lauren and her friends had started that rumor, just to intimidate people.

But if they had, it wasn't totally working. A lot more people came in Tuesday morning with old-style sneakers, in all colors and plaids and patterns now. After Kennedy's text went around, kids must have rushed to the mall last night, to get theirs. There were more colored sneakers than boots, today.

Definitely more.

When I saw her in the morning, Bethany was surprisingly low-key. When I asked how she was, she said, "I'm okay." She seemed abashed. It was like she realized the boot girls had used her weakness, which was also her strength — that she was confident on camera, that she felt she had something to say. I felt bad for Camilla, a decent girl who had clearly been used. It would have been easy for Nicole to tell her to get the interview for the project, then later upload it for editing.

But at lunchtime, Bethany came to our table seething.

"The *principal* called me in. She said 'How could you *say* that?' I told her I didn't! I told her what happened. She didn't believe me! Can you *believe* that?"

Elliot nodded. "Yup."

"You have to prove it to her," I said. "That's how she is."

"Prove to the principal that I didn't say I love having *sex?*" Bethany sighed, exasperated. "This is ridiculous. And you know what? I am *not* taking this lying down."

Elliot, Janelle and I started sputtering when she said that. Bethany looked baffled; then she got it and started gasping, hand over her mouth — and now we were all laughing. Out loud. It was great. People were staring. I *liked* that they were staring.

Turner came up. "What?"

We waved at him, breathlessly. Janelled hiccuped, and that set us off again.

"Well, anyway," Turner said. "Bethany, you want to do something?"

She gulped, and nodded.

"Just don't do it lying down," I said, and the rest of us fell apart again.

Turner looked at us like we belonged in a home. "Come on," he said to Bethany. "You don't need lunch, right?"

"I'm a girl, I don't eat. What are we doing?"

"We're going to recreate the interview and the edit. Then we'll take that in and show the principal."

"Okay!"

We fell into a last chuckle-burst as Turner hustled away. Bethany turned to us, put her thumbs in her ears, and stuck out her tongue. Then she grabbed my ham and cheese sandwich and took a big bite. I said, "Hey!" But she was already gone.

At the end of school I was standing outside Mrs. Capelli's office, waiting for my friends. Turner had reshot Bethany's same comment in the same hallway spot, at lunchtime. He was so skillful that ten minutes after the final bell, he had recreated the evil edit. Then he and Bethany marched in to see the principal. They'd been in there a while.

When they came out, I could tell from their faces something had happened. I wasn't sure if they were happy, though. They looked more surprised.

I said, "Well?"

Turner's eyebrows went high. "We have three minutes on the Morning News."

"What — they're going to say something?"

"No," Bethany said as a slow grin spread over her face — "she's giving us three minutes. We can show the video we made, comparing what I really said with the lie. *And* we can film a comment. As long as she approves it, it goes on the air. On tomorrow morning's news.

"I have to go — my mom's waiting," she said to Turner, "Pick you up later, okay? Bye, Russell!"

We watched her hurry out. I said to Turner, "What about the Morning News committee?"

"The principal's bypassing them," Turner said. "She said, 'I want this mess defused fast. It's a huge distraction.' We're gonna do a *great* three minutes. Then, obviously, it goes in the project. It all goes in the project."

"What'll you say in the comment?"

"I'm not saying anything. It's up to her," he said, glancing at the front doors that Bethany had pushed through.

We walked out there and stood on the steps. It was a blustery spring day. Bethany's mom's silver SUV was pulling away. Everyone else was gone. Rain spattered around us, and on us.

"So," Turner said with a sneaky grin. "You have a *girl*friend."

"Uh ... what?"

"It's that girl who sat with us, right? The one who started the sneaker thing."

"Um, yeah."

"I knew it. Bethany and me both saw it. She looks at you that way."

"What way?"

"I don't know. *That* way."

We started walking. The rain was spattering harder. I said, "What about you two?"

"Who two?"

"You and Bethany. Does she look at you that way?"

Turner stopped and looked at me sort of searchingly. Then he started walking again.

"What?" I said, "What'd I say?"

His shoulders were clenched, like water was going down his back. As I caught up, he kicked a pebble, staring down. He said, "There's something I'm sort of ... I don't know. Messed up about. If I mention it, with all this crap going on, I have to know you won't say anything. To anyone."

I nodded.

"I have to *know*," he said.

"I won't say anything. To anyone."

He kicked another pebble. The rain made darker circles on his black sweatshirt. He said, "I just ... I don't know how to say it. Girls are like friends to me, okay? But they're just ... I mean ... I don't know. I really don't."

I didn't understand. And then I sort of did.

"Oh," I said. "I think maybe I get it."

He looked up. "I just feel really ... I mean so far, I haven't really felt

..." He turned red and stepped away. "Never mind."

"No. It's okay. It is."

"I just don't *know*," he said again. "But this year, it's kind of gotten weird. It's probably why I want to be behind my camera all the time, you know? I haven't wanted to think about ... other stuff. To be totally honest, it kind of got confusing ..."

He took a deep breath.

"Around Cam. I mean, we were absolutely just friends, but ... when that rumor came out, he was *so* pissed, because it totally wasn't true. About him. But me ... Russell, I just don't know. I'm just ... kind of ... confused."

His eyes were pleading. I knew that whatever I would say right now would be really, really important. And, of course, I had no clue what it should be.

"Hey," I said. "People our age get confused about stuff like that."

"Yeah, but ..."

"It doesn't matter."

But that wasn't right. It *did* matter. That's why we were talking about it. So I started babbling.

"Look, I don't mean it doesn't *matter*, but ... I mean ... okay, the sneaker thing, what's that about? It's like people are finally tired of being scared they'll get pointed at and called different — that someone'll say something's *wrong* with them and everyone else will laugh. But I mean, if you just are who you are — if you say this is me, this is my color or whatever — then you're all right. You know? It's like ... it's like a power."

I was pretty sure I hadn't made any sense at all. But Turner's face relaxed.

"So," he said, "if I was ... different ... we could still be friends?"

"Are you kidding me? Are you *kidding* me?"

I shoved him. He kicked another pebble. He said, "Thanks, man."

"I didn't do anything."

"That's what you think."

My call alert sounded on my way home. The screen said it was Elliot. I didn't want to get the phone wet, so I ducked into Convenience Farms.

"Yello."

"This is no damn game any more," he said. "They just went too far."

He was growling. Not like a kid; like an angry man. I said, "What happened?"

"Those girls started a new rumor," Elliot said. "In school today. This one is so low, they don't even text about it. It's all *whispers*."

"What is?"

"They're saying Emily plagiarized her music. They say she stole it."

"They said *what?*"

"See, if you sent that in a text, someone might call you on it and you'd have to back it up," he said. "But if you just whisper in people's ears, it starts going around, and nobody has any proof — because it's a lie — but that doesn't matter. It just keeps going around."

"How's Emily?"

"She won't talk."

"Uh oh."

"She won't talk to me, she won't talk to anyone. Russell, this girl's been through some stuff."

"I know."

"There's no *way* they're getting away with this. You mess with Emily, you're gonna deal with me."

The amazing thing was that when he said that, I didn't feel like laughing.

"Call Bethany," I said. "Mrs. Capelli just gave her and Turner three minutes on tomorrow's Morning News. They made a video showing what Bethany really said, when she got interviewed about dating, and how those girls perverted it. Bethany gets to add a comment, to broadcast on the show. Call and tell her what happened."

"Right." He hung up.

I was staring out at the rain when the call alert sounded again. This time, it was Cat.

Please, I thought — *no more drama. Not right now.*

"Russell, where are you?"

"I'm at Convenience Farms, out of the rain."

"Stay there. CC will come pick you up."

"What? Cat, listen ..."

"Russell, something really serious has happened."

"What? Did he hit you?"

"No — it's not me! It's *you*. Well, it's sort of me, too. But Russell, you have to come over here. You were right."

"I was? About what?"

"About her — Serena. Russell, you won't believe what she says I have to ... just stay there, all right? CC will come in five minutes."

I texted Elliot: **Call me.**

A few seconds later he did.

I said, "Did you talk to Bethany?"

"Yeah. It's a start. But I'm not done with these people."

"Apparently I'm not either. Are you home?" Elliot lived right up School Street, past the basketball court.

"Yeah."

"Doing anything?"

"Math supposedly. Why?"

"I'll come by in a couple minutes in a red Audi, to pick you up. We're going to Cat's house."

"All right. Why?"

"Apparently there's more."

"More from those girls?"

"Yes. Cat says it's major."

"I'll be outside my door."

"She's evil," Cat said. "I can't *believe* I trusted her."

"It's not so wrong to trust somebody," Elliot said.

"But you *told* me," she said to me. "You said she wasn't what she seemed. I thought she was my friend. She seemed so ... interested. Now I know why."

CC had slid some plates of different things in front of us, before leaving us alone in the kitchen — but I didn't even notice what those dishes were. All I remember is the storm that by now was downpouring outside, and the warm humid kitchen, and Cat gulping in air like she was trying not to drown.

"Tell us what happened," I said. "It's all right. Just tell it."

Cat took a breath. She folded her hands on the table.

"She said she needed to talk to me, after school. I said, 'Do you want to get together?' She said, 'No, I will call you.' I thought, okay, we'll talk. Then when she called, she said people were ready to have me in the group. The real group. I said, 'What do you mean, the real group?' She said, 'We're the ones who make the decisions around here. What we say is what happens.'

"I was confused — I didn't know what to say," Cat said. "I'd been just happy to have this friend! Then Serena said, 'First, we need you to do one thing. This is a very serious thing, and it will prove you're serious — that we can trust you and you belong in the group.'

221

"I said, 'What do you mean?' I honestly didn't get it. She said, 'To-morrow after school, you need to make sure Russell Trainor meets you after band. He'll be at his locker and it'll be open, because that's what he does — he stands at his locker while he waits for you to come out.' I said, 'How do you know this?' And she said, 'We know everything.' Just like that: 'We know *everything*.'

"Then she said, 'We're going to give you something. You'll be put-ting it in his locker.' I said, 'Why? What is it?' She said, 'You do not want to know that. You just need to do what I tell you.'

"And I said, 'I'm not going to do that! Russell is my friend!'"

Cat took a deep, shuddery breath.

"For a second," she went on, "Serena didn't say anything. Then, in a kind of nice voice like she was being my true friend and looking out for me, she said, 'Here's something really interesting. I'm in touch with your mom, on Skype.' I said, 'My *mother?*' She said, 'Oh yes. She's actually kind of worried about you. I just want to make sure, since she and I are talking, that she doesn't find out you've got an older boyfriend that you're sneaking off and having sex with three days a week after school. It would be really *awful* if she found out about that, don't you think?'

"Now I know why she acted so *caring* and *interested*," Cat said. "That girl just wanted to find out what would really get to me. Then she goes and finds my *mom*."

"It's partly my fault," I said.

"No it isn't — you warned me. How could I be so *stupid?*"

"The question," Elliot piped up, "is what do we do now?"

We looked at each other. That was the question.

I asked Cat, "What did you say to her?"

"I was so appalled and horrified, I didn't say anything. She said, 'To-morrow when lunch period starts, you go to the under-the-stairs place. You know it, right? Go there exactly when lunch starts, when everyone else is heading for the caf.' When I still didn't say anything, Serena said, 'You heard me, right?' I said 'Yes.' She said, 'Fine. See you then.' And she hung up."

For a while we just sat there, thinking.

Elliot said, "If you go, they'll give you what they want you to put in Russell's locker."

I nodded. "Sounds like it."

Cat said, "What do you think it is?"

"I don't know," I said — "but I don't think you want to have it. It's got to be something nasty."

"Or dangerous. Or illegal," Elliot said. "Something."

"You know what?" Cat sat up straight. "That girl thinks she's got control over me, because she thinks she found the one thing I'm most scared of. But first of all, it's a lie — she's assuming something that isn't true. And second, I am not going to do anything bad to you, Russell. I won't even *pretend* to do it."

"Pretend to do it," Elliot said. "There's an idea."

We looked at him, and waited.

"Well ... it might be an idea," he said. "Somehow."

"You could just not go," I said to her.

"But if I don't go, they might find some other way to give you whatever it is. Put it in your backpack, or something."

"How?"

"I don't know," she said, "but they're very clever. And they have lots of" — she made quote marks with her fingers — "'friends.'"

"She's right," Elliot said. "Not cooperating won't guarantee they're stopped." He kept on thinking, chin in hand.

"You know what?" he finally said. "My family's a little weird."

I had to laugh. "Your family's a little geeky," I said. "It's you that's weird."

"No, that's just it — we love technology. Last year, remember how I used to get picked on a lot? When I was obsessed with dinosaurs? I admit I was a little strange."

"Yeah," I said. "Last year."

"Right. So a couple of times, kids actually snuck up at nighttime and did stuff to the house. One time they wrote 'Freak' with soap on the living room window. If it'd been me, I'd have written it backward, so you could read it from inside, but ... anyway. Another time they put a bag full of dog poop on the front steps, and rang the doorbell."

"They did? What happened?"

"Well, my mom said we had to get a dog. To watch the house."

"But you still don't have a dog," I said.

"No — my dad's allergic to dogs! So they argued, and discussed, and finally they decided on a low-light surveillance camera."

"A ... what?

"It's a webcam," Elliot said. His eyes were sparkling. "It's motion-activated, linked by wireless to my dad's computer. It cost like 200 bucks, but if anyone came in the front yard at night, it would switch on silently and film them."

"Has it done that?"

"Not really — kids kind of stopped coming around to do stuff. But you'd never believe how many raccoons are out there, at night," he said. "They finally took the camera down, because all we were getting was raccoons. The thing just sits in a closet."

I said, "What about the poop?"

He squinted. "The what?"

"The bag of dog doo those kids left. Did anybody step on it?"

"No! We're the Gekewiczes, not the Stupids."

"So," Cat said, "the point of all this is ..."

"The point *is*," Elliot said, "we borrow the webcam. We put it under the stairs, where you're supposed to meet those girls. It's small and black, and thin — you wouldn't see it, especially in that dim light. I can set it up. I'll put tape over the red recording light. As soon as someone comes into the space, the camera goes on. We'll be somewhere else, watching on my laptop on the school's wireless. I can load in the webcam software tonight."

"But," I said, "she needs not to take this thing they want her to take. It could be dangerous."

"I know," Elliot said. "You just want to get them on camera *offering* it to you," he told Cat.

"But," she said, "would that be enough? They could claim later on that it was just ... dog poop. Or something."

I nodded. "She's right."

"Hmm," Elliot said.

"I'm going to take it," said Cat.

"What? No."

"Yes. I'll take it. I'll act like it's fine. Then we'll have it, whatever it is. For evidence."

"We'll need to hear what they say," I said. "That could be critical."

"The webcam has a microphone," Elliot said.

"Can we save the feed?"

"Of course — it's auto-save software," he said. "Without that, a surveillance cam is kind of pointless. But," he said to Cat, "what if what they give you is dangerous?"

"If we have it recorded, I'm not worried," Cat said.

"I am, a little," I said.

"Yeah," Elliot mused. "Also, it's possible everything might not work exactly right. I mean, I can link to the camera using my password on the school wireless — but when can I get under the stairs to set up the camera?"

"It's too risky," I said. "I don't think ..."

"We have to do this," Cat said. "I have to. If your thing doesn't work, I'm just going into the principal's office with whatever they give me. I don't care."

"Wait — I know," Elliot said. "I've got math second block; I won't go. I'll tell Mrs. Mooney I have a dental appointment. Don't worry, she loves me! I'm *great* at math."

"But you'll need a note," I said.

"No, I won't. You only need a note if you're leaving school. I'll walk fast through the hall, all earnest and serious like I'm on some official nerd mission. Which I *will* be."

"Yeah," I said, "okay." I was starting to see it. "If you go under the stairs in a class period, no one'll be there."

"Then at lunchtime," he said, "we'll just log on."

"This *has* to work," I said. "If it doesn't, Cat could be left holding the bag."

Elliot grinned. "What if it's dog poop?"

"It won't be," I said. "They've been cooking up something serious. I think those nasty new things about Bethany and Emily were really distractions. Get us all stirred up about those, then spring the trap."

"Could be," Elliot said. "Well, surprise."

I said to Cat, "Can you really do this?"

She nodded. "Absolutely. And you know what? I'm glad we're doing this together. You two were my first real friends here. It's like old times."

"And," Elliot said, finger in the air, "we shall *nevah surrendah!*"

"Where do you *get* that?" I said. "From your game?"

"No, Winston Churchill said it. He was the prime minister of England in 1940, when they had to fight the Nazis all by themselves. He told the people, 'We shall fight on the beaches! We shall fight on the landing grounds! We shall fight ...'"

"Elliot."

"'In the fields!' What?"

"Can we focus?"

"I am focused. It's just that saying, 'I need a ride to my house so I can put the software in my laptop' doesn't have the same ring."

"Emily," I reminded him. "You're doing this for Emily."

225

"Right." He got serious. He said to Cat, "Can I get a ride to my house? I need to put the software in my laptop."

"Sure," she said, smiling. She went to get CC.

38.

Docudrama

The next day, when Turner's truth video had finished on the Morning News, the camera shifted to Bethany, sitting at a desk. She looked, surprisingly, a little nervous.

"I want to say something about myself," she said to the camera, a little too quickly. "You might be thinking, 'Oh Bethany DeMere, get over yourself.' And actually, I wouldn't totally blame you."

Kids in my homeroom stopped talking. Someone snickered. We all looked at the TV.

"Recently, something happened to me," Bethany said. "At the time I thought it was the worst possible thing that could happen — but now ... well. What happened was, I got pushed out of the most popular group." She swallowed. "You may have heard about that. It was embarrassing, you know? Actually, to be honest, it was humiliating. But now I think it was the maybe best thing that could have happened.

"See, for a long time I tried so hard to be Ms. Popular Perfect. I never felt relaxed. I had no real friends. The people I was with, it's like we were all wearing masks — like you're trapped in this mask and every day you're scared someone might rip it off and say, 'Look, everyone! She's a *fake!*'"

Bethany almost shouted that. People jumped.

"Well, so. When I wasn't in that group any more, suddenly I had to deal with people sort of ... like on my own," she said. "I started seeing myself in other people's eyes. I kind of saw someone people didn't really ... like that much. Or trust."

Bethany shook her head. "Can you imagine? But then I started to *like* what was happening. All of a sudden I didn't have to look at you like you were clothes and hair and status stamped on your forehead. I could just *be* with people. At first it was awkward, but it was also kind of amazing. I started to feel like I could breathe.

"Then I started seeing what people will do when they're so scared in *their* masks. I saw how some people will tell any lie, hurt anyone however bad, just so they can feel like they're safe from being exposed for one more day. You saw, just now, what some people did with a little interview I gave for a school project. But yesterday, those same people also did something else.

"They started a whispering campaign," Bethany said, "about a girl who never hurt anyone. This girl has a special creativity, something that's been really inspiring. To us. You know. A lot of people even started wearing a certain something because of this person's inspiration.

"But some people couldn't stand to see that. So they started whispering that this girl wasn't really real — that what she created wasn't actually hers. Nobody could prove this, because it's not true, but they started saying it anyway. And because this was another spicy rumor, people started to pass it along. Because that's what we do, right?

"So here's what I have to say. Everyone's scared, okay? It's *normal* to be scared. But we don't have to be controlled by that any more. I can't tell anyone what to do — and whatever you want to think about me, that's fine. But I need to tell you, what's being whispered about this one girl, that is a total lie. So let's make a statement. If you feel like I do about this, then let's ... just ... wear the *shoes.*"

As she said this, Bethany, who always had to look just right, lifted up her foot and plopped it on the desk to show everyone she had on brand new, old-school funky sneakers. They were bright yellow, like her hair.

The anchors came back on, thanked Bethany and Turner, and signed off. Someone in my room snorted, in a mocking way. But someone else said, "Wow."

The backpack Elliot took under the stairs when he cut second-block math had inside it the webcam, small and black and flat, and a roll of black duct tape. He taped the camera to the bottom of one of the stairs, at eye level in the murkiest part of the space. Now he and I sat in the computer lab, which was otherwise empty as the rest of eighth grade herded off to lunch.

An image appeared on his laptop screen. The space under the stairs was dim and grayish, but we could see it fine. Catalina stepped into the viewframe. She slowly turned around, peering, then saw the camera. She gave us a wink.

"Test," she said. "Test."

I pushed my phone's auto-dial for her cell, to transmit the signal that everything worked. She had her cell set on vibrate — and you could see she got my signal, because she reached in her pocket and my call disconnected. If anything went wrong at our end, we would buzz her again.

"This is like Mission Impossible," I said. "Does the camera self-destruct?"

"Everything will if those girls spot it," Elliot said.

Cat stood, hands on her hips. She didn't look scared. She hadn't seemed scared at all, today. Then two dark shapes ducked in.

"Okay," I whispered.

When they stood up, we could see that one was Serena. The other was Cayenne Sheffield. *The one who'll do anything.*

Cayenne had a backpack. Serena did not.

"Let the docudrama begin," said Elliot.

I think those people who lift weights in the Olympics must have a similar experience. I mean, you go through all this preparation and suspense, and there's a lot of risk — will you lift that thing, or will it break your neck? But the thing is, you get up there and try to do it and bam, in a few seconds it's over. Either you succeeded or you failed.

This was like that. Or it would have been, if Cat hadn't done what she did.

Serena nodded to her assistant. Cayenne unzipped her backpack along the top, reached in and pulled out a paper lunch bag. Its top was folded over.

Cayenne held out the bag. Cat reached out and took it.

"If this *is* a bag of poo," I said, "I'm jumping on it and leaving it there."

Then Serena said, "Today, after band. At his locker. Talk with him, flirt with him, be upset — whatever. Just distract him, then drop this in there. Once you've done that, close his locker door and say, 'Let's go.' Make sure he comes with you right then."

Cat said, "Do you think that'll work?"

"Trust me, you can make that loser do anything you want — and you do *not* want to be caught with this." She glanced at the bag that hung from Cat's hand.

The girls turned to go. Then Cat said, "Actually, no."

They turned back. Serena said, "What?"

"I need to know what this is," Cat said.

"No you don't," Serena said. "You totally do not."

"Oh, but I *do*."

Cat started unfolding the top of the bag. Serena said, "Don't!" and grabbed for it.

"*Back* off," Cat said, pulling the bag away. "If this is something dangerous, or poisonous or whatever, I would never want to put it in my friend's locker, would I?"

"It's not poisonous," Serena said tensely. "You need to do what I say. I *told* you."

"You *tried* to tell me," Cat said. "You're supposed to be so good at figuring people out, Serena, but you actually got a couple of things wrong. First of all, you don't know the real truth. And second, I'm not scared of you."

"I will *ruin* you," Serena said. "I told you what I'll do."

"Oh right, you mentioned my mom? But my mom and I know each other really well. And when I tell her what you tried to do, my mom will know just the kind of person you are. See, my mom and I *trust* each other. I don't know if you even know what that is."

Cayenne was looking amazed, first at Cat and then at Serena.

"We're not talking about me," Serena said. "We're talking about what you are *going* to do."

Cat shrugged. She went back to unfolding the top. "Let's just see," she said.

She reached in, and pulled out something that drooped from her hand. They were all three looking at it. Elliot said, "What is it?"

"I don't know. I can't tell ..."

Cat took the thing in two pinched fingers, and let it unroll. It was a plastic ziploc bag. She was staring, motionless now, at something dark and crumbled-looking that filled the bottom of it.

"Holy crap," Elliot said. "That looks like ..."

"Oh," Serena said, and smiled: "You are gonna be in *sooo* much trouble." She jerked her head at Cayenne, and they ducked out of there fast.

Cat stooped over to the camera. She held out the bag.

"I think it's marijuana," she said. "What do I do now?"

"Whoa," said someone behind us.

Elliot and I spun in our chairs. Mr. Dallas was bent over behind us, peering at the screen.

He said, "Is this some kind of skit?"

"No," I said.

He peered closer. Cat was motionless on screen, waiting for an answer. He said, "Is that really ..."

"I think it might be," I said.

"In *school?* What the *hell?*"

Elliot asked, "How much did you see?"

"I've been here since those two girls went in there," Mr. D said. "I was admiring your focus, at first."

"Catalina was supposed to put that in my locker," I said. "To get me in trouble. Those two girls, the group they're in — they really hate us."

"Have you recorded this?" Mr. D asked.

"Every bit," Elliot said.

"Are you using one of our cameras?"

"No — it's from home," Elliot said. "A night-vision webcam."

"Okay. I want you to store that file, name it and burn it to a CD. Do this right now."

On the monitor, Cat had set the baggie down carefully on the floor. She was looking at us with pleading eyes.

"What about her?" I said. "She needs help. She's scared." I pulled out my cell.

"Right," said Mr. D. "Call her and tell her to stay there — then go wait with her. Absolutely do not touch that stuff, and don't let anyone else in. We're going to take a CD to Mrs. Capelli's office."

"Right," I said, pulling out my phone.

"Well," I said as we left the principal's office hours later, "now we know why Lauren went out with Baked Corrigan."

It was the end of the day. We'd had the police, Serena's mom (either she didn't have a dad, or he couldn't come), and Cayenne's parents in the main office. All three of us had given statements. So had Mr. D, who was adamant about what he'd seen. But it was the webcam video that clinched it.

Serena and Cayenne had been taken to the police station. No handcuffs, but they'd been escorted out through the main hall by three cops. One of them was the officer who'd talked to my mom and me, outside Richie's house. We nodded at each other.

Now Cat, Elliot and I stood in the hall. Basically, we exhaled.

"I was wondering something," I said to Cat.

"What?"

"How did you think to stay there and open that bag on camera? That wasn't in the plan."

"I realized if I didn't show myself opening the same thing they gave me, those girls could have said we'd switched bags," she said. "They are excellent liars. And we'd have had no proof."

Elliot nodded. "Wow."

"I can't believe they made up that list of names," I said. "Even for them that was evil."

We figured Serena's plan was to make an anonymous call — to the cops? the principal's office? — saying to look for drugs in my locker. She denied it, of course, but she and her friends had it set all up.

When Mrs. Capelli and Mr. D got to the space under the stairs, Cat and I were sitting on the floor with the paper lunch bag and the plastic baggie on the floor between us. Ms. Capelli didn't touch the baggie — she left that for the police, who were on their way. But she lifted the open end of the paper bag, and looked in.

"There's something in here," she said.

"If it's contraband I wouldn't touch it," Mr. D said.

"No — it's a piece of paper." She pinched her fingers in, and pulled out a folded white sheet.

On the paper — it had come through a printer — were the names of the Out Crowd:

Buyers
Elliot Gekewicz   4 grams
Turner White   3 grams
Janelle Burd   2 grams
Bethany DeMere 5 grams
Emily Behrens   1 gram

"Hey," I said. "Bethany made it into the cool group."

The principal didn't think that was funny. It wasn't, really. I just had to be me.

Now we pushed open the outside doors. It was a softly sunny spring day. And he was standing across the street, leaning against his old tree.

Cat had walked down one step before she noticed him. She stopped dead.

"Oh my gosh," I said. "It's Wednesday."

Richie stood up straight. He waited.

Cat turned back to us. "I have to go talk to him," she said.

"Did you know he was here?"

"No! But ... will you wait? I'd feel better if you could see us."

"Go," I said. "We're here."

She went down the steps and rushed to him. She went to hug him, but he caught her arms. He just held them, not hard I think, as he kept her standing there in front of him.

Richie was talking. Cat listened. She nodded. He had on his old jacket, his armor that hadn't protected him. Richie looked into her face as he talked.

I couldn't see Cat's expression, but she sagged. Her knees buckled. She took a step back and said something. Richie nodded. She fell into his arms, and they hugged for a long time.

Then Richie kind of gently set her back where she'd been standing. She turned and started walking our way. She turned back to him. He nodded to her.

Cat walked across the street and came up the steps. Her face was colored very deep, and her eyes were soft.

"He wants to talk to you, Russell," she said.

I looked across the street again. This time, he was waiting for me.

"Hey," I said.

"Hey."

I stood in the shade, in the place where she had always come to him. He wasn't looking at me. He wasn't looking at anybody.

I said, "Did you just break up with her?"

For a long time he kept looking off. Then he nodded, and met my eyes.

"It's the only thing I can do," he said. "You know?" He turned up his empty hands. "It's the one thing I can do for her."

"You know," I said, "you don't have to go through this alone. There are people you can talk to. Like that lady — on that card I gave you. Remember?"

He nodded. "We'll see," he said, and took a breath. "I just need to ask you something. Maybe I need to tell you something, too."

I waited. Felt the tension. What was this?

"You've been a friend to her," Richie said. "Right through all of this. I know it. I ... appreciate it."